Graham
the recei

Teddy's call had not come as a surprise, since he'd already received a report of the "accident." But her brave attempt to make light of what had been a very close brush with death had shaken him.

He picked up the phone again to call her father and inform him of the situation. Taking his cue from Teddy, he downplayed the seriousness of the incident, but it was obvious that the man was badly shaken, too.

As well he should be, Graham thought angrily after he'd hung up. Hadn't the man ever considered the possibility that his daughter could be dragged into this? Did he think he was dealing with Boy Scouts?

Graham paced the small study for a few minutes, debating with himself over what course of action to pursue, then let his heart make the decision for him.

ABOUT THE AUTHOR

Saranne Dawson is a voracious reader and has an avid interest in current events, which she says stems from "living in the middle of nowhere" in central Pennsylvania. With a master's degree in public administration, she works as a human services administrator. In her spare time, Saranne sews, bikes, plays tennis, gardens and tends three "hopelessly obnoxious and pampered cats."

Books by Saranne Dawson

HARLEQUIN AMERICAN ROMANCE
180–INTIMATE STRANGERS

Don't miss any of our special offers. Write to us at the following address for information on our newest releases.

Harlequin Reader Service
901 Fuhrmann Blvd., P.O. Box 1397, Buffalo, NY 14240
Canadian address: P.O. Box 603,
Fort Erie, Ont. L2A 5X3

Summer's
Witness
Saranne Dawson

Harlequin Books

TORONTO • NEW YORK • LONDON
AMSTERDAM • PARIS • SYDNEY • HAMBURG
STOCKHOLM • ATHENS • TOKYO • MILAN

Published November 1987

First printing September 1987

ISBN 0-373-16222-7

Chapter One

Teddy Sothern stood up in the speeding boat, peering over the top of the windshield with an eager, happy smile on her face. The wind made a rippling coppery flag of her hair as she watched the horizon, unmindful of the racket of the powerful inboard engine and the rhythmic slappings of boat against water. The man in the pilot's seat beside her chuckled.

"You've looked this way every summer of your life, do you know that?"

She turned briefly from her examination of the horizon to smile at the handsome gray-haired man beside her. "That's because I've felt this way all my life. But you can't tell me to sit down anymore."

He chuckled again and let out the throttle some more, causing Teddy to wobble only slightly before she regained her balance. Her sky-blue eyes, hidden at the moment behind oversized sunglasses, never wavered from their attention to the water ahead.

Then, far out at the edge of the Atlantic's gray-green waters, barely visible in the haze, she saw an indistinct dark hump of land. A sigh of pleasure escaped softly before she sank down into her seat.

The fact that this summer would not be as peaceful and lazy as all others had been didn't trouble her; all that mattered was that she was once again here. In the rugged beauty and solitude of Matiscotta island, Teddy Sothern felt she could handle anything.

The boat made its way swiftly across the watery gap that separated them from their destination, and with each noisy moment that destination grew more distinct. Teddy stood up again as the blur took shape and remained standing as individual features came into focus.

Huddled near the shoreline just north of the island's center was a small cluster of houses—a few constructed of weathered shingles, but most of them in sparkling-white frame. Before them, boats of every size and shape rode at anchor in the harbor. Beyond the houses, the land rose into a dark forest that from this distance looked black.

The houses were all summer homes now, though in years past there had been permanent residents on the island. Many of the Maine coastal islands had once held permanent populations of hardy residents, but a decline in the fishing industry combined with the lure of the mainland had taken them away.

Here, as on some of the other islands, though, the old families had clung to this spot, even if only for a month or so during the summer. One branch of Teddy's mother's family had been residents here for over a hundred years, and at about the time of Teddy's birth thirty years ago, their home had been bequeathed to her mother. Despite the fact that the family who had summered here for these thirty years was named Sothern, the house continued to be called the Holbrook house.

When she saw that her father was on a bearing for the town docks, Teddy turned to him with a frown. "Are we docking in town?"

He gave her a rueful look. "I'm afraid so. That big storm last month damaged our dock. It must have been that one, because Amos said it was fine when he came out just before that. It did a lot of other damage, too."

Teddy nodded. Like most of the island's other hundred or so summer residents, she followed the progress of the violent North Atlantic storms known locally as nor'easters from the relative safety of her Connecticut home. She knew the one he meant because the TV news had been full of reports of damage along the mainland coast as well.

"It'll get fixed—in due time, of course." Ted Sothern added the latter with a smile.

She returned the smile. Island time was slow time. All repairs were handled by a small cadre of mostly retired summer residents—dedicated craftsmen who could not be hurried. Each year they repaired or replaced damaged properties in a never-ending battle with the elements, taking a quiet pride in their work while accepting the fact that it was probably only temporary.

The man to whom her father had referred, Amos Moody, was the island's self-appointed caretaker. Each winter he made regular visits to Matiscotta from his Rockland home to check on things, then came out to stay before the others arrived. He had keys to every home on the island, and a minor flap had occurred just a few years ago when a new family had balked at such an intrusion. The following winter several pipes had burst in their improperly winterized home and the resultant damage had quickly changed their minds.

Amos apportioned the work among himself and the other craftsmen according to the immediacy of the problem, and there was no haggling over bids. A damaged dock didn't rate at the top of the list; hence, they waited.

Ted throttled back and they came into the harbor, making their way among the other boats already anchored or tied up there. Teddy scanned the craft, looking for boats belonging to island friends. She saw the one that belonged to their closest neighbor and her father told her that their dock had virtually been destroyed. The boats themselves spent the winter at the marina in Rockland, even though many owners, like the Sotherns, had boathouses at their private docks.

She leapt nimbly out of the boat after tossing the bumpers over the side, then tied the boat securely to the pier. The neighbor with the destroyed dock approached them, and after greeting him Teddy left the two men to commiserate on winter's ravages.

Directly across from the harbor was the one nonresidential structure on the island—a combination general store, post office, gas station and community center of sorts. The first stop on everyone's agenda, it was rather like registering at a hotel.

The wind off the Atlantic was raw and Teddy stepped gratefully into the faintly kerosene-scented warmth of the crowded store. In the midst of a jumble of goods sat an antique potbellied stove, before which sat two older men playing checkers. It was a portrait of Americana and it never failed to amuse Teddy, even as she cherished it. So few things remained unchanged in this world, and she was everlastingly grateful that Matiscotta was one of them.

Both men looked up at her entrance, announced by a jangling bell over the door, and their weathered and creased faces broke into smiles of welcome. Amos Moody was the first to speak.

"Well, I see you made it back again, Teddy. No man with you yet, either, I notice."

Teddy repressed a smile at the wonderfully familiar sound of their incomparable downeast accents. Teddy, who normally found it quite easy to mimic accents, had never quite mastered this one with its unusual vowel pronunciations and its unique rhythms.

"One of these years, Amos, I'm going to surprise you," she replied, having long since grown accustomed to his teasing about her single status.

Amos turned to his checkers partner. "Must be something wrong with those professors down there in Connecticut, to let a girl like our Teddy get away from them."

The other man nodded solemn agreement, and Teddy refrained from pointing out to them that the fault was hers, not that of her faculty colleagues.

"Teddy! Your daddy said you were coming today!"

Teddy whirled around at the sound of the jolly female voice and was quickly engulfed in a warm hug and the delightful aroma of baking. When she was finally released, she sniffed appreciatively.

"I don't suppose that could be sticky buns I smell, could it?"

The store's proprietress beamed. "It could indeed. Your daddy already put in his order."

She cast a quick glance toward the door, then lowered her voice. "He looks good, Teddy. Putting his suffering behind him, I think."

Teddy nodded as a wave of sadness brushed over her. It was here that she still missed her mother most. Last summer had been difficult for both her father and her, after Ann Sothern's death late in the winter. But even so, neither of them had suggested that they should stay away from Matiscotta. The painful memories might be stronger here, but somehow, so was the power to heal.

"He should think about getting married again," the woman went on, with all the certainty of one who has spent more than forty years in that state.

Teddy smiled. "I think he has other things on his mind at the moment."

"Yes, I guess he does at that. Going to be a busy summer. Did the senator talk him into it?"

"No. Or at least Dad says not. Uncle John might have had something to do with it, though." And another shard of cold sadness pierced her at the mention of that name.

The woman nodded sympathetically. "We heard about him, of course. The world just isn't safe anymore, is it? That's what makes this place so special."

Teddy's Uncle John, her mother's brother, had been one of those men known as political kingmakers: men who never held public office themselves, but who were frequently responsible for the rise and success of those who did.

In truth, she really didn't know whose idea it had been for her father to run for the senate, but she did know that Uncle John had immediately set about raising the necessary funds and putting together a talented campaign staff. Then, a little more than a month ago he had become the victim of a vicious mugging and murder as he left his Hartford law office late one night.

Teddy lingered in the store, listening to gossip and news of other island families, only a few of whom had yet arrived. An occasional customer came in and greeted her warmly, and over at the stove the checkers match was concluded with the usual good-natured joshing about cheating. Amos got up and pronounced himself ready to return to work on the shingles at the Weston place. By the time her father came to collect her, Teddy could feel herself slipping into the rhythms of the island and shedding her academic skin for another summer.

Father and daughter strolled across the street to the parking lot at the docks where their ten-year-old Volvo sat waiting. He had already loaded her luggage into the rear of the wagon.

"No problems with Old Faithful?" she asked as she smiled affectionately at the Volvo.

"Not a one," her father responded proudly.

On the mainland, Ted Sothern favored large domestic sedans with every possible convenience, but here on Matiscotta, he drove something far more practical. The only way to take a car off the island was the once-a-month Maine State Ferry Service, so cars lived and died here, tended by a retired mechanic who disdained such "modern gewgaws" as power windows and dashboard computers.

They left the small cluster of houses behind and drove south as the road temporarily wound inland. It was a small island, a little more than three miles long and not quite three miles wide at its broadest point. A gravel road wound about, connecting all the scattered homes along the irregular coastline. The winter had taken a toll on it, too, but the Volvo was very forgiving of the as-yet-unfixed potholes and washouts.

They rounded a bend and both the sea and a house came into view, the latter perched on a bluff some seventy-five feet above the shoreline. Teddy smiled happily.

"Was there any damage to the house?" she asked, peering at it closely.

"Nothing, except for a few loose shingles early in the winter and Amos has already replaced them. Pointed out every one to me, too," he finished with a smile.

They left the main road and moved up the driveway to the big shingled structure, weathered to a mottled dark brown with bright-blue shutters. Teddy focused on the shutters, which were far more than decorative. During the long winter months, they were closed to protect the glass from the storms, and despite the use of the best marine paint they generally required repainting every few years. It was probably time again. Their last painting had been two years ago, the result of a joint mother-daughter project. Teddy's father had joked at the time that they were both egocentric, painting the shutters the exact shade of their eyes. Teddy squeezed out the sadness again, deciding that she'd paint them some other color this summer.

She got out of the wagon and surveyed the house, making her own unnecessary check for damages as she recalled the story her mother had always delighted in telling about a summer in her own childhood. The Holbrook family had come out to the island to find that a late winter storm had torn away a portion of the roof, thereby providing a wonderfully cozy refuge for a large flock of crows. They hadn't much appreciated being evicted, she had said with dry humor, and had hung about all summer long, waking their erstwhile landlords at dawn with their cawing.

The bittersweet memories continued to assault Teddy as they carried her belongings into the house. The front door was unlocked, as always. Only at the end of the season did anyone on the island remember where their door keys were. A locked house would have been an insult to neighbors who were prone to stopping by with fresh garden produce or freshly caught fish. Many times they had returned from their wanderings to find dinner awaiting them in the kitchen sink.

Ted carried her bags upstairs to the bright corner room that had been Teddy's for as long as she could remember. Two windows opened to a splendid view of the sea and another faced the dark fir forest, resulting in a mixture of aromas that Teddy could recall at will during the long winter months in Connecticut.

"Drinks on the terrace whenever you're ready," her father announced from the doorway as he was leaving. "After that, I'll cook us a big steak to start things off right."

Teddy nodded with a smile as she began to unpack her things. The summer officially started with a gin and tonic for her and a martini for her father, followed by a thick porterhouse steak, medium rare. Gin and tonics and sand between her toes and the scents of pine and salt water: of these things had summer always been made. That continuity meant even more to them now as they settled into a life without mother and wife.

A short time later she joined her father on the broad terrace that ran nearly to the edge of the bluff. The breeze off the ocean was cool, but neither of them considered moving indoors or even into the shelter of the screened porch off the living room.

Summer did indeed come to the Maine coast, but it was a very late and temporary visitor. Warmup suits or jeans and sweaters were more frequently seen here than were shorts and halters or bare sundresses. And for those intrepid islanders who had to have their ocean swims, wet suits replaced bikinis and swim trunks. The water temperature, even at the height of the summer, rarely reached sixty degrees.

"The Boswells are making noises again about opening an inn," Ted said as Teddy settled herself into a chaise, drink in hand.

"Hmmph!" She snorted. This subject came up every year or so, to the amusement or disdain of the other residents. With its lack of nightlife, cold waters and the absence of even a single tennis court or golf course, Matiscotta was hardly likely to turn itself into Miami Beach North.

"Well, even if they actually do it one of these years, it won't change anything," she said reassuringly. "The only people who would vacation in a place like this are nature lovers—and they'll fit right in."

"Amos Moody said he hoped maybe they'd put in one of those nudie beaches." Ted grinned.

Teddy threw back her head and laughed. "Amos would have to import a couple of backup pacemakers if that happened."

The easy conversation and laughter continued throughout most of the waning evening. Both father and daughter delighted in each other's company, anticipating a deepening of their special relationship over the coming summer months.

Teddy was, from her father's point of view, a perfect amalgam of her parents. She had her mother's copper curls and bright-blue eyes, her father's long, lean body, her mother's sense of fun and quick wit and her father's keen mind and candor. All in all, he thought, if fate had chosen to give him only one child, he had certainly got the very best.

From Teddy's point of view, *she* was the lucky one. She had been given a lively, lovely mother and a father who remained the standard by which she judged all men. That none had yet measured up was self-evident in her continued unmarried state.

Still, there were things about her father lately that she just didn't understand—chiefly, his startling decision to enter politics. She was about to open that particular subject when he did it for her in a surprising fashion.

"I've hired a new campaign manager, Teddy. He'll be arriving the day after tomorrow."

Teddy stared at him. "I thought that I was going to be your campaign manager." After all, she'd taken a semester's leave for that purpose, after Uncle John's death.

Seeing his daughter's less than pleased reaction, Ted backed off a bit. "Well, maybe campaign manager isn't the right title for him. You'll still be in charge of the operation, but I needed someone with more experience to advise me."

Teddy remained silent since she couldn't really fault his reasoning. The only experience she'd had had been some volunteer work in the ill-fated campaign of a woman who'd run for congress from Teddy's home district. And it probably was true that her enthusiasm exceeded her abilities by a bit. Such had often been the case with Teddy.

"Jack Oldham recommended him. He worked in Jack's last campaign, and he's from Connecticut."

Teddy wrinkled her slightly upturned nose. "That's no recommendation as far as I'm concerned. You know what I think of his politics."

Senator Oldham, another island resident, was a close friend of her father's and a longtime senator from Maine. In Teddy's opinion, he exemplified everything she detested about politics. He swayed with every political breeze and had never, insofar as she knew, given a straightforward answer to any question put to him.

"He knows the game, Teddy," her father responded mildly, having heard his daughter express her opinion of the senator many times before—occasionally even to the man himself.

"I suppose," she sighed, acknowledging that it was a fait accompli. "Is he going to be here all summer—this new manager, I mean?"

"Most of it, I imagine. We have a lot of work to do."

Teddy made a sour face. She had known that this summer wouldn't be as peaceful and relaxing as past ones, but she had hoped they would have a few quiet weeks together before they were thrown into campaign preparations.

"Teddy, for my sake—because we need him—try to get along with him."

Teddy narrowed her eyes suspiciously. "And what makes you think that I won't get along with him?"

"Well, I suspect that you're already prejudiced against him, and I'm afraid that he's probably, ah, not your type."

"Oh?" Some very unpleasant images of the new manager were beginning to form in her mind. One of those blow-dried, wire-rimmed glasses, capped-teeth types, no doubt. The modern version of the snake-oil salesman.

"I'm not going to say anything more," her father sighed. "Just remember that we need his expertise."

"TEDD-EE!"

She continued to sit there, curled into the lee of a huge sand dune, invisible from land and barely noticeable from the sea.

"Tedd-ee!"

She got up reluctantly and dusted off the seat of her jeans. So much for solitude. Teddy had a feeling that that commodity wasn't going to be much in evidence this summer, and it was the thing she liked best about Matiscotta. A hundred or so people distributed on nearly a thousand acres left a lot of empty space, and islands had a lot of shoreline to wander.

Their unwanted—by her, at least—houseguest was due to arrive today. That was undoubtedly why her father was calling her, and certainly explained her slowness of response. She just didn't want a stranger staying here for the summer, crowding her space.

Her uncle's presence in the house would have been perfectly acceptable; he had often visited for part of the summer. But she was already disposed to look unfavorably upon this Graham McKinsey person. What on earth did a Graham McKinsey look like, anyway? Try as hard as she could, she couldn't quite put a face and body to that name, and therefore continued to expect the worst.

She clambered up to the top of the dune and waved at the figure walking along the beach. "Over here, Dad!"

Father and daughter met at a rocky outcropping near the boundary of their property.

"I was wondering if you could go over to pick up Graham. He just called to say that he'll be in Rockland in an hour and a half."

Teddy shrugged unenthusiastically. "I suppose so." Spitefully, she wondered if the man could swim, or if he might be subject to seasickness. She'd noticed some whitecaps out there today, thanks to a stiff breeze.

Ted Sothern flung an arm across his daughter's shoulders as they started back to the house. "Your enthusiasm underwhelms me. Don't let your nose get out of joint over this, Teddy. You do understand why I had to hire him, don't you?"

He waited for a response that didn't come, then went on. "It isn't just that I need someone with experience. I also don't want to hurt Jack Oldham's feelings. We haven't always seen eye to eye on things over the years, but he's a good friend and wants to help even though he knows that I'd oppose him on some issues if I win."

Teddy knew he was right. She'd heard some of those arguments over the years and had even taken part in some herself. But to the senator's credit, he appeared willing to put friendship ahead of politics. She smiled and hugged her father around the waist.

"I do understand, Dad, and I'll do my best to work amicably with Mr. McKinsey. You really do want this, don't you?"

He threw her a surprised look. "Didn't you think I did?"

"I wasn't sure, really. I mean, you were never all that interested in politics before—even though you like to argue it with the senator. But your decision still caught me by surprise and I guess I haven't quite adjusted to it."

Ted was quiet for a moment. "Well, I suppose it must have come as a surprise to you, but I had thought about it before. The company has gotten so big that it seems to run itself these days, and ever since I took it public, I just haven't felt the same about it. I needed something else—a new challenge."

"Well, to be honest, I never understood that, either. Your decision to take it public, I mean."

"Corporate finance isn't your field, honey. At a certain point, that almost becomes inevitable if a company is to continue growing."

He was probably right, but she didn't quite understand why that growth was necessary. And how many times had she heard him proclaim that he would never take it public, that he wanted to keep it manageable? Besides, why should that have made such a difference to him, in any event? After all, he continued to hold a majority of the stock.

She didn't ask any more questions because she sensed that he didn't really want to talk about it. As they walked back to the house arm in arm, Teddy mused about how little people actually know about those closest to them, even after a lifetime together. Perhaps in some perverse way, that very closeness prevented a deep understanding. Decisions such as these made her uneasy, as though this familiar and beloved figure might in some sense be a stranger to her. Was it possible that her father suffered from some inner turmoils about which she knew nothing?

A little over an hour later, she was maneuvering the boat expertly up to the dock in Rockland. She cut the engine and vaulted onto the pier to secure the lines, then glanced at her watch. He probably wasn't here yet, but she scanned the waterfront anyway. Her father had told her that McKinsey would recognize her, since he'd seen her photo when he'd visited his office. No one approached her, so she checked the parking lot and was about to return to the dock when she spotted a familiar figure about to enter the phone booth. He saw her at the same time, and they started toward each other, grinning.

"Alex! I thought you weren't coming up for another two weeks." Teddy was delighted to see her old friend and island neighbor.

"I decided that I needed a break now, not later. Are you going over?"

Teddy nodded. "As soon as Dad's new campaign manager arrives. Want a lift?"

"Yeah. I was just about to call the folks." He frowned. "I thought *you* were the new campaign manager."

"So did I," Teddy replied ruefully, then proceeded to explain to her old friend in no uncertain terms just how she felt about this usurper named Graham McKinsey.

GRAHAM PAID THE TAXI DRIVER, took his bags and set them down, then surveyed the dock area. He spotted her immediately. She had her back to him, but the odds were definitely against there being two redheads here at the same time.

He smiled at the cascade of coppery curls that billowed in the ocean breeze. Under ordinary circumstances he would have been looking forward to meeting Teddy Sothern. He'd had a special weakness for redheads ever since the age of eleven, when he'd fallen in love with the little redheaded girl who'd sat in front of him in school.

But he reminded himself that these were not ordinary circumstances, and he should be hoping that she was only visiting, rather than staying for the entire summer.

He picked up his bags and started toward her, wondering who the guy was with her. They were locked into an animated conversation and paying him no attention at all. He watched her vivacious gestures and thought that his initial impression from that photo had proved to be correct. Not even the formal pose of a studio portrait had been able to disguise that joie de vivre he'd sensed immediately.

"Looks like this must be your passenger, Teddy," Alex said as he peered back over her shoulder.

Teddy turned rather reluctantly, having temporarily forgotten all about Graham McKinsey. She squinted into the late afternoon sunlight and could see little more than a silhouette. Then she brought her sunglasses back down to her nose and took a better look as the man started out onto the pier. What began as a falsely welcoming smile changed instead to a slight frown.

He stopped a few feet away and set down his bags. "You must be Teddy." With what he hoped was discretion, Graham took in that long, lithe body that hadn't been a part of the photo. The sense of an opportunity missed was already bothering him and he hadn't even met her yet.

Teddy finally managed a grin and extended her hand. "Welcome to Maine, Mr. McKinsey. This is Alex Johns, one of our neighbors who's hitching a ride out with us."

His grip was firm and slightly calloused and sent something skittering through her briefly before she got herself under control again. Whatever she'd expected a Graham McKinsey to look like, it certainly hadn't been this. And neither had she been at all prepared for her disturbing reaction to him.

Graham turned to shake hands with the other man, certain that her reaction had matched his and knowing that he had no right to be so pleased about it. He also couldn't quite prevent that slight bristling of the predatory male sizing up possible competition.

"Well, let's be off," Teddy said briskly as she began to cast off the lines. "Those look like thunderheads moving in and there aren't any hatches to batten down on this boat."

Graham chuckled, a low, wholly masculine sound that reverberated annoyingly through her. Then he tossed his bags into the stern storage compartment and leaped in to take the front passenger seat.

Teddy slid into the pilot's seat rather self-consciously, having taken note of the athletic grace with which her guest moved. That irritating disturbance ran through her again. There was something entirely too male about Graham McKinsey. It was, she thought, a quality far more easily sensed than actually seen. It was also vaguely threatening, as though some sort of response in kind might be unwillingly dragged from her.

She started the engine and began to back away from the dock, stealing another glance at him as he turned sideways to talk to Alex, who had cast off the stern line and climbed into a rear seat.

Initially, she would have characterized his looks as being rather nondescript, but perhaps that had been too harsh a judgment. There was nothing really wrong: medium-brown hair that was slightly wavy, flecked with gold and definitely not blow-dried, a straight nose that might be just a bit too long, a wide mouth beneath a very attractive mustache, and a firm chin with just a hint of a dimple. He was wearing wire-rimmed sunglasses that hid his eyes, but she imagined them being a warm, dark brown.

Then there was that body: that was what lifted him way out of ordinariness. He was, she judged, just over six feet and wearing a well-tailored suit whose easy lines had disguised a lean, hard body beneath. Teddy had become accustomed to the tricks of good tailoring that could hide all but the worst defects, and therefore it had come as somewhat of a shock to learn that in the case of Graham McKinsey, no such defects existed.

No muscles bulged anywhere, but there was just no doubting that this was a man in peak physical condition. His unhesitating leap into the boat had reminded her of TV adventurers who were forever vaulting into cars that way. How was it that a political campaign manager could behave like this?

She guessed that he was probably in his late thirties, an age Teddy privately regarded as being the very best for a man. Before that, they often seemed rather unfinished, and after that, it was usually just a long slide into paunchy, balding middle age. She rather wished that he'd already begun that slide.

She told herself that curiosity about a man with whom she would be working closely and who would, furthermore, be sharing her home for the summer was quite natural, but she sensed that in this particular case that interest bordered on the unseemly. All her antennae seemed to be aquiver, and she was already mentally cataloguing her defects of the moment: messy hair, no makeup, a tattered old sweatshirt.

The simple truth was that she would have preferred to have found the obnoxious, glad-handing, blow-dried type she'd been expecting. Not that she wanted to spend the summer with a creep, but at least it would have made things a lot simpler. As it was, she was already being forced to deal with an elemental awareness of him—an inner response over which she seemed to have no control. In short, Graham

McKinsey was already spelling trouble and they weren't even on Matiscotta yet.

"Will you be spending the summer here, Teddy?" The object of her thoughts inquired suddenly as he shifted his gaze and caught her staring at him.

Teddy was doubly startled: first, because he had caught her staring at him and she feared he might have tuned into her thoughts, and secondly, because she'd assumed that he was already aware of her role in the campaign. What had her father told him . . . or *not* told him?

"Yes," she answered, returning her attention to the water and at the same time edging the boat's speed toward recklessness. "I'll be working on the campaign, too."

She missed the brief flicker that would have told her of his displeasure at that news. "You teach political science, don't you?"

She nodded without turning. "But I've taken a semester's leave to help Dad. After Uncle John's death, I thought he could use my help."

Graham detected a certain bitterness in her tone, but he didn't know if it was the result of her uncle's violent death or because his own arrival on the scene cast her into a lesser role than she had planned. His brief reading of Teddy told him that she was unaccustomed to anything other than the starring role. He decided that his problems were multiplying even before he had landed on the island. Without much hope—and with considerable regret—he wondered if he could get rid of her.

"Have you ever worked on a political campaign before?" he inquired.

"Yes," she responded with a trace of defensiveness. "Two years ago I volunteered in a congressional campaign."

"Whose?"

"Ellen Stone, in Connecticut. She lost." Teddy's tone hadn't changed.

"She lost because she wasn't aggressive enough, among other things," Graham pronounced. "Politics is a game where nice guys really do finish last, even if they're women."

"If she'd been more aggressive, the press and the voters would have labeled her a pushy woman."

"Some might," Graham admitted. "I know that it's hard for a woman to find that balance."

"Well, it shouldn't be," Teddy replied indignantly, speeding up to the point where Graham began to wonder for the first time about her piloting skills.

"I don't deal with what should be," he shouted above the racket of the straining engine. "I deal with what is. And you'll have to do the same if you expect to help your father."

She turned briefly to him, those remarkable blue eyes blazing. "Is this supposed to be my first lesson in politics, Mr. McKinsey?"

His response to that quick flash of anger was a slight smile that skewed his mustache. Idealism and fire, he thought: a potent combination.

"Since we're going to be spending a lot of time together, I suggest that we dispense with the formalities. I'm Graham and you're Teddy. Is that all right with you?"

She gave him a quick look and a brief nod that told him eloquently that nothing was all right at the moment, and she didn't expect it to get any better, either.

Graham shifted in his seat to resume his conversation with Alex, but his gaze flicked from time to time to the woman beside him, who was now studiously ignoring him. Teddy Sothern wore her emotions for all the world to see; that much was already very clear. At the moment, he could feel the hostility emanating from her and could see it in the rigid set of her body as she concentrated on breaking the sound barrier.

Congratulations, fella, he told himself ruefully. *Ten minutes with her and you've already got her hating you.* He knew he should be pleased about that since it might prompt her to leave, but all he felt was a sharp twinge of regret.

Teddy was thinking that it was a pretty safe assumption that they weren't hitting it off too well. He must certainly have gotten the message that she wasn't exactly thrilled with either his presence or his philosophy. Furthermore, something told her that he wasn't overjoyed at the prospect of working with her, either. Did that mean that he considered her to be a threat? She rather hoped so, because that was just what she intended to be.

Graham McKinsey might have arrived in a sexy package, but he still didn't fool her one bit. He was exactly what she'd feared he would be: the cynical professional politician. No doubt he'd try to push her father in whatever direction the prevailing political winds were blowing. It was very easy to see why Senator Oldham had recommended him.

She fully intended to fight him, but she didn't make the mistake of thinking it would be easy. Her father had already decided that Graham McKinsey was indispensable to the campaign, and the man himself showed no indication that he'd be a pushover. All that self-assuredness signaled a man who generally got what he wanted.

They docked in town and Teddy was once more treated to a display of that athletic grace as he leaped out of the boat to help secure the lines. She would have preferred to see him fall into the water.

Alex went across to the store to check in with the locals—registering, he called it—and after both men's bags had been stashed in the back of the Volvo, Teddy stood there in a self-conscious silence with Graham, hoping that Alex wouldn't be too long. The less time she spent alone with this man, the better, as far as she was concerned.

Perhaps he sensed her discomfort, because he began to ask questions about the island, which she answered with formal politeness. Alex returned before that topic was exhausted and they all piled into the wagon. Teddy carried on a gossipy conversation with Alex and ignored Graham completely until they had deposited Alex at his home.

"Our house is just down the road," she told Graham as she backed down the driveway. The statement was actually made to reassure herself that she wouldn't have to be alone with him for very long.

"Is your father at home?"

"Yes."

"Then pull over here for a minute."

Teddy was so startled that she briefly lifted her foot from the accelerator before she realized what she was doing. "Why?"

"Because I think we should talk now while we have the chance."

She pressed on the accelerator again as an uneasiness stole over her. "I'm sure we'll have plenty of time to talk later."

"Pull over, Teddy."

It was an improbable order cloaked in velvet softness and she hesitated again. Then her curiosity got the better of her resentment and she eased the wagon off the road before turning to face him with a determinedly cool expression.

"All right. What is it that you want to talk about?"

"Had you planned to run your father's campaign?"

Once more Teddy hesitated—this time because she was beginning to see how her behavior thus far must appear to him. "Yes, I had. Otherwise I wouldn't have taken a semester's leave. Uncle John had things already set up and I felt that I could handle it. But then Senator Oldham forced *you* on Dad." She made no attempt to hide her disgust at that turn of events, her promise to her father notwithstanding.

"The senator didn't force me on your father, Teddy," Graham replied in a quietly reasonable tone. "He simply recommended me because I have the necessary experience."

"Dad didn't want to offend him," Teddy persisted, annoyed at his failure to rise to the bait she was proffering.

"You're an only child, aren't you?" he asked.

"Yes, but what does that have to do—" She stopped and threw him a disgusted look. "Knock it off, Graham. I'm not a spoiled Daddy's girl. I'm a busy professional who has made a sacrifice and then discovered that perhaps it wasn't really necessary. I have nothing against you personally...yet." She gave him a look that told him she fully expected that to change in the very near future.

Graham's response to all this was another annoying smile that made her forget again about her promise to her father.

"Anyway, if you're so good, why weren't you already working on someone else's campaign? I know the senator isn't up this time, but there must have been plenty of other candidates you could be working for."

"I'd decided to take some time off to do other things," he replied levelly. "Mainly some writing."

"About what?" Teddy couldn't picture him as a writer any more than she could see him as a campaign manager.

"Politics. What else?" Then he gave her that half smile again. "Don't worry, Teddy. I'm good."

She put the wagon into gear. "Well, I guess we'll just have to see about that, won't we? For Dad's sake, you'd better be right."

Chapter Two

They faced each other across the width of the kitchen, each of them armed with a glass of orange juice. Those of a military bent might say that the battle hadn't yet been joined, but there had indeed been skirmishes of the kind designed to test the opponent's strengths—and weaknesses.

Graham McKinsey had been a resident in the Sothern household for five days, which was about five days longer than Teddy would have preferred. In that time, she had learned that he was highly intelligent and well-read and that he possessed a keen, sardonic sense of humor not unlike her own. Teddy liked those qualities; in fact, they were right up there at the top of her list.

Furthermore, she had already given up trying to deny to herself that Graham McKinsey was indeed very attractive. He exuded virility the way lesser men give off waves of seductive cologne. Normally, Teddy found such men totally unappealing, since they generally suffered from the exaggerated machismo mentality of a Rambo. But much as she might have wanted to fit Graham into that mold, she couldn't quite manage it. His machismo—if indeed it could be called that—was unstudied, unaffected, disturbingly real. Or so it appeared to her at this point.

But—and it was a very big but—Graham carried pragmatism to new heights, virtually turning it into an art form. In five days of increasingly desperate searching, Teddy had yet to discover one iota of idealism in him. It was becoming abundantly clear to her why the senator had recommended him so highly. And it was becoming equally clear that this combination of assets and liabilities spelled disaster.

Graham had accepted the glass of orange juice she'd handed him, suspecting that she would have preferred to throw it at him. His ruse was working, to the extent that she obviously disliked him. But he doubted that it would have the desired result of sending her away. Neither could he bring himself to be too upset about that, even if it did make things much more difficult.

Teddy was disconcerting, even to a normally unflappable man like Graham. Many times during these past five days she had pinned him with those remarkable blue eyes and virtually demanded that he open his soul to her. She seemed to be prodding at him, seeking inconsistencies, seeking the truth behind the lies—and thereby forcing him to retreat even further from the truth.

She was one hell of a woman; there was no doubt about that. There was nothing halfway about Teddy Sothern. He had long since forgotten that brief impression—or perhaps hope—that she was nothing more than a spoiled brat. Everything about her pleased a man who had always been very discriminating about women—often with the unfortunate result of long periods of celibacy.

He liked her mind and the quick flashes of humor that he suspected would be even more frequent if he wasn't there. She had a nimble brain and a quick tongue, although use of the latter sometimes preceded use of the former. Still, even that lent her an insouciant charm that he thoroughly enjoyed.

She also continued to please his eyes, which were never far from her for long. Teddy wasn't really beautiful, but it took intense concentration to notice that fact. What she was was vibrant.

Her features were unremarkable, except for those brilliant-blue eyes and that tangle of red-gold curls. Of course, there was also that generous, vulnerable mouth, to which his attention was constantly being drawn by her habit of chewing on her lower lip when she was thinking. He could very easily imagine himself doing the same thing, just as he could imagine that firm, nicely curved body beneath the baggy clothes she nearly always wore. She obviously wasn't one to flaunt what she had—and he liked that, too.

"I don't suppose that it will come as a shock to you that I disagree with your approach to the campaign," Teddy said as she drained her juice glass and set it in the sink.

"I pride myself on being rather discerning in such matters," he responded, doing the same.

She gave him that uncomfortably direct stare for a moment before turning her attention to the coffee maker. "Well, I guess it shouldn't come as a shock to me that politics is a dirty business. But it doesn't have to be that way. Ellen Stone didn't run that kind of campaign."

"Ellen Stone lost," he stated bluntly. "You're an idealist, Teddy. The time for nobility doesn't come until after the election. If it comes at all, that is."

"'The end justifies the means,'" she quoted disgustedly. "I just can't accept that."

"The man who said it first was a master of the game. As a professor of political science, you know that. And I know you can't accept it. That's why you teach theory instead of practicing the game."

The fact that he was undoubtedly right did nothing at all to improve Teddy's disposition at the moment. So she decided to attack from a different angle.

"Why is it necessary to bring in that image maker?" Distaste was evident in every syllable as she glared at him. "Dad's image is just fine as it is. He's a highly successful businessman and he's always been very civic-minded. He doesn't need any gloss."

"That's for Jacobsen to decide. He knows his business. And image is all-important these days. The White House has proved that beyond a shadow of a doubt."

"You are easily the most cynical person I've ever met," she pronounced disgustedly as she poured the coffee. "Furthermore, I haven't yet heard you express opinions of your own on any subject."

"My opinions aren't important. I'm not running for office."

"But you must have opinions, Graham," she persisted as she handed him some coffee. She knew she was still probing for that elusive quality of idealism.

"Of course I have opinions, but they don't count here. What counts is getting your father elected."

She decided to try another tack in her foolish quest. "Would you work for someone whose opinions you disagreed with?"

He shrugged. "I have, although the disagreements weren't really fundamental."

Teddy was ashamed of herself for grasping at even the smallest hint of principles. She forged on, irritably aware of the fact that he seemed to find all this vaguely amusing.

"But why won't you at least tell me your opinions?"

"Because you won't like some of them and then we'll be at loggerheads even more than we are now," he replied with a smile. "It won't help your father for us to be fighting all the time, Teddy, however interesting it might be."

The slight inflection on that last phrase brought Teddy's head up sharply. He was leaning casually against the counter, but the intensity of his dark eyes belied that easy posture. She met his gaze for just long enough to assure herself that she'd accepted his subtle, unspecified challenge, then looked away.

So he knew what she knew: despite their almost constant bickering—or perhaps even partly because of it—something disturbingly sensual had begun between them. It could be found in a glance such as this, or in a self-conscious movement, or in a subtle relaxation when one or the other left the room.

Teddy considered briefly the possibility of bringing that challenge out into the open, then decided against it. Instead, she picked up her coffee and a danish and took herself off to the screened porch, assuming that he would join her father in his study.

Teddy could feel her body begin to relax as she settled down at the table on the porch. Graham's presence in this household was a torment to her, preventing the relaxation she had always associated with summer on Matiscotta. Day by day, she became frustrated. There were all those things about him that she liked very much, and yet there was also the cynicism she couldn't stand. It was, she thought, rather like finding a dress that was perfect in color and style and then discovering that it just didn't fit.

That analogy seemed uniquely appropriate. Something about Graham McKinsey just didn't fit, either. Very shortly after his arrival, she'd had a fleeting but powerful impression that he was an impostor. It was absurd, of course, and undoubtedly the result of his failure to live up to her worst expectations. He was obviously experienced and besides, he'd been personally recommended by Senator Oldham.

She sipped her coffee and continued to think about him. She didn't like his attitudes, but she was being ever more powerfully drawn to him. The next few months could be unpleasant indeed if she had to spend them in the throes of a tug-of-war between her mind and her body. But she quickly soothed herself with the thought that the attraction would surely wear off in time. And in the meantime she could certainly handle it.

Inside the house, Graham started toward Ted Sothern's study, then paused when he saw Teddy out on the porch, where a ray of sunlight bathed her head in a burnished coppery glow. He glanced toward the study. Business beckoned, but at the moment pleasure beckoned even more strongly. He'd never before permitted the two to coexist. Of course, in his profession, that hadn't been difficult. Until now.

Knowing that he was making a mistake in encouraging something that couldn't be finished, he still found his feet carrying him toward the porch.

Teddy swung her curly head around briefly as he came up behind her and then sat down opposite her. It happened again, that little frisson of awareness. She tried hard to ignore him.

"You know," Graham said, oblivious of her attempt, "it might be a good idea for us to get away from work for a while. Why don't we take the afternoon off and you can show me around the island?"

Teddy swung her gaze to him suspiciously. "You don't have to humor me, Graham. I couldn't get you fired, anyway. If I thought I could, I'd have done so by now."

He laughed in that low, quiet way that she alternately found endearing and irritating. "I'm not really concerned about that. Let me phrase it differently. I'd very much like to have you show me around the island."

She hesitated, wondering just what his game was now. Besides, their bickering at least provided a framework for their relationship, and she wasn't at all certain that she wanted to step outside that framework.

"You wouldn't need a guide. It's impossible to get lost on Matiscotta. And in any event, there's really nothing to see, unless you happen to like deserted beaches and pine forests and birds."

"I do."

Teddy snorted. "You don't look like the nature-loving type to me, Graham."

He made an exaggerated gesture of helplessness. "See? That's just what I mean. We don't really know each other apart from our disagreements over politics. For all you know, I could be the type who spends every weekend with binoculars dangling from my neck, out looking for the elusive yellow-bellied sapsucker."

She laughed in that manner that so delighted him because it made her whole being come even more alive. "Okay, you win. If Dad doesn't need us this afternoon, we'll explore the island."

THEY HAD WALKED only a short distance along the gravel road when the afternoon silence was broken by a noisy old pickup truck. They moved to the side of the road to make way and the driver, Amos Moody rolled to a stop alongside them and greeted Teddy cheerfully, then peered closely at Graham.

"Snuck one in on us, did you, Teddy?" he asked in his downeast accent.

Teddy quickly realized that this was a continuation of their conversation at the store about her lack of a man.

Outwardly at ease, she laughed and introduced the two men. But inwardly, there was a certain unease about being linked with Graham, however jokingly.

The situation was pretty bad, she thought as the two men talked, when a teasing remark could produce such a reaction. And yet, there it was.

Finally, Amos's truck rumbled off down the road and Graham stared after it, then turned to her with a grin. "Now *that* is what I call local color."

Teddy laughed. "Amos takes a proprietary interest in this island and all its inhabitants. Since he actually carried on a conversation with you, I guess you must be acceptable. If he doesn't like someone, all he says is 'ayuh' to everything."

"What was that remark about your sneaking me in?" Graham asked as they continued along the road.

"Oh, Amos thinks that I should have found a man by now. He waits every summer for me to show up with someone." Teddy managed to keep her tone light.

"And you never have? Brought anyone here, I mean?"

"No, I like to be alone here. I have my fill of a social life at home." Luckily at that moment she saw the path she wanted and gestured to it as a means of derailing this particular conversation.

"We'll leave the road here and I'll show you my favorite spot on the island."

Graham followed her but refused to accept the change in conversational topics. "Isn't there anyone in your life now?"

"No," Teddy said in a tone she hoped would end the discussion.

"Why not?" He persisted, showing again his stubbornness could easily match hers.

"Because knights in shining armor don't come along all that often."

"That's true enough," Graham agreed. "Beautiful princesses don't come along very often, either."

Their eyes met and they both laughed. But there was no doubting that something more serious lay beneath that laughter. A first step had been taken: an admission that they were both free. Even as both of them denied it to themselves, they were pleased.

They climbed uphill through a thick forest redolent of pine and the tang of salt air. The sunlight barely penetrated the heavy forest, resulting in a dimness that was almost like twilight. That semidarkness and the utter stillness around them seemed to heighten further their awareness of each other.

They stayed apart, sensing the importance of that distance between them. There was a self-consciousness in each step they took and an attempt to deny it through small talk. Teddy half tripped over an exposed root she hadn't seen and Graham was almost struck by a low branch that had escaped his attention.

Teddy nearly sighed aloud in relief when they finally broke out into the open at the top of the hill, leaving behind that verdant intimacy. She strode quickly to the very edge of the rocky outcropping and made a sweeping gesture as she turned to Graham.

Below them, at the base of a sheer, rocky cliff, lay a fringe of forest and rock-strewn beach, and an endless expanse of water. None of the island's houses was visible from this vantage point, which added to the primitive beauty of the scene.

Graham came up to stand beside her on the small, flat space, close enough so that his elbow brushed against her arm as he pushed his hands into the pockets of his jeans. Teddy recoiled slightly from his touch, then hoped that he hadn't noticed.

She watched him as he stared in silence at the scene and wondered if he could truly appreciate it or if he was, as she had earlier stated, just not the nature-loving type. She had to admit, though, that he seemed to be very much in his element, standing there in jeans and sweater with the wind ruffling his hair. A rugged man in a rugged land, she thought. He looked more at home than she did.

Then he turned to her and smiled. Teddy returned the smile, but somewhat uncertainly. For just a moment, it seemed to her that the mask of cynicism he wore most of the time had slipped, permitting her a brief glimpse of a persona he had kept hidden. And perhaps he sensed that he might have given too much away, because he turned away abruptly and gestured to the right below them.

"What's that dock over there for? I don't see any house."

Teddy followed his gaze, already wondering if she'd imagined that brief change in him. "There isn't a house there anymore. If you look closely near the edge of the woods, you can just make out a corner of the foundation. The house burned several years ago, probably as the result of a lightning strike during a spring storm. I understand that the family has put the property up for sale. Probably relatives of an island family will buy it. It's a nice property—the most isolated on the island."

Teddy knew that she was probably giving him more information than he'd wanted, but she couldn't seem to stop babbling. Running through her brain at the moment were some perplexing questions. Was there more to this man that she'd seen thus far? And if there was, why was he taking such pains to hide it?

As they stood there, looking down at the lonely dock, a figure appeared, walking out from the woods and testing the pier gingerly before going out onto it. Graham frowned.

"That looks like your father."

Teddy had already recognized the familiar sweatsuit-clad figure. She'd bought him two stylish warmup suits, but he, like Graham, continued to wear the old regulation gray sweats.

"It is Dad. He's probably out for a bike ride. I'm glad that he's back to his exercise regime. It's a good sign. For a while there, I was worried about him."

"What do you mean?" Graham asked.

Teddy shrugged. "Well, as you probably know, my mother died just a little over a year ago. He handled her death well at first—better than I did, actually—but I guess it just caught up with him later, that's all. I spent that summer here with him and he seemed to be okay, but by last fall, it must have hit him because he became so...sort of distant and distracted a lot of the time. I went up to see him on weekends regularly and a lot of the time I wasn't even sure that he wanted me there."

She paused, chewing at her lower lip as she watched her father, who stood with his back to them as he stared out to sea.

"At Christmas he announced his intention to run for the senate, and I decided that that must have been what was on his mind. But even after that he seemed distracted a lot of the time. And I still don't really understand his decision to get into politics. He'd never seemed all that interested before, except as an observer."

She looked away from her father and gave Graham a rueful smile. "Sometimes I wonder just how well I know him, even after all these years. I remember Mom's saying the same thing when he decided to take the company public. That really shocked us, since he'd sworn that he'd never do it."

"Why did he?"

"He said it was because he needed to raise capital, but that didn't make sense to either of us because Mom had plenty of money and would have put it all into the company if he'd let her."

Graham absorbed all this without comment, then asked, "I take it that you have no interest in the company yourself?"

"If you mean a financial interest, yes, I do. There's stock in my name. I've had some since I turned eighteen, and then more was transferred to me when Mom died. In theory, I'm on the board."

"In theory?"

"I refused to attend any board meetings. As long as the company sells to that five-sided funny farm on the Potomac, I won't have anything to do with it."

"You mean the Pentagon?" Graham asked with a smile.

Teddy nodded. "Under the terms of the stock bequests, I can't sell it—except to Dad. And he refused to buy it. So I refuse to attend board meetings. Stalemate."

"The company is making an important contribution to national defense, Teddy," Graham said placatingly.

"So I'm told," she responded dryly. "But a microelectronics company doesn't *have* to sell to the Pentagon. They could be making that contribution to peace, instead of to war."

"A strong defense is the best possible contribution to peace."

"Aha!" Teddy exclaimed. "That's the first political opinion I've heard you express, Graham. And you were right. I don't like your opinions. You sound just like Dad."

Graham chuckled. "You two must have some real arguments."

"Oh, we do indeed. According to him, I've been arguing with him ever since I learned to talk." She gave Graham a wry grin, then looked down to see her father disappearing back into the woods.

"But I love him anyway," she went on.

Graham said nothing, but unconsciously he began to edge away from her. It had been a mistake to spend any more time than was necessary with her. He was only tormenting himself, and thanks to this father she loved, she would one day truly hate him.

Teddy cast a sidelong glance at Graham as he moved away from her. Once again, she could sense that something had shifted in his mood. It seemed strange to her, because he just didn't seem like the moody type. In fact, there was a reassuring solidity to Graham that she'd seen from the beginning.

"We'd better be heading back," he said rather abruptly as he started back toward the path.

Teddy hesitated, then followed him silently. She wanted to know what was troubling him, but she felt certain that he would brush off the question. It was mysterious, she thought, how she could sense subtle shifts in his moods, even though the man himself remained more or less a stranger to her.

But I want to know him, she said to herself as she stared at his broad back. *I must find out what makes this man tick.*

The descent was steep in places and made even more difficult by the wet ground. Graham went ahead to find the surest footing. Teddy followed, paying less attention than she should have to the terrain as she wondered if she was becoming obsessed with him.

Suddenly, some stones rolled beneath her foot and she began to skid in the mud. Before the startled cry had even left her lips, he had whipped around and grabbed for her, taking her full weight as she hurtled forward.

Teddy was stunned: first, by her near fall, and secondly, by the speed with which he had prevented it. There was something almost frightening about his lightning-quick re- action, almost, she thought briefly, as though he were ac- customed to a life filled with sudden danger.

They stood there at eye level because she was on higher ground. He had grasped her about the waist, and now con- tinued to hold her. She was still gripping his arms and rest- ing against one muscled thigh. Neither of them seemed able, or inclined, to move.

The moment passed when she might have thanked him or they could have simply laughed it off. Indecision hovered in the charged atmosphere. Five days of sharing the same house and working together had certainly made him less of a stranger to her, but these few hours today had somehow reversed that process. She was certain that he wanted to kiss her, but was hesitating for some unknown reason. Teddy wondered about that. Up to this point, Graham had seemed to be unshakably sure of himself, and she knew full well that she was scarcely indicating that she wanted to keep him at a distance. Not at this moment anyway.

Nervously, she gnawed at her lower lip, drawing his gaze there immediately. His fingertips dug briefly into her waist, and then he shifted, moving his leg away from her. Teddy quickly took a few steps away from him, caught between relief and regret. She waited for some flippant remark from him, then wondered if he might be waiting for the same from her. Certainly neither of them had yet been at a loss for words in each other's presence.

But they were now. She finally managed to murmur her thanks after he inquired solicitously if she was all right. They quickly continued on their way, making awkward at- tempts at further conversation.

Teddy's curiosity was growing by leaps and bounds. Just who and what was Graham McKinsey? How could she reconcile the self-assured man with the hesitant one who had failed to seize the opportunity presented?

Teddy knew darn well that he found her attractive. She hadn't reached the age of thirty without gaining that sort of knowledge. Furthermore, she also knew that she had just sent out some signals of her own.

So where, she wondered, did they go from here? That they would indeed go somewhere, she had no doubt.

But if Teddy had no doubts, Graham had enough for them both. From the beginning, it hadn't been easy to keep his attraction to her under control, but he hadn't realized just how tenuous that control was until an unforeseen incident had very nearly shattered it.

Then too, perhaps he'd been counting on her to keep them apart. If so, he knew now he could forget about that. In that moment when he'd held her, she had wanted just what he'd wanted. Graham let himself enjoy that knowledge for a few moments, then began to worry again.

More than once in the past few days, he'd had the uncomfortable feeling that she was seeing right through his carefully calculated cynicism. Incapable of dissembling herself, Teddy seemed to have the ability to spot it quickly in others—and his whole mission here was based on deceit.

Graham McKinsey was nervous. A long, notably successful career seemed to be hanging by a thread, a thread controlled by a very desirable redhead who seemed capable of penetrating his very soul.

They walked back to the house talking about safe things: island flora and fauna, the history of her mother's family on the island, their respective travels. Such carefully casual conversation was important to them both because it put them back into their previous roles of two strangers thrown together by force of circumstances. They outdid each other with polite questions and amusing anecdotes.

But all the while, beneath the oh-so-careful casualness, an inexorable force was growing. Although both of them tried hard to ignore it, neither of them succeeded.

A short while later, Teddy again watched Graham slip into the role of tough politician. And she thought of it as being just that: a role. It annoyed her to think that she might be seeking so desperately to believe there was more to this man. Deceiving herself had never been her style.

As she half listened to him discuss the key issues with her father, she studied the latest polling results that showed Connecticut voters' opinions. One result caught her attention immediately, and she interrupted their discussion, waving the sheaf of printouts at them.

"Look at this! The survey shows that nearly half of the voters support nuclear disarmament. And when you add in the undecided, it's more than a majority. There's no need to soft-pedal that issue."

Graham shook his head. "First of all, the way the question is worded was misleading, so the results are suspect as far as I'm concerned. And secondly, Ted will leave himself open to charges of hypocrisy because he built his fortune on defense contracts. Besides, as I told you before, Teddy, defense-related industry is a major source of income in Connecticut. If Ellen Stone had remembered that, she might have won. People are very willing to sound noble to pollsters, but it's a different matter if they think their livelihoods are being threatened."

"But—"

He shook his head more firmly. "Forget it, Teddy. We're not touching that issue, except in the vaguest possible way. Ted's most likely opponent is strong on defense, and we can't afford to sound weak.

"I know that Ted plans to have you make some campus appearances on his behalf, but if you're going to get up there and start spouting disarmament, we'll just have to forget about it."

Teddy bristled. "I'm getting pretty damned tired of your brand of pragmatism, Graham. Especially since I don't believe one word of it."

For one instant, she was sure that she had struck a nerve. But that glimpse of vulnerability she thought she'd seen transformed itself quickly into his familiar, cynical half smile. They glared at each other until Ted Sothern moved in to ease the tension.

"Graham's right, honey. It's a divisive issue, and I would sound like a hypocrite."

"But you agree with me," Teddy protested. "You said so just the other day, before *he* got here." She sent Graham a withering look that he met with bland indifference.

"I *do* agree with you. Up to a point. But I also said that we have to negotiate from a position of strength."

"We're already muscle-bound," Teddy said disgustedly. "All those billions and billions of dollars wasted while—"

"I think we'd better forget about those appearances of yours," Graham interrupted calmly, without bothering to look up from the clipboard upon which he was making notes. "You're a loose cannon."

"And you're a cynical bastard," Teddy snapped at him as she flung herself out of her chair and stalked toward the terrace doors.

The brief silence behind her was ended by Graham's low chuckle. Infuriated, Teddy yanked the sliding door open and went out into the cool night. It was all just as she had feared. Senator Oldham, that master of obfuscation, had sent his henchman to turn her father into one of his own kind. And it was working.

When she heard the conversation resume behind her, she started to go back, then stopped and finally turned to the path that led down to the beach. The night was cool and she wasn't dressed for it, but at the moment, it felt good. She was very close to her boiling point and would surely reach it if she went back in there now.

In the living room Graham watched her start toward them, then abruptly head toward the beach. He had to restrain himself from getting up to follow her. He'd wanted to antagonize her; he'd certainly accomplished his goal. Provoking Teddy was rapidly becoming the only way he could keep them apart. But lying to her was becoming an increasingly risky business. She didn't just see through him; she saw into him. He looked back at Ted to find the older man smiling at him.

"I guess I don't need to tell you that Teddy has the proverbial redhead's temperament. And you struck a nerve. She's been involved in the disarmament movement for years. She won't even have anything to do with the company for that reason."

Graham just nodded. He knew all that, of course, which was exactly why he'd chosen that particular issue.

"She's never been one to hide her feelings, either, or to consider the consequences of her actions, for that matter," Ted went on in a tone that bespoke great affection for his daughter. "Her mother and I always thought that it might have been best we didn't have any other children. Teddy has been more than enough."

Graham smiled, but it was no more than a polite facade. He'd already had ample evidence of the love between father and daughter, and a surge of uncharacteristic self-pity washed over him as Ted got up and walked over to the terrace door.

"If I know her, she'll sit down there on the beach fuming over this until she catches cold."

TEDDY WAS INDEED feeling the cold by now, and she was still fuming. A "loose cannon," was she? Graham had to know that she'd never do anything to jeopardize her father's election.

Then, as she slowly began to calm down, she wondered if those words might have been a deliberate provocation. She mulled over that possibility as she sat there, only partially sheltered from the chill ocean wind.

Damn him anyway, she thought disgustedly. He was just taking up too much space in her life. She had far better things to do than to spend her time trying to understand a man who was deliberately being obtuse.

"Teddy!"

Guiltily, she jumped up. "Over here, Dad!"

Her father came up to her, his normally pleasant features etched with concern. "You'll catch cold out here, dressed like that."

"Better to catch cold out here than to boil over in there," she replied with a rueful grin.

"You and Graham aren't exactly hitting it off, are you?" he asked dryly.

"Not exactly," she admitted in the same tone even as images of that afternoon flitted through her mind. "But don't worry. I'll patch things up with him—even if I would rather pop him one."

Ted smiled at his daughter and flung an arm across her shoulders as the two of them started back toward the house. "He knows his business, Teddy. That's what counts."

"You like him, don't you?" she asked curiously.

"Yes, I do. But I suspect that he may be more of a man's man than the type women usually go for."

Teddy found that assessment interesting. "And exactly what is a 'man's man'?"

"Oh, that's kind of difficult to describe. What I meant was that he's the kind of man most other men would feel comfortable with."

"And women might feel threatened by?" Teddy finished.

Ted laughed and squeezed her shoulder. "Some women, maybe, but not you."

Teddy prudently changed the subject. "Dad, I want to make those campus appearances for you. And you know I wouldn't do or say anything that would cause problems for you. Are you going to let him stop me?"

"He wasn't serious, honey; he was just making his point. Graham's inclined to be a bit blunt at times."

"Tell me about it."

"But then, so are you." He grinned.

Teddy laughed and hugged him. "And that's why you're not getting any closer to grandfatherhood."

"I can wait. Any man who's put off by your honesty isn't a man I'd want for a son-in-law, anyway."

"You could look at it this way," Teddy teased. "When you do finally have a grandchild, he or she could turn out to be another holy terror like me."

Her father groaned loudly. "Do you remember the time you 'painted' the stairs—carpeting and all?"

Unfortunately, Teddy did.

"I had painted that one wall in your mother's and my bedroom that blue shade she loved so much, and made the mistake of going downstairs and not taking the paint with me. You wanted to be helpful, so you painted part of another wall, then started to carry the paint can downstairs and it slipped and spilled the whole way down the steps, on the new wall-to-wall carpeting your mother had just had installed.''

"I never did like that carpeting." Teddy grinned. "It was the color of mud."

"For good reason," her father reminded her with a chuckle.

They were both laughing when they walked into the living room, where Graham still sat on the sofa, scribbling on his clipboard. Before he could do anything more than look up at them questioningly, Teddy went over to him, bent down and gave him a quick kiss on the cheek. The pleasant tickle of his mustache still lingered on her cheek as she turned to her father.

"See? I told you that I'd kiss and make up."

She turned back to Graham, knowing that she'd caught him by surprise and thoroughly enjoying that fact. He gave her a slow, lazy smile.

"Just imagine what I can look forward to when we really get into it," he drawled.

Chapter Three

Graham's feet pounded rhythmically on the packed wet sand. He was later than usual this morning because he'd been up late the night before. The sun was already burning off the remnants of the morning mist and promising the warmest day yet.

He reached the end of the strip of sand in front of the house and broke his stride to vault over some rocks near the shoreline. The beach wasn't really a good place for a serious runner because there were no really long, unbroken stretches of sand, but he enjoyed it anyway, considering it to be more of an obstacle course than a track. Although there was less reason now to keep himself in peak physical condition, he still enjoyed testing his agility and endurance. He also admitted unhappily that he needed such diversions just now.

Dedication to his work hadn't kept him up late last night. Or perhaps in an unusual sense, it had. He still couldn't shake from his mind that portrait of father and daughter when they'd come back from the beach. A mission that had seemed only a short time ago to be so clear-cut had become entangled in a web of emotions that had denied him sleep long into the night. And then, when he'd finally fallen asleep, he'd tossed and turned with dreams that alternated between ugly nightmares and erotic fantasies.

The nightmares he'd dismissed upon awakening this morning, but the fantasies lingered on, tormenting him still. Teddy was just so damned desirable in every way. He was shocked at the depth of his feelings on the basis of such a brief acquaintance. In the past, he'd occasionally met women who'd turned him on immediately, but that had been physical and nothing more. This was more.

He found himself noticing the smallest, most inconsequential things about her: that habit of chewing her lower lip, the way her coppery curls were flattened on one side in the morning, even the way she curled herself into her favorite living room chair.

Not that he overlooked the more obvious things, of course. There was that lithe body that moved always with self-assuredness, but not too much self-awareness. And that quick wit that sometimes—like last night—caught him off guard and seemed to demand that he match it.

But most of all, there were the quicksilver, ever-changing moods of a woman who didn't know the meaning of dissembling. Teddy Sothern stared at the world from those remarkable blue eyes and told it quite firmly that it had better learn to accept what it saw. She challenged him, delighted him—and haunted his every moment.

The supreme irony, he thought bitterly: after years of searching, he might well have found the one woman he truly wanted—and she was the one woman he could never have.

Should he take himself out of this now? That question had been hammering at him for the past few days. He could do it, even if it would cost him dearly, but what good would it do, really? Eventually, she would learn the truth and the end result would be the same.

Despite his exercise and the warmth of the day, Graham felt a bone-deep coldness settling in for a long, long stay. Even for a man accustomed to being alone, this was a particularly sharp-edged loneliness.

Ahead of him lay another obstacle course of dark rocks, beyond which he knew was a wide strip of sand. Seeking to rid himself of his morose thoughts, he vaulted up onto the highest of the rocks, spun around in midair and vaulted down again onto the sand—to encounter two small boys who were staring at him with openmouthed admiration. He grinned at them rather sheepishly and guessed immediately what was running through their minds. They probably thought he was Superman in a sweatsuit.

"Do me a favor and don't try that, okay? It takes a lot of practice on something softer than rocks."

The older of the pair, whom Graham judged to be about eight or nine, finally managed to find his voice. "Wow! Are you a football player or something?"

"I played some football in high school and college," Graham acknowledged with a grin as he noticed the large pile of sand behind them that appeared to be on its way to becoming a sand castle. "I see you've got a construction project going."

The younger boy gave him an answering grin. "Yeah. We're building a fort for our Masters." He was clutching one of the toy figures.

Graham walked over to have a look, amused at the juxtaposition of space-age toys and fairy-tale castles. He had two nephews about the ages of these boys and that similarity was strangely soothing to him this day. For a few minutes, at least, he could afford to be himself again.

TEDDY TUMBLED OUT OF BED and peered out at the day, then quickly pulled on some sweats for a pleasant bike ride.

Despite the fact that she had vowed to get to work today on a scholarly paper due in the fall, and despite the fact that there was campaign work aplenty, her thoughts had nothing to do with either of those things.

She opened the door to her room and saw immediately that Graham's door was also open and the room was empty. She walked over and stood in the doorway. The bed was neatly made, and other than a shaving kit and wallet on the dresser, there was no evidence of him. Graham McKinsey was a very neat man; she'd already noticed that about him. In fact, there was very little she hadn't noticed about him. That lean, hard body, those warm, dark eyes that always seemed to follow her own movements, the quiet voice that nevertheless managed to cut through the most heated discussions between her and her father—all the tiny shadings and nuances of speech and behavior that were so appealing.

She went downstairs and quickly drank a cup of coffee before going out to get her bike from the garage. Her father's bike was already gone and Graham was probably off on his morning run, since she hadn't seen him down on the beach where he usually did his calisthenics.

She wheeled the bike out of the garage and hopped on, then nearly tumbled off as the pedals spun freely. With a muttered curse, she got off and examined the gears. Something was definitely wrong there, but given the fact that she had a negative mechanical aptitude, she didn't know how to put it right. The bike she kept up here was very old and she supposed she should have replaced it long ago. Probably her father could fix it, but he wasn't around.

Forced to give up the bike ride, Teddy headed instead for the beach. She saw immediately that Graham must be down here, since a single set of footprints in the wet stand led off up the beach. She greeted the prospect of running into him with something less than enthusiasm. It seemed to her that she was best advised to limit her contact with him to their shared work. At least until she could decide what to do about him. Clearly, some sort of plan was called for. It just wouldn't do for her to keep reacting to situations and letting him dominate her thoughts.

She jogged on the sand, then crawled over the rocks, keeping her senses open to the serenity of the place. But each time she permitted herself to notice those footprints, some of that serenity slipped away. Still, she moved on, not really wanting to encounter him just now, but doing nothing to prevent it, either. She finally saw him as she reached the top of the next outcropping of rocks.

To her utter amazement, she saw that he was playing with the Marsden boys, building a sand castle or fort. She just stopped where she was, paralyzed by the unlikelihood of the scene. Never would she have believed Graham McKinsey to be interested in playing with children. And yet there he was, with his back to her as he scooped up handfuls of sand and carried on a spirited conversation with the boys.

For the briefest of moments, Teddy had a nearly overwhelming urge to flee before she was spotted. She couldn't shake the feeling that she had stumbled upon something she wasn't intended to see. It was an absurd thought and was gone as quickly as it had come, but it left behind an uncertainty that kept her rooted in place until the younger boy spotted her and called out to her.

She started down off the rocks as Graham turned around. He stood up quickly and, she noted, seemed somewhat chagrined at having her discover him there. But before either of them could say anything, the younger boy claimed her attention. He was a special favorite of Teddy's and knew it, too.

"Teddy, are you gonna stay and help us build the fort and then make up some stories?"

Teddy saw the glimmer of amusement in Graham's eyes before she turned her attention to the little towhead. "The fort's almost finished," she pointed out. "And you can make up good stories yourselves."

"Yeah," the boy answered reluctantly. "But yours are better. Couldn't you make up another one about the giant spiders?"

"Yeah," the other boy chimed in. "That was great. We could have them spinning their webs around the fort this time."

"Giant spiders?" Graham echoed with a spreading grin.

"Teddy hates spiders," the older boy explained to Graham. "And she made up this story about giant ones that spin webs that burn."

"Acid webs," Teddy explained. "I even had nightmares over them myself."

She turned back to the boys. "We have to get to work, but you two can make up a spider story and tell it to us next time."

"I don't want you to have nightmares, Teddy," the younger boy said with an expression of adult concern that made both Teddy and Graham smile. She assured him that she'd think only nice thoughts before she went to sleep.

"Would you do that trick for us again, Graham?" the older boy asked as they said their goodbyes.

Teddy gave Graham a puzzled look that drew a slight flush from him. But before she could make any inquiries, Graham told the boy that once a day was all he could manage at his age, and then warned them not to try it.

"What trick, old man?" Teddy teased curiously as they started back down the beach.

"Oh, nothing," he said in an embarrassed tone. "I used to fool around with gymnastics a bit and I can still do some of it. They're cute kids."

She decided to let him change the subject. "They are, but they're also little devils, especially the younger one. He's pulled some stunts that even I had never thought of."

Graham went on then to talk about his nephews and some of their escapades, and as Teddy laughed along with him she realized that once more she was being given a brief glimpse of a very different man.

By the time they reached the house, she was ready to blurt out a question about why he felt it necessary to hide that side of his nature. But when they entered the house, her father was waiting for them, and Graham's mood shifted abruptly again. In a few minutes, all traces of that other man were gone, and once more, Teddy was left wondering if she had only imagined him.

A trip to campaign headquarters in New Haven was planned for the following day, but that afternoon Teddy announced her intention of remaining on Matiscotta. She had plenty of work to do, she told them, but her real reason was that she both wanted and needed some time to herself.

She was accustomed to spending part of her summer alone on Matiscotta; her father's work had always taken him back and forth and her mother had frequently gone with him. She had enjoyed this solitary time as much as she'd enjoyed her parents' company.

But this time she very quickly saw that she might as well have gone with them. If she'd hoped to set Graham aside and view the situation with some degree of objectivity, she soon discovered that had been wishful thinking. He was there even when he wasn't there.

Teddy sensed uncomfortably that she was in the grips of a full-blown obsession. She didn't understand Graham

McKinsey, and it had somehow become absolutely essential that she do so. Furthermore, she was not a patient person.

But by the time she took the boat over to Rockland to meet them, she had decided that patience was the only response possible. They would be working together closely for months, and sooner or later, she would figure him out. But she fervently hoped it would be sooner.

The two men were waiting on the pier when she roared into the harbor, late as usual. Her father hugged her with a mild remonstrance about her speed, and when he released her, she saw Graham watching them with a strange, indecipherable expression. His greeting was no more than politely cordial, and she responded in kind. She would give exactly what she got as far as he was concerned.

THE DEEP LAUGHTER BEGAN as soon as Graham had raised and focused the binoculars. Teddy smiled as she squinted to see them better herself. She was pleased that Graham appreciated the puffins, although in truth, she hadn't yet met anyone who didn't react that way to the rare birds.

There were several dozen of them, she estimated, perched on an islet that was really no more than a rock. They didn't require much land space because they were sea feeders—so efficient that the once-thriving colonies had been decimated years ago by jealous human fishermen. Now, thanks to conservation efforts, they were rebounding.

From where the boat bobbed in the water perhaps a hundred yards away, the puffins bore a strong resemblance to small penguins: fat black bodies with white bellies. But a closer look revealed the distinctive brightly colored beaks that seemed to cover most of their faces.

"It's an appropriate name for them," Graham said, still smiling as he finally lowered the glasses.

Teddy nodded. "One of the local bird experts told me that the name is no coincidence. They were named puffins because they appear to be puffed up."

She accepted the glasses he held out and then brought them into focus. The birds were totally ignoring the boat now, but Teddy knew that if she moved it closer the whole flock would take flight.

"Each year, there are more of them," she pronounced with satisfaction. "I suppose that sooner or later the fishermen will start to complain again."

Graham took one last turn with the binoculars before Teddy began to edge the boat away from the rock. As she swung in a wide circle to head back to Matiscotta, he felt a surge of regret. These times the two of them spent together away from work had become very precious to him. He felt as though he were building up a supply of memories to draw upon in a future he didn't want to contemplate.

He turned around for one last glimpse of the puffins, then caught Teddy's eye as he turned back again. They smiled at each other and his heart skipped a few beats before settling down again. It happened often now—those fleeting moments of sharing that allowed him for just a few moments to forget his purpose here.

Even their working relationship was changing. They still had noisy disagreements from time to time, something he knew would have happened regardless of circumstances, given their different political views. But he had backed off a bit from playing the part of the politician—partly because he feared she would call him on it and partly because he wanted to let her see more of his true self.

For her part, Teddy had become less strident in her idealism, giving occasional indications that she understood his point of view, even if she wouldn't accept it. They were making their adjustments to each other, he thought—a sure sign of a deepening relationship.

He watched her curls blow in the breeze and glint in the sun and reflected that if circumstances had been different, they might already be lovers. Dozens of times each day, there were subtle signals sent out by one of them and received by the other. Given Teddy's capacity for blunt honesty, he wondered why she hadn't confronted him with the issue and demanded to know why he continued to hold her at arm's length.

That arm, he admitted with an inner smile, was getting damned shaky. He wasn't at all sure that it would hold out long enough for him to finish his job here. And yet he was increasingly certain that it must.

"Dad says that the work on our dock will be done in a few more days," Teddy said conversationally, turning to him and catching him staring at her with that unreadable expression he wore so often.

He nodded, then turned away again and she felt that uncomfortable silence move in between them again. It happened too often, and nearly always after a time like this, when they had so obviously enjoyed each other's company.

Teddy's impatience with this state of affairs was growing. Sometimes, she felt as though they were becoming closer, but then Graham would retreat once more into polite formality. Moreover, she'd noticed that the formality didn't extend to her father, with whom Graham had developed a close relationship that often seemed to exclude her. Both of them had a large supply of off-color jokes that she knew came out when they thought she was out of earshot, and Graham seemed to have a great interest in the company, too. Ted Sothern had invited him to join his regular poker sessions that provided the chief amusement for the men of the island. They both returned from these sessions surrounded by an aura of cigar smoke and male collegiality.

Teddy might have felt rather put out at this state of affairs if it wasn't for the fact that his times with Graham seemed to be the best part of her father's life at the moment. The rest of the time Teddy noticed a certain pensiveness in her father, a continuation of the unhappiness she'd thought he'd put behind him when he'd decided to run for office. At the moment, though, this observation was nothing more than a vague, buzzing worry at the edges of a mind that had focused itself on the man beside her in the boat.

She brought the boat up to the town dock, where Graham jumped out to secure the lines. He reached out to help her alight and there was that all-too-familiar surge of magnetism as hands clasped and eyes met. Teddy, who had been the one to suggest this excursion, now perversely decided that she wanted to be away from him.

"I think I'll stay in town for a while," she decided aloud as they headed for the Volvo. "You take the wagon and I'll walk out later, or hitch a ride."

Graham gave her a mock serious look. "I don't know about that. I may be forced to dock your pay for excessive absenteeism."

"You do that," she challenged. "But just remember who's working into the night writing inspiring speeches while you two are out playing poker."

Graham smiled. "For shame, Teddy. You're beginning to sound cynical."

"It must be rubbing off."

"They are good ideas, and you know your father's speech patterns better than anyone else. I've seen some really fine speeches turn out badly because the writer didn't take into account the way the candidate would deliver them."

Teddy chose to ignore the compliment. "I still hate all this image business, you know."

"I know," he said in a strangely serious tone. "And I wouldn't have it any other way."

She didn't quite know how to respond to that and was still seeking a response when his hand came up to brush away the curls that had blown across her cheek. Warm fingertips caressed skin that was still cool from the boat trip and once more, brown eyes met blue in an eloquent silence.

His hand began to curve itself around the slim column of her neck just as the moment was shattered by a car pulling into the lot. Both of them started nervously, then moved slightly apart. Teddy said a hasty goodbye and hurried off to the general store, knowing that his dark eyes were following her. After a few moments, she heard the Volvo starting up, and then found that her feet had touched earth again. Where they'd been before that, she didn't want to consider.

By the age of thirty, a woman should know herself, Teddy thought disgustedly, and she certainly should be well past such giddy foolishness. Those years should be well behind her, the years when every girl seems to have a dangerous attraction to the wrong man. And every ounce of sense she possessed was telling her that Graham McKinsey was indeed the wrong man.

Of course, she rationalized, it was rather difficult to avoid a man with whom you were both working and sharing a house. She paused briefly at the steps to the store and stared after the departing Volvo, half hoping that there might be some truth in that old saying about familiarity breeding contempt.

"Ayuh, looks like an interesting summer, Teddy."

Teddy whirled around to see Amos Moody coming along the sidewalk from his own small house next to the store. She knew he must have seen her with Graham. Those old pale-blue eyes never missed a trick.

"Now why would you be thinking that, Amos?" She grinned, cocking her head to one side.

Amos's eyes drifted off briefly in the direction Graham had taken. "Seems like a nice fella. Not married and a good poker player, too."

Teddy laughed. "I'm glad you approve, but he's here on business, you know."

"Ayuh." He nodded solemnly, only his eyes revealing a glint of amusement. "But I always did think a man should mix business and pleasure whenever he can, and it looks like he just might think the same."

Teddy thought not. In fact, it was possible that that was just the problem. Contrary to Amos's opinion, she was beginning to think that Graham might prefer to keep the two sides of his life quite separate.

"Well, I'll be sure to keep you posted, Amos," she said as she pushed open the door into the store.

"Won't have to. It's a small island," came the taunting response from behind her.

"Hello, Teddy," the proprietress greeted her cheerily. "Your ears should be burning, because we were just talking about you. Liza was just in here. She said she was going out to see you."

"Liza?" Teddy repeated in pleased surprise. "What on earth is she doing here?"

"Just passing through. She's off to London tomorrow."

"I didn't know that the senator had arrived," Teddy said with a frown. "Dad said he wouldn't be here until day after tomorrow."

"He isn't here yet. Liza stopped by to open up the house and to take a break between Vancouver and London. She just left here a few minutes ago."

Teddy thanked the woman and hurried back outside, hoping to catch her old friend before she left the village. She hadn't seen Liza in nearly a year, not since her brief visit here last summer. The two women had been friends since childhood. Liza was Senator Oldham's niece and had spent her summers here with her uncle and his family. She was a computer systems analyst with a major Canadian bank and though they were separated by the breadth of the continent and demanding jobs, they still kept in touch regularly.

She searched the street and had just about given up when she spotted the Volvo wagon that was a near-perfect match for their own island car. For a man who expostulated regularly on the importance of buying American, the senator became very practical when it came to his island car.

Stepping quickly into the street, Teddy raised her hand in a wave that brought the wagon to a halt beside her. Liza's dark curly head poked through the open window.

"Teddy! I was just on my way out to your place."

The two friends embraced clumsily through the window and agreed that they both looked better than ever. Then Liza asked Teddy to come back to the Oldham house with her.

"I told Aunt Helene that I'd open up the place. Their housekeeper's been sick, so she won't be coming till they do. And I have to leave at the crack of dawn to get down to Boston for my flight to London."

"Why London and for how long?" Teddy asked, wishing that Liza could stay.

Liza waved a hand airily and grinned. "Oh, I'm so incredibly brilliant that they're sending me over to straighten out some problems in the system at the British branches. I expect it to take me the entire summer. Or until I get tired of London," she added impishly.

"No one gets tired of London."

"True. I may have to program in some glitches that will pop up from time to time, preferably in the spring and summer."

Teddy got in and they drove away, chattering about their island friends, none of whom had arrived yet accept for Alex Johns. Then they were at the Oldham house, a rambling structure that, like Teddy's own home, occupied a beachfront promontory. It was the largest and one of the oldest homes on the island.

"Come in and I'll put you to work while you tell me all about the trials and tribulations of being a campaign manager," Liza said with a grin before turning serious again. "Have they caught the man who murdered your uncle?"

"No," Teddy said with a shrug. "The detectives tell us that the trail has grown cold by now and there isn't much likelihood that they will catch him."

They walked into the big, empty house in a brief silence, then Teddy went on. "Anyway, I've been more or less demoted. Now I'm called campaign coordinator, thanks to your uncle."

Liza turned around with a surprised look. "What do you mean?"

"He persuaded Dad to hire the man who managed his last campaign," Teddy said as her mind raced on to the certainty that Liza must know Graham. She had worked in the senator's campaign, too.

"Tom Buckley?" Liza asked. "But I thought that he was in charge of Uncle Jack's senate staff now."

"Who's Tom Buckley?" Teddy asked in confusion.

"Uncle Jack's last campaign manager."

"Oh." Teddy digested this, trying to recall exactly what her father had said about Graham's role in the senator's campaign. "No, not him. His name's Graham McKinsey."

Liza frowned, obviously trying to place the name. Teddy felt confused and somewhat uneasy. Through her mind flitted that brief early impression of Graham as being an imposter. But that was clearly ridiculous; the senator himself would be here in a few days. Still, Graham wasn't exactly forgettable—to her, anyway.

"I don't recall anyone by that name," Liza said finally. "What's he look like?"

"He's thirty-seven. A little over six feet, with reddish-brown hair and a mustache. And a terrific body; he's a real fitness nut. Not really handsome, but he does have something." Just what that something was was still open to question.

Liza was still frowning thoughtfully. "I wasn't so engrossed in getting Uncle Jack re-elected that I wouldn't have noticed someone like that. I wonder what he did."

"I would assume that his role must have been a major one. He doesn't act like a minor functionary, that's for sure."

"Am I getting vibes that something's going on between you two?" Liza asked with a grin.

Teddy laughed. "Yes, but don't ask me what it is. I don't like him at all in some ways—but I must admit that he turns me on." She paused, then added, "Maybe."

Liza's grin grew wider. "Now that's what I like to hear: a woman who knows her own mind. Graham McKinsey," she repeated. "Funny, I just can't remember him. Of course, I was only there for part of the time."

"Well, why don't you come over for dinner and meet him? Maybe that will refresh your memory." Teddy had intended to invite her to dinner in any event, but now she saw a chance to lay to rest her unnatural fears. There had to be an explanation somewhere

Liza readily accepted and the two women moved on to other topics as they aired and dusted the house. Still, Teddy's mind kept returning to her friend's failure to recognize Graham. It just didn't make sense. If Graham had played a major role in the senator's campaign—something he himself had alluded to a few times—then surely at least his name would be familiar to Liza. It wasn't as though it were a very common, easily forgotten name.

She was still preoccupied with this revelation when she set out on foot for home, after refusing Liza's offer of a ride. It took a while before she realized that what was bothering her even more than Liza's failure to remember Graham was her own unsettling reaction to that failure. She found that she was all too ready to believe that Graham might be lying, when that was clearly impossible. Senator Oldham was due to arrive in a few days and Liza herself hadn't worked in the entire campaign. Still, the uneasiness persisted.

The house was empty and Teddy had just gone to the kitchen to get a can of soda when she heard the sound of laughter and the two men came in. Graham had written off her concern about her father's mood to campaign jitters and Teddy now decided he must be right. It had to be that overactive imagination of hers.

Both men came into the kitchen, looking windblown and relaxed and carrying with them the clean scent of sea air.

"I see that you two have been working hard in my absence," Teddy teased, directing her remarks to her father and avoiding the eyes of the man behind him.

"Oh, we have," Ted assured her. "We both think better outdoors."

"Guess who's coming to dinner?" Teddy stated, then went on at her father's questioning look. "Liza. She stopped by on her way to London."

"Did Jack come early, then? I wasn't expecting him for another few days."

"No, his plans haven't changed. Liza's here alone, and unfortunately, she's leaving first thing in the morning." Teddy finally turned to Graham.

"Liza is the senator's niece. We're old friends. She worked in his last campaign, too, but she said that she didn't know you. I guess I must have misunderstood Dad. I thought he said that you were the senator's campaign manager."

Teddy somehow managed to keep her tone very casual, but she virtually held her breath as she watched him closely and awaited his response. He had gone to the refrigerator for a beer as she'd started to speak to him, and he now turned around to face her.

"I don't recall her, either—and I wasn't the manager. I acted as a special consultant to Tom Buckley, who managed the campaign."

"Oh." Teddy let herself relax a bit as she saw his calm, unruffled behavior. But in the next breath, she admitted that Graham was probably completely imperturbable. As Amos had pointed out earlier, he played a good game of poker.

TEDDY INTRODUCED Graham and Liza several hours later. If Graham was at all disturbed by the presence of the senator's niece, he hid it well. Their conversation about the senator's campaign was disappointingly brief, but Teddy could not, in truth, say that Graham had tried to avoid the subject. For her part, Teddy could think of no subtle way to force the issue. Liza seemed to harbor no suspicions at all that Graham was not who he said he was, and that left Teddy in the very uncomfortable position of acknowledging her own irrationality.

When Liza reluctantly left early because of her dawn departure the next day, Teddy walked out to the car with her. Her old friend gave her a wicked grin.

"If you decide that you're not interested in Graham, you can wrap him up and send him to me anytime."

"Then you don't have any doubts that he is who he says he is?"

"What are you talking about?"

"I mean, you don't think he could be lying about having worked in your uncle's campaign?" With each word, Teddy felt more and more foolish.

Liza stared uncomprehendingly at her. "How could he be lying, when Uncle Jack will be here in a few days?"

Teddy shrugged uncomfortably. "You're right. I don't know what it is about him that bothers me."

Liza laughed. "I do. He's obviously interested in you and he's also obviously right for you."

"Oh, really?" Teddy asked archly. "And just what makes you think that?"

"I just feel it," Liza said. "There's a chemistry between you two."

There was indeed, Teddy thought, recalling those many times when a glance or an accidental touch had sent the world spinning away.

"Well, time will tell," she said finally.

Liza nodded. "You have months together to see what happens." She started to get into her car, then paused and turned around with a slight frown.

"Graham doesn't seem like the type to be in that business, does he?"

Teddy agreed with her, the two women said goodbye and the Volvo drove off. She rather wished that Liza hadn't spoken those last words that so closely mirrored her own thoughts on the subject of Graham McKinsey.

But Liza had been right about something else, too. They did have plenty of time to decide if there was more than just chemistry between them. The only problem was that Teddy knew she wasn't a very patient person.

GRAHAM LAY IN BED and frowned into the darkness. The evening had gone off well enough. There'd been no slip-ups, despite Teddy's attempts to precipitate them. Still, he was in an unpleasant quandary. Teddy didn't trust him for some reason; he was sure of that. On the other hand, she was attracted to him; that was equally obvious. The solution, of course, was to encourage her in that attraction so that she'd forget her suspicions.

But therein lay danger. How could he encourage her feelings for him and still control his growing desire for her that could only result in pain for them both? Graham just wasn't a man who could take affairs of the heart lightly.

No answers had presented themselves by the time he drifted off to sleep, and cold reality gave way to warm fantasies.

Chapter Four

"Hot dogs?" Graham looked aghast. "But this is Maine!"

"So?"

"Maine," he repeated. "As in Maine lobsters. We haven't had them yet."

"Then pretend. That is, unless you want to make a trip over to the mainland to buy them—and then cook them yourself."

"All you do is throw them into a pot of water," he scoffed.

"Like I said: if you get them, you cook them. I'm not going to touch them, let alone throw them into a pot."

"But you wouldn't mind eating them?"

"Of course not; I love lobster. But I prefer to distance myself as much as possible from the living animal."

"I suppose there's some logic to that," he said, shaking his head.

"Suppose what you will," Teddy replied with mock acerbity. "If a wienie roast on the beach doesn't suit your tastes, you can always stay up here and open a can of soup."

"When does the housekeeper arrive?" he asked with a groan.

"Day after tomorrow. But she's much better at cleaning than she is at cooking."

"Will there at least be some potato salad to go along with them?"

"Potato salad comes from a deli, and since there's no deli on the island, I'm afraid you'll have to make do with potato chips. I'm sure you'll like the dessert, though," she added with a wicked grin.

"I'm afraid to ask."

"Marshmallows, toasted over the fire until they're charred on the outside and gooey on the inside. A gourmet delight."

"I prefer mine lightly toasted."

Teddy sniffed disapprovingly. "You do have plebeian tastes, Graham."

But despite his disapproval—or perhaps because even hot dogs were preferable to canned soup—Graham helped her carry it all down to the beach, where Ted Sothern was already busy piling wood into the pit that had been dug years ago above the high-tide line.

Father and daughter exchanged smiles and Teddy felt pleased with herself for having suggested this picnic. Wienie roasts on the beach had always been a summer tradition, but when they'd done it last summer, the first time without her mother, it had been sad for them both.

The old rhythms were returning at last, Teddy thought, and Graham's presence somehow helped. The desire to initiate a guest into their traditions had allowed them both to set aside their loss.

Teddy had suggested it this morning, after a not-quite-overheard phone call had moved a simmering concern about her father into the forefront of her mind. She watched him now as he discussed the fine art of fire building with Graham and decided that she had perhaps overreacted.

She'd gotten up earlier than usual and had gone for a solitary bike ride. When she'd returned to the house, she'd seen Graham down on the beach, busy with his calisthenics. Watching him from the screened porch, she'd been thoroughly enjoying the display of grace and athleticism when the phone had rung.

Uncertain about where her father was at the moment, Teddy had started to turn to answer it when it was cut off in mid ring. Her father's office was located at right angles to the screened porch and the window was open. She heard his voice saying hello and turned her attention back to Graham.

Little curls of frankly sensual heat had just begun to unfold themselves in her when her attention was once more dragged away from Graham. After the initial greeting, her father had suddenly lowered his voice.

Ted Sothern had a pleasant voice, an asset for any aspiring politician, but the voice she could now just barely hear had sounded anything but pleasant. He was clearly angry, but it sounded to her straining ears like an anger being held in check. Unfortunately, no matter how carefully she listened, she hadn't been able to make out any words.

Business problems had been her initial guess. She knew little about his business, but it was a safe guess that he wasn't always the pleasant, amiable man she'd seen all her life. Otherwise, how could he have achieved such notable success in what she knew must be a highly competitive field?

Still, she was quite sure that the company had to be doing well, what with the Pentagon virtually shoveling money into it. And besides, her mother had left a sizable estate, most of which had gone to her father, with a trust fund set up for Teddy herself. Ann Holbrook Sothern had come from a wealthy Maine family whose money had initially been acquired generations ago in the timber business. By contrast, Teddy's father was the son of hard-scrabbling Vermont farmers.

So it just didn't make sense that her father could have any serious financial problems, though of course, business problems didn't necessarily have to be financial. Nevertheless, the problem continued to worry her, especially in light of her father's continued moodiness.

They all sat down on the beach with drinks as they waited for the fire to be right for cooking. The conversation was casual and easy, with the two men engaging in one of their periodic attempts to outdo each other with terrible puns.

The surprising closeness of the two men and the enforced intimacy of sharing a house and working together in this relaxed setting were making Graham seem less and less a stranger in their midst. He had, Teddy thought, a definite knack for fitting himself into their lives very comfortably—a somewhat surprising trait for someone with his forceful manner.

Teddy had finally given up her earlier, absurd suspicions about Graham, even though she was still inclined to think that his individual pieces didn't add up to a credible whole. Senator Oldham had arrived the day before, and his familiar greeting to Graham had dispelled Teddy's remaining suspicions. The noisily gregarious senator was inclined to greet everyone like he or she was a dear old friend, but the fact remained that he obviously did know Graham, and therefore, Graham must be just what he claimed to be.

The sun was dropping low over the water, casting golden paths across the quiet ocean by the time they had finished their drinks and begun to cook their dinner. Teddy watched Graham's shadowed face as he squatted beside the fire to cook his hot dogs—two of them, she noticed, despite his complaints.

There are so many layers to this man, she thought. Too many layers. Complex or secretive people were always troubling to her. And yet . . .

Graham looked her way suddenly and caught her staring at him. Across the sparks and tongues of flame, they smiled at each other. She was never quite sure what was in those smiles, and that was part of the problem. Sometimes, it seemed to her to be nothing more than camaraderie—two people thrust together by force of circumstances. Yet, at other times, she was very sure there was much more.

After they had feasted on hot dogs and potato chips and argued over the relative merits and nutritional value of medium rare marshmallows as opposed to well done, Teddy's father surprised her by asking her to fetch her guitar and play for them.

"She's good, Graham," he said proudly. "She's even played professionally."

Teddy rolled her eyes. "The full extent of my professional career was to play for one semester while I was in college, for tips in a local hangout."

"I'd still like to hear you," Graham said with that familiar half smile.

Reluctantly, Teddy got up and dusted off the seat of her jeans. "Very well. But I must warn you that my singing isn't up to my playing, and three hot dogs doesn't improve it, either."

"Ahh, but then, there's that pound of marshmallows you ate," Graham reminded her. "That should lend a certain sweetness, if nothing else."

Teddy dumped the remainder of the potato chips over his head, then quickly sidestepped the grab he made for her and went off to get her guitar. The sound of laughter followed her into the darkness, and she wondered what he might have done if she hadn't gotten away from him. The thought of being tumbled to the sand by Graham McKinsey did not displease her.

As she entered the house, the phone began ringing. She hurried into her father's study to answer it and was rewarded by silence on the open line. So she said hello again in a somewhat louder tone. After another few seconds of silence, a cold, prickly sensation began to crawl along her spine. Someone was there; she was sure of it. In fact, she thought she could hear the faint sound of breathing. When a third, less certain hello also went unanswered, she slammed down the receiver forcefully, hoping that the prankster ended up with an earache. Then she shivered lightly and hugged herself as she stared at the phone.

Any woman who lived alone feared such calls, and although Teddy was certainly no shrinking violet, she was also no exception. But this was Matiscotta, a place where she had always felt safe, and furthermore, she wasn't actually alone.

As she shrugged off her unease, her mind went skittering back to that phone call of her father's this morning, and the unmistakable anger in his voice. Could it be the same caller, someone who hadn't wanted to identify himself to her?

She was just reminding herself about the pitfalls of an overly active imagination when her glance fell on the yellow notepad on her father's desk. Ted Sothern was an inveterate doodler, and a talented one at that. When she was a child, he had often amused her by drawing her favorite cartoon characters.

Her admonition to herself rang hollowly as she stared at his latest work. The sole drawing on the pad was a large box, inside of which was a crudely drawn figure of a man. Despite the sketchiness of the figure, there was no doubting who it represented. Her father's untamable cowlick was an old joke within the family. No matter how his hair was cut and no matter what he used to hold it down, those stray locks invariably popped up by the end of the day. The cartoon figure inside the sharply drawn box had an exaggerated cowlick.

A man in a box? Was that how he saw himself? But what could the box represent? Had he changed his mind about the senate race, yet felt constrained to continue? That seemed to Teddy to be the most likely explanation. But what about that phone call this morning, and now, possibly, this one, too?

She stared at the doodle for a few moments longer, then finally snorted her disapproval at herself. That call this morning had probably meant nothing more than that someone at the company had incurred his wrath. As to this call, it was probably just a wrong number, or maybe even a mistake in the island's antiquated telephone system. As for the doodle—so what? She doodled herself occasionally, though with far less talent, and she'd certainly hate for someone to put interpretations on them.

A few minutes later she rejoined the two men, toting her precious Martin. "Sorry it took me so long. There was a phone call."

"Oh?" her father inquired with what Teddy immediately thought was a slight edge to his voice.

"I guess it was a wrong number, although they didn't have the courtesy to tell me so." As she explained, she tried discreetly to gauge her father's reaction.

She had removed the guitar from its case and Graham now interrupted to ask if he could see it. Still undecided about her father's reaction, Teddy turned her attention to Graham and handed over the guitar.

"Very nice," he pronounced. "About twenty years old, isn't it? You must have started young."

Teddy was too startled to explain that she had gotten it about fifteen years ago, from a cousin who had given up playing. "Do you play?" she asked incredulously.

He handed it back to her with a grin. "Doesn't everyone who grew up in the sixties?"

Teddy leaned forward and stared at him disbelievingly. "Are you trying to tell me that you were a hippie, Graham?"

He chuckled as he shook his head. "Not quite, but it wasn't for lack of trying at one point."

"I don't believe it!"

"Neither did I, after a while. Besides, I looked like hell in long hair."

Teddy began to tune the guitar as she tried to fit this latest bit of information into the increasingly complex puzzle that was Graham McKinsey. He'd actually told her very little about himself, despite some not-so-subtle attempts on her part to pry details out of him. By the time she was ready to play, she had decided that he was just teasing her. Flower children did not metamorphose into hardened cynics. On the other hand, though, she wasn't convinced that that cynicism was real, either.

Then she dismissed the pointless speculation as she settled in to her singing and playing. Although she rarely sang anymore, she did play often to keep up her skills. The guitar had always been a sort of self-therapy for Teddy. Whenever she was upset about something, she would take out the Martin and lose herself in her music.

After a few easier tunes, she plunged into Mason Williams' "Classical Gas," a difficult and intricate piece she loved. She played it flawlessly and was pleased when she saw the respect and admiration in Graham's eyes. Then she moved on to some Baez and Dylan and Lightfoot, hoping that her voice sounded better to her small audience than it did to her.

She had all but forgotten her father in her desire to prove her skills to Graham, and so was startled when he got up a moment after she had stopped playing. She looked up at him questioningly and he came over to bend down and place a kiss on the top of her head.

"Thank you, honey. I enjoyed that, but I've got to get back to work."

Teddy opened her mouth to protest, but he was gone quickly. She stared after him, frowning with concern.

"You're very good, Teddy." Graham's compliment brought her attention back to him.

"Thanks. Now it's your turn." She extended the guitar to him. Annoyed at her father's sudden departure, Teddy transferred some of that to Graham, convinced that he couldn't really play.

But he accepted the instrument and then retuned it expertly. "I don't sing," he warned as he began to strum some chords.

Her annoyance gone in a flash of surprise, Teddy laughed. "That's okay. Neither do I, as you now know."

Graham grinned at her. "Oh, I don't know about that. I thought I detected a hint of Joan Baez there, beneath all the marshmallows."

Then she watched in continued amazement as his long fingers moved nimbly over the strings, faltering only once on a particularly intricate chord. After listening for a few minutes, her expression grew puzzled.

"I don't recognize that."

"No reason why you should," he replied equably as he continued to strum softly. "It's never been published."

"You mean you composed it?" she asked, almost prepared for anything by now.

"That's right."

Teddy lapsed into a stunned silence as he finished the tune. It was soft and unabashedly romantic, even haunting at times. Here and there she caught echoes of some recognizable melody. It might not be wholly original but it was far more than she could have done. She knew that because she'd tried many times to compose, with no luck at all.

When he had finished, she cast about for something appropriate to say, then finally stated simply, "I'm impressed."

"Exactly my intention," he responded dryly as he put the guitar aside.

"Were you really a hippie, Graham?"

He laughed. "In the strictest sense, no. But I hung around with some for a while and I was involved in some peace marches."

"Peace marches?" she echoed. "But I thought you said that you'd served in Vietnam?"

"I did. Obviously, the peace marching didn't work, and Canada's too cold for my tastes."

"I don't understand you," she said, more plaintively than she'd intended.

"Oh?" His inquiry held a gentle mockery. "I thought you had me all figured out from the beginning."

"Well, I did," she admitted. "But you keep changing."

Graham merely smiled at her as their eyes met in the dim, ruddy glow cast by the dying fire. Teddy suddenly became aware of their isolation, but even as the romance of the spot began to tug at her, she remembered her father.

"Is something bothering Dad?"

It seemed to take a few seconds for Graham to reply, making Teddy wonder if he, too, had been thinking of the lovely intimacy of the scene.

"Not that I'm aware of. What makes you ask?"

"Oh, I don't know," she temporized, unable to bring herself to explain the reasons for her concern lest she sound silly. "He just seems preoccupied."

"That's understandable. He's got a lot to think about."

"You don't think he's regretting his decision to run, do you?"

Graham threw her a surprised look. "No, of course not. What makes you think that?"

"Nothing, except that I know something's bothering him."

"It's not uncommon for successful businessmen to seek new challenges," Graham pointed out.

"Mmm, I suppose so." Graham's lack of concern made her feel much better. As close as the two men were, he would surely know if something was wrong. She smiled at him.

"You've been good for him, Graham. He likes you a lot."

He stared at her for a moment, then turned his face to the sea as he nodded. Teddy had the strange impression that he hadn't appreciated what had been intended as a compliment. Then, when the silence threatened to become uncomfortable, he turned back to her again and began to talk about his college days and the beginning of his own interest in politics.

Teddy realized that he had said more about himself this evening than he had in all the time she'd known him. She couldn't account for this sudden change, but accepted it happily. Still, to her, he remained a collection of disparate pieces that just didn't fit together. When he had finished, she asked a question that had been on her mind for some time.

"What do you plan to do with the rest of your life?"

"More of the same," he replied with a shrug.

"I don't believe that, Graham."

"Why not?"

"Because I don't. I find it hard to believe that you've been doing it this long." She was unable to come up with a reason for her feelings, but she was sure that he was lying.

There was just no way she could see this man drifting from one campaign to another, working for politicians.

A half smile played across his mouth as he stared back at her. "I see," he said laconically. "You prefer your men to be upwardly mobile, is that it? By forty, they should at least be company vice presidents?"

Teddy did not fail to notice the phrase "your men." She was also, once again, tantalizingly aware of their isolation on this moon swept beach with its softly lapping waters. Nevertheless, she chose for the moment to ignore both.

"I can't stand men like that."

"Oh? Then maybe it's the tweedy academic type you prefer, dedicated to teaching and research?"

Even in the semidarkness, she could see a twinkle in his eyes. It seemed to her that Graham was flirting with her, and she fought down an urge to giggle at the unlikelihood of that. A man like Graham was hardly going to engage in such games.

"It seems to me that this conversation has been straying a bit. All I said was that I don't believe you intend to continue as you are."

"And all I was doing was pointing out that you don't believe it because you don't want to believe it."

"And just why wouldn't I want to believe it?" she asked recklessly, aware of a small, throbbing pulse that was accelerating in her throat.

Graham just sat there watching for a moment, his face shadowed. Then his mustache curved into a lopsided grin that made her throat suddenly constrict.

"You're not very good at dissembling, Teddy. And I'm quite good at reading vibes, especially the ones you've been sending."

She thought about giving in to self-righteous indignation, then thought about ignoring his taunt. She compromised. "We're living and working together. It's only natural that there should be a...mutual attraction." That, she thought, was a subtle way of letting him know that he wasn't the only one capable of reading vibes.

His grin remained. "I can think of a lot of women I could be in this situation with, without 'mutual attraction' being involved. And I'll bet you could do the same as far as men are concerned."

She couldn't refute that, so she didn't.

"Actually, I haven't decided yet what I think of you, Graham." He said nothing to that, so she went on. "And since you haven't yet made a pass, I can only assume you feel the same. We're going to be 'living and working together' for months, so there's no hurry, is there?" Teddy was rather proud of how reasonable she sounded, considering the havoc that was being wreaked upon her by the night and the beach and the man across from her.

"Right," he said, his expression still not changing.

"On the other hand, I think that we're both mature enough to handle it if we do get, uh, involved. Don't you?"

"Definitely."

"You aren't contributing much to this discussion, Graham," she pointed out in a voice that was growing huskier with every syllable.

"Moonlit beaches and sexy redheads have a way of destroying my conversational abilities."

And there the conversation floundered. The night seemed to close in about them and the soft, rhythmic sounds of the ocean hovered sensuously in the background. The dying fire hissed and crackled and sent occasional sparks flaring into the blackness.

Teddy was intensely aware of all this—and of the man who sat quietly across from her. The atmosphere was heavy with waiting. When he finally got to his feet, a delicious thrill skittered through her. He crossed the short distance between them unhurriedly, then extended a hand down to her.

"We'd better be getting back to safety while we still can," he said with gentle mockery.

She gave him her hand and then felt a strange light-headedness as he drew her to her feet. That strong, calloused hand became her only anchor to reality. She could actually feel his hesitation, but then, instead of dropping her hand, he reached for the other one and held them both as he searched her face very solemnly.

Teddy, too, was hesitant. The pieces of the puzzle that was Graham McKinsey floated about in her mind: the cynical manager who counseled telling the people what they wanted to hear, the blunt-spoken man who had no use for soft words, the playful builder of sand castles, the creator of beautifully romantic music. Which was real—or was any of it real? For someone whose life was frequently marked by lack of caution, Teddy Sothern was very careful now.

Graham slid his hands slowly up along her arms and across her shoulders until they came finally to rest against the curve of her neck. Her caution gave way under undulating waves of sensual heat that spread downward from his touch. She met his gaze unwaveringly, even though a small residue of uncertainty remained.

Still moving with agonizing slowness, he cupped her face, and at the same time took a half step toward her, until only two layers of clothing separated them. Despite her jeans and sweater, Teddy felt naked—and very vulnerable.

At some point in those breathless seconds, the kiss became inevitable. She stretched upward just as his face bent to hers, and a small, primitive sound worked its way out of her throat when his bristly mustache touched her sensitive skin a heartbeat ahead of the coming together of their mouths.

That tiny sound was a catalyst that sent his arms around her to draw her into the warm shelter of his body. Fierce possessiveness vied erotically with gentleness as the kiss deepened into exploration.

And yet she could feel his restraint even as his tongue flicked out to curve about hers hungrily. The leashed passion fed the flames of her own desire, making her want what was being held back. There was one brief scary and exhilarating moment when she sensed that his self-control was about to break and take them both beyond that barrier—but then he abruptly broke off the kiss. Teddy was left slightly dazed, with the imprint of his hands and mouth still lingering as he took a few steps backward and jammed his hands into the pockets of his jeans as though that was the only way he could control them. He avoided her confused gaze for a few seconds, then finally gave her an ironic grin.

"I'm glad to see that we don't turn each other on. I was a bit worried about that for a while there."

The tension and disorientation that had followed his abrupt behavior drained away from her and she, too, managed a smile. "So was I. But I'm sure we have nothing to worry about."

His dark eyes flicked briefly to the beach around them. "I think we'd better get the hell out of here before we're tempted to reenact that old film. You know the one I mean."

She, too, stared at the moonswept beach where the waves lapped gently at the sand. She knew. "Burt Lancaster and Deborah Kerr. I don't remember the name of it."

They smiled at each other rather uncertainly until he took her hand and they started slowly back toward the house.

"So when does the water up here warm up enough for swimming?"

"It doesn't," she replied absently, still lost in the images he had evoked. "You have to wear a wet suit."

"Oh, well, in that case I guess we're safe. Wet suits would ruin the whole thing."

GRAHAM ECHOED Teddy's good-night, then contemplated a second cognac as he watched her curvy bottom move rhythmically up the stairs. He was afraid that he'd have to drain the bottle if he expected to get any sleep tonight.

The past few hours spent in what he'd thought would be the safety of Ted Sothern's company hadn't done much to dispel the moments on the beach. He still couldn't quite believe that he'd been able to stop. Not that he was a man lacking in self-discipline, but never before had temptation come in such a warm, yielding package.

To force his mind away from yet another replay of those moments, he thought about Teddy's comments about her father. He'd lied to her, of course, since he was very much aware of Ted's recent distraction. And unlike Teddy, he knew the reason behind it.

The pressures building within Graham were both complex and powerful. Success, he was sure, was within his grasp. It could be over very soon. Professionally, he was highly pleased about that. But that dull, heavy ache inside him told him that his professionalism was in grave danger.

He should never have allowed that scene on the beach to take place, because one small step could so easily lead to another. That kiss had whetted his appetite to an extent he wouldn't have believed possible. He'd foolishly—and nearly disastrously—believed he had better control than that.

He stared at the empty staircase, letting his mind travel up to her room, where even now she was probably shedding her clothes and crawling between the sheets. He actually started to get to his feet before reason settled him down again.

Guilt temporarily took the place of desire, leaving a bitter taste in his mouth that not even the cognac's fire could dispel. Teddy had been pleased that he was getting along so well with her father. And Ted was equally pleased to observe their growing interest in each other; he'd seen that in the older man's eyes when he and Teddy had returned from the beach, no doubt with invisible bits of passion still clinging to them.

The bald, ugly truth was that he liked Ted Sothern and was at least halfway in love with Teddy—and he was here to destroy the one and incur the lifelong hatred of the other as a result. Graham knew that he was in the worst predicament of his life, one from which there was no escaping.

He drained his glass and dragged himself upstairs, where he paused for a moment outside her closed door. The warmth and softness of her, the clean-smelling tangle of silken curls, that little moan of arousal: all of it lay just beyond that door.

Graham McKinsey would have described himself, quite rightly, as a man of honor. His personal integrity had never been questioned—by him or by anyone else. He had lived his life thus far by adhering to a few basic principles. They included never knowingly causing pain to others and never using innocence to his advantage.

It came as a very ugly shock to him that his thoughts at the moment were something far less than honorable. He moved quickly into his room and closed the door firmly.

Chapter Five

Teddy managed a farewell smile and wave as she backed off from the pier. Then, as soon as she had put the boat into a wide turn toward Matiscotta, the smile turned to a grimace accompanied by a noisy sound of disgust. Two days under the same roof with Art Jacobsen had been far above and beyond the call of duty.

Jacobsen was a media consultant, and Teddy had learned very quickly that her suspicions about that profession were well-founded. And yet, she thought sadly, it was through people like him that politicians got themselves elected. Image was all-important; substance just didn't count. That loathsome man had actually stated just that.

She took out some of her frustration on the boat by pushing it to its limits on the choppy waters, but she was still steaming when she returned to the house. Unfortunately for Graham, he happened to be the one in her path, since her father had gone over to the senator's home.

"Five more minutes with that creep and I would have been forced to conduct a burial at sea," she raged.

"Your restraint was admirable—and greatly appreciated," Graham responded dryly as he looked up from his ever present clipboard.

"He actually made *you* sound like an idealist," she went on, still fuming and not about to be mollified by humor.

Graham chuckled and tossed aside the clipboard as he watched Teddy pace about the room, gesturing disgustedly. The truth was that he was as glad to see the man go as she herself was, although for a rather different reason. The man's incessant lusting after Teddy had very nearly driven him past the limits of his self-control. He was somewhat embarrassed at his possessiveness where Teddy was concerned and couldn't help wondering how much worse it might be if she was actually his. There was, he thought, a very primitive streak to his feelings for Teddy.

"I had the impression that he found you very interesting," he said with forced casualness as she came over and flung herself down on the other end of the sofa. "But he did seem to back off a bit after a while."

Teddy gave him a wicked grin. "That could be because I told him that if he made one more move on me, he was going to need to have his teeth recapped."

Graham threw back his head and roared with laughter. "And here I was beginning to think that you might have needed my protection."

"On the contrary," she said wryly, "*he's* the one who might have needed protection. I know darned well that Dad couldn't stand him, either."

"I know, but he served his purpose," Graham said placatingly. "He did make one or two good suggestions."

Teddy drew her long legs up onto the sofa, then rested her chin on her knees. "I still think that something's bothering Dad. I've even heard him up and about during the night, but he denies that anything's wrong. Has he mentioned anything to you about business problems?"

Graham immediately switched from thoughts about taking her into his arms to a consideration of how he could get her out of here.

"No, from what he's told me, the company's in fine shape. What makes you think he has business problems?"

"Just a guess," she said with a shrug. "I don't know what else it could be, and I know it's not the campaign. He really seems to be looking forward to that."

"Well, to take your mind off all your unnecessary worries, and to reward you for your amazing forbearance these past few days, let me take you to dinner on the mainland tonight."

Teddy felt a little tremor of pleasure and nervousness at that prospect. "But what about Dad?"

"I already mentioned it to him and he said that he'd have Mrs. Watson fix him something before the poker game."

"Don't you want to play poker?" she inquired. He certainly seemed to enjoy that all male atmosphere, to Teddy's disgust.

He gave her a deliberately provocative smile. "I haven't reached the point yet where I'd rather play poker than spend the evening in the company of a beautiful woman."

His teasing remark practically begged for some sort of flippant response, but Teddy had become strangely tongue-tied. She just didn't know how to handle these occasional flirtations. Graham's behavior toward her since that night on the beach had been frustratingly proper. Even in the rare moments when they'd been alone, absolutely nothing had happened. Furthermore, it seemed to Teddy that he was going to great lengths to insure that they *weren't* alone together. And yet, here he was, suggesting that they spend the evening together. It was unsettling, to say the least.

"Okay," she said finally. "We'll go to a pound."

"A what?"

"A lobster pound," she explained. "And contrary to what you may be thinking, they're not homes for stray lobsters. They're the best place to go for lobster up here. You'll like it."

And so, in honor of the occasion, Teddy put on a skirt for the first time since her arrival on Matiscotta. Her summer wardrobe consisted of jeans and sweats, with gym shorts and T-shirts appearing at the brief peak of summer. It was her small personal rebellion against her professorial wardrobe. She selected a soft, floral-printed challis skirt that ended at the lower calf and topped it with a matching summer sweater that dipped to reveal her light tan. When she came downstairs to join Graham, he looked her up and down, then grimaced elaborately.

"I knew you had legs there somewhere, but I was hoping to see more of them."

Teddy gathered up the full skirt to mid-thigh and did a modified cancan kick down the final step. "There you are: legs. But that's the last you'll see of them unless the weather turns warm. Fashion has decreed legs to be nonexistent."

"Is this the same woman I once heard proclaim that she didn't believe in following the whims of fashion?" he asked in mock astonishment.

"I don't follow fashion, unless it suits me," Teddy replied, wondering if he ever forgot anything she said. This was not the first time he had quoted her own words to her. Flattering though it might be, it was also very disconcerting.

While she went off to inform her father that they were leaving, Graham was belatedly considering the implications of spending an evening alone with her. But after two days of watching Jacobsen making moves on her, he felt an overwhelming need to reestablish what could only be called territorial rights.

And what rights did he actually have, he wondered: the right to hurt her as well as himself?

Still, his hands off behavior toward Teddy could last only so long, and then need won out over principle. He was very much aware of the dangerous cycle he had been establishing. First, he would hold her at arm's length by being certain they didn't spend time alone together, and then his need for her would overwhelm him and he would deliberately seek that which he was denying himself.

When she returned, he ceremoniously offered her his arm and they strolled down to the newly refurbished dock. Despite their casual banter, both of them were feeling slightly off balance.

They crossed to the mainland, where Teddy had arranged for a taxi to take them to her favorite pound a short distance out of town. When they pulled in to the well filled parking lot, she watched Graham's surprised expression with amusement.

"Somehow I doubt that this place made the *Mobil Guide* to dining in Maine," he remarked with a mixture of amusement and dismay.

Teddy laughed, having expected him to react this way. Pounds were never elaborate. Most, like this one, would hardly warrant a glance from passing motorists, unless they happened to be particularly knowledgeable about Maine.

Out in front of the rather ramshackle building were four large metal drums set up on iron grates over wood fires. Steam issued from the open tops, filling the air with a pungent mixture of salt water and seafood. Graham strode over and peered in.

"The lobsters are cooked in salt water and seaweed," Teddy explained. "I'm not sure if that's what makes the difference, or if it's the fact that they were caught only hours

ago. The pound is owned by a local lobsterman and his
family—very much a Mom-and-Pop operation.''

Although there were wooden picnic tables set up under
the trees, on this cool night most of the patrons were eating
inside. Teddy led them in, then smiled again at his continued befuddlement. If the *Mobil Guide* people had somehow managed to find this place, they certainly wouldn't be
awarding any stars for ambience. The walls were bare, the
floor was covered with a serviceable linoleum, and the cus-
tomers sat at card tables covered with checkered vinyl ta-
blecloths. Amidst the distinctive sounds of down-east accents
and the cracking of lobster shells, they found an empty table. A cheerful teenaged waitress appeared instantly.

Graham was obviously suppressing laughter as the girl
told them that the dinner included potato salad and baked
beans and rolls. Then she asked how many lobsters they
wanted, after explaining that the day's catch had yielded
rather small ones. Teddy asked for two, and Graham, still
fighting laughter, ordered three. As soon as the girl had departed, Graham gave in to his mirth.

"I believe you *did* express a fondness for potato salad,"
Teddy commented dryly.

He nodded, still chuckling. "But with hot dogs, not lobsters."

"Up here there isn't much difference." Teddy grinned.
"And wait till you see what a cheap date I am." Since there
were no menus, he didn't yet know that lobster dinners for
the two of them would cost no more than a modest dinner
for one at a fine city restaurant.

In this unusual and relaxing atmosphere, their initial sense
of strangeness vanished as though it had never been. They
talked about anything and everything, picking up threads of
earlier conversations and probing ever more deeply into

each other's psyches. The campaign wasn't mentioned once by either of them.

To the other patrons of the pound, they made an interesting pair: the vivacious redhead who seemed to be in perpetual motion, and the rugged, quiet man whose dark eyes never left her. There was more than one knowing smile and some inner sighs for lost youthful love.

Although Teddy had been able to ignore past and future during their leisurely dinner, on the way back to the dock she found herself wondering again how and why this man could change so dramatically. Tonight, he had been a charming and attentive date; tomorrow, he might well become distant and formal again.

Even more troubling to her was her own reluctance to do anything about this strange state of affairs. Normally one to confront things head-on, she found herself temporizing this time.

Perhaps, she thought, she didn't confront him because deep inside she was content to let matters between them remain as they were. With that admission, Teddy recognized the profound difference between her relationship with Graham and other relationships in the past. She was, she suspected, teetering on the brink of something very large here, something truly frightening, and perhaps for the first time in her life was feeling a most strange emotion—caution.

She accepted his hand to alight from the taxi and met his eyes briefly as their bodies touched. A pleasant warmth traveled through her, a warmth that could, at any moment, flare up into passion.

Yes, she decided, they were definitely better off keeping things on a friendly, casual basis. There was no hurry, after all; they had plenty of time. But from somewhere deep inside her came the sound of mocking laughter.

They started across the lot toward the piers and Teddy looked up at the night sky. The moon and stars had vanished and the breeze was freshening. Storms were predicted for later this night, and even as she peered into the darkness, a few fat drops began to fall. She had just turned to Graham when a familiar voice hailed her out of the darkness. She smiled with pleasure when she saw the rotund figure approaching them at his usual half trot.

"George!" she exclaimed. "I wondered when you were going to show up."

He hugged her enthusiastically and kissed her resoundingly on the cheek, smelling as he always did of the the cigars he'd begun to smoke when they were teenagers.

"The temperature hit ninety in the Big Apple today, and that's my exit cue. Looks like I showed up at a good time. I was about to call Dad to come over for me, and I know he doesn't like to make the trip at night. You are going out tonight, aren't you?" He paused to take in the silent man beside her.

Teddy assured him that they were and then introduced Graham. George was one of her very favorite islanders, and one of the few that she saw regularly during the winter, too, since he lived in Manhattan. He was the only son in an eccentric family of writers and artists who'd been on the island for several generations and were referred to by Amos Moody as "our very own crazies." George himself was a sculptor of increasing renown, whose critically acclaimed one-man show Teddy had attended only a few weeks before her departure for Matiscotta.

The rain began to fall more heavily and the wind started to blow in earnest and they all scrambled into the boat, whose canvas canopy Teddy and Graham had fastened before their crossing earlier. Teddy started the engine, thinking that she didn't blame George's father for not wanting to make the crossing at night. She didn't like it much herself, if the truth be known. As soon as they had left the ring of light within the harbor itself, the oppressive blackness closed about them, sliced only in small swaths by the boat's lights.

Darkness on the water, she reflected, had a different texture to it from darkness on land. One could almost feel the heaviness of black sky above and the menace of fathomless, inky depths below, with only a frail, small boat to protect the intruders from the void.

At such times her eyes played tricks on her, conjuring up all sorts of obstacles in their path. There was no real danger, of course; Teddy knew that. They were well inside the commercial shipping lanes, and in any event the big ocean-going vessels were lit up like small cities at night. Likewise, any small craft like theirs would have both running lights and bright spotlights. But facts had a way of becoming lost in a mind whose imagination could be easily aroused by the heavy darkness.

When the lights of Matiscotta finally pierced the blackness ahead of them, Teddy let out a sigh of relief that brought a questioning look from Graham. She gave him a sheepish smile.

"I've never liked crossings on dark nights. I start to imagine all sorts of things."

From the rear seat, George piped in in a teasing voice. "Still wishing that we had our own Nessie up here, Teddy?"

Teddy groaned loudly and George explained to Graham, "When we were kids, Teddy read about the Loch Ness monster and became convinced that he must have a cousin somewhere around here. She used to drag us up to that lookout of hers to see if we could spot him. Then, after she gave up on that, she switched to ghost ships."

"Well, at least the ghost ships are a bit more plausible," Teddy put in defensively. "A lot of ships did sink around here."

George went on, regaling Graham with tales from their childhood, embellished in his inimitable fashion. Graham appeared to enjoy such stories, just as he had on the numerous occasions when her father had dredged up some long-forgotten incidents.

He's learning so much about me, she thought. *And I still know so little about him.*

In the meantime, she homed on the lights of the village and town dock and then began to turn toward the far end of the island where George's family had their own dock.

"I hope the dock lights are on," George commented, leaning forward to peer out into the gloom.

Teddy hoped so, too. She was forced to remain several hundred yards offshore, because this part of the island had treacherous rocky shoals that were all but invisible on a night like this. The wind had picked up sharply during their crossing, raising whitecaps that created spots of white in the blackness, and the boat was therefore less maneuverable. If the dock lights were on, she could drop George there; if not, she would probably be forced to return to the town dock and leave him there.

Despite her close concentration on the task at hand, Teddy had still noted a slight tension emanating from Graham. To his credit, though, there hadn't been any demand that he should be the one to pilot the boat. In view of his powerfully male nature, Teddy found the absence of machismo rather unusual and very welcome. Too many men were inclined to assume that certain tasks such as driving a car or piloting a boat were their exclusive province, despite the skills of their female companions. And in Graham's case, there could easily be an assumption that this was true, since he projected an aura of competence and confidence in everything he did.

"Hah!" George exclaimed just as Teddy let out a sigh of relief herself. The darkness was suddenly broken not only by the dock lights, but also by lights blazing from the house itself. She throttled back and eased up to the dock in the rising swells, with George tossing out the bumpers to protect the boat.

George clambered out with his bags, then leaned down to thank Teddy. "Take it easy. The rain's getting worse."

Rain pummeled the canopy with a staccato sound, and the wind buffeted the boat. Teddy considered, then rejected, the idea of leaving the boat here and going home by land. George must have been thinking the same thing, because he offered them the use of the family's car.

"Thanks, but we'll be okay," Teddy replied, only belatedly realizing that she hadn't consulted Graham. She glanced quickly at him.

"You're the captain," he said with a shrug.

They bade George goodbye and headed back out into the stormy seas. Teddy explained to Graham that she intended to continue around the island the long way, since that would keep them on the leeward side of the island for most of the trip. Graham accepted that with a nod.

Teddy gave him a smile. "You surprise me, Graham. No macho declarations that *you* should be the one running the boat?"

"I bow to your expertise," he replied equably. "Besides, you know these waters and I don't."

"That wouldn't have stopped a lot of men," she commented as she fought her way to a safe distance offshore.

"In my profession, machismo can be an occupational hazard."

No sooner had these words left his mouth than Teddy, who wasn't even watching him at the moment, sensed a strong tension in him. The feeling was further strengthened by the fact that he immediately began to ask questions about George and his family.

Machismo an occupational hazard for a campaign manager? That, Teddy thought, was a very strange comment. Even as she obligingly filled him in on the island's resident eccentrics, she was wondering what on earth he could have meant.

She might have pursued the remark if it hadn't been for the fact that piloting the boat soon claimed all her attention. The hilly geography of the island resulted in freak winds even here on the leeward side, and the seas were running as heavy as any Teddy had ever encountered. Time after time as they inched along, she had to throttle back to ride out large swells, and the incessant drumming of rain on the canopy only contributed to the sense of imminent danger.

Despite her intense concentration on the task at hand, Teddy's attention was drawn sharply to Graham as he suddenly got up and crawled over the seat into the stern of the boat, then reappeared with two bright-orange life jackets. She had thought about them herself, but after his show of faith in her, she hadn't wanted to alarm him.

"Don't think this is any reflection on your skills, but you know what they say about an ounce of prevention," he commented as he slid back into his seat again.

Then he moved closer to her to fit the jacket over her and secure it. Already tense from the strain of piloting the boat, Teddy reacted powerfully to his touch. For one brief moment the darkness became intimate instead of malevolent, and Teddy felt reassured by his calm, stolid presence.

"I'm not insulted," she said with an embarrassing huskiness in her voice. "It's a good idea."

She turned to him briefly and they exchanged smiles that told each other eloquently there were other things they'd rather be doing on such a night. The silent message was so startlingly clear that the words might as well have been spoken. The relentless staccato beat of the rain took on an urgent, sensual quality.

Then Graham settled back into his own seat and donned the other jacket and Teddy leaned forward to peer out through the windshield. She was trying to find landmarks that would give her their present location, but it was very difficult, given the darkness and the heavy rain. She continued to watch, seeking a distinctive array of boulders that spilled out into the sea not far from the tip of the island.

"There they are," she breathed in satisfaction when she finally made out the dark shapes off to port. "Now I know where we are."

Graham saw them too, and recalled that they were close to the tip of the island. They now had less than a mile to go, he estimated, but most of that would be made in the full fury of the storm.

Teddy was competent and he wasn't really worried, but he acknowledged that he would still be greatly relieved to see their dock. He thought with considerable amusement that Teddy would be less than pleased with him if she knew that he was indeed suffering from wounded male pride. He hated being the helpless one, forced to rely on her skill and knowledge to keep them safe.

He also knew that his discomfort over this state of affairs had been largely responsible for that stupid slip of the tongue earlier and wondered if he'd covered it adequately, or if she would bring up the subject again once they were safe on land. It was difficult enough to continue his deception, but outright lying to her could prove impossible.

The boat continued to rise and fall with the angry sea, surging forward through relatively calm waters, slowing to accommodate itself to the swells. Graham watched Teddy as she maneuvered the boat with great expertise. She was tense; he could see that in her posture and her grip on the wheel. But she was handling it well. For a woman whose emotions could often seesaw dizzyingly, she had that rare capacity to remain calm in the clinch.

The dim interior lights cast her profile into soft shadows and subdued that red-gold hair, creating an effect not unlike firelight. Graham began to drift off into fantasies about soothing away that tension before a crackling fire.

"What...?" Teddy's sudden outburst brought him back to reality quickly.

She was leaning forward and peering intently toward the shore with a puzzled expression. He followed her gaze, saw nothing, and turned to her questioningly.

She didn't answer for a few seconds as she continued to stare into the darkness while the boat edged its way along, about a hundred yards offshore.

"It must have been my imagination," she said finally. "But I would have sworn that I saw the running lights of a boat in there for a moment, just after we came around that bend."

Graham looked back again into the darkness. "I thought this part of the island was deserted."

"It is, but there's a dock in there where I thought I saw the lights. Remember the dock you asked about when we were up at the lookout?"

Graham remembered, all right, and he also remembered who they'd seen on that dock. Cold reality washed away the lingering traces of his fantasies.

"Maybe I'd better have a look," Teddy said uncertainly. "If someone is in there, it must be because they're having trouble, and there are no houses within a half mile of that dock."

"If someone was in there, they wouldn't have switched off their lights. They'd certainly have seen us," Graham pointed out with what he hoped was convincing logic. "You probably saw some sort of crazy reflection brought on by the rain."

"You're right," she agreed. "And if there is anyone in there, the worst that will happen is that they'll get drenched going for help."

Graham relaxed as Teddy throttled up and continued on their way, but his mind was already working on just how he could discreetly learn what time Ted Sothern had left his poker game.

Teddy laughed. "Blame it on George and all that talk about my ghost ships. No one could possibly be in there on a night like this."

Someone who had urgent business on the island and had believed the forecast that the storms weren't due until later certainly could be there, but Graham did not disabuse Teddy of her certainty.

The last half mile to the dock was the worst of all, but Teddy continued to demonstrate a calm competence. Still, she heaved a loud sigh of relief when she had maneuvered the boat into the calm of the boathouse and cut the engine. They both climbed out, then paused as they listened to the deafening sound of the rain pelting the metal roof.

"Maybe we'd better stay put until it lets up," Graham suggested.

Teddy nodded and sank gratefully onto the wooden deck that ran along the edge of the boathouse. Then she began to swivel her head in an attempt to alleviate the tension in her neck and shoulder muscles.

Graham knelt behind her and circled her neck with his hands, then began to knead it slowly with strong, sure fingers. Teddy sighed appreciatively as his closeness and gentle touch began to transform the tension into something far more pleasurable. She leaned back against him, her head cushioned against his hard chest.

"Thank you for dinner and a very pleasant evening. I enjoyed it, even if the trip back was a bit hairy."

He continued his gentle massage and leaned down to kiss her ear. "Does that mean that you'll be willing to see me again?" he asked teasingly as his warm breath fanned against her sensitive skin.

"Oh, I don't know, Graham. Don't get pushy. After all, I barely know you," she rejoined flippantly in an effort to counter the havoc he was wreaking upon her senses.

You don't know me at all, Graham thought miserably. *And when you do, you'll hate me.*

He remained silent, still massaging her neck, until he could stand it no longer. Then he got up and moved a short distance away from her before seating himself on the deck.

Teddy looked at him curiously, wondering if it was a time for another reversion to formality. He was staring at the boat, and his face, in profile, looked grim. Exasperated, she pulled herself into a cross-legged position and leaned forward determinedly.

"Graham, what is it with you? I can't take much more of this Jekyll and Hyde business."

He turned toward her. The single overhead bulb in the cavernous boathouse cast his face partially into shadow, but Teddy was nearly certain that she saw a momentary fear there, before his expression became annoyingly bland.

"What Jekyll and Hyde business?"

"Don't play dumb with me, Graham McKinsey. You know very well what I'm talking about. You come on to me, and then you back off as though I had the plague. You've done it before, and you did it again just now."

A half smile played across his rugged features. "I thought I was just helping you to relax."

"Hah!" She scoffed. "And I suppose that's all you were doing that night on the beach after the wienie roast, too?"

He said nothing and after a moment, she went on. "I know darned well that you're not shy, and you know I'm interested. So I repeat my question: what's with you? I don't like playing games."

"It isn't a game, Teddy, however much it might seem that way."

There was another brief silence, and Teddy sensed that he might be about to tell her the truth. But when he spoke, she was certain he had changed his mind.

"We'll be working together for months under hectic circumstances, and I just don't think this is the time for involvement."

"Hmmph!" Teddy snorted, letting him know that she didn't believe him. "Have you got a girlfriend stashed somewhere, Graham?" He'd never said that he didn't, although he had certainly implied that was the case.

"No, no *women* friends," he teased, mocking her occasional outbursts of feminist rhetoric.

Teddy knew he was trying to tease her away from the issue at hand, but she also knew that whatever the truth was, she wasn't going to hear it now. She'd wear him down sooner or later, and perhaps it was for the best that it be later. After all, she wasn't yet certain about her own feelings, was she?

He tried to initiate a discussion about the recommendations of the loathsome media consultant, but Teddy answered him in monosyllables. Finally, he gave up and reached for her hand, cradling it in his as he ran a calloused thumb across her soft, fleshy palm in slow circles.

"Sometimes I think that my initial impression of you was correct, after all. Maybe you are a spoiled brat who has to have her own way."

She tried to jerk her hand away, but he merely tightened his grip. "Wanting to know the truth does not mean being spoiled."

He smiled and shifted himself into a cross-legged position that brought his bent knees against hers. Then he leaned slowly forward until his mouth was hovering scant inches from hers.

"The truth is that you are, beyond a shadow of a doubt, the most fascinating and delightful woman I've ever known."

Before she could respond to that, his mouth covered hers with a gentle insistence that escalated quickly into demand. One hand continued to hold hers in a firm grip, and the other curved about her neck, holding her imprisoned as he sent his tongue on sensuous little forays into the warm, moist recesses of her mouth.

The rain hammered insistently on the roof, urging them on. The damp chill of the night was held at bay by two heated bodies moving as closely together as their awkward positions would permit. But even that awkwardness had a strange eroticism, holding them apart even as their mouths promised so much more.

Finally, with a frustrated groan, Graham slid his arm around and beneath her and lowered her to the wooden deck. Teddy murmured her approval and wrapped her arms about his neck to draw him close.

Tentatively, then with growing boldness, they began to explore each other. Both of them ached with the need to touch, to bring reality and fantasy together. She slid her hands beneath his jacket to encounter the heated hardness of a chest barely covered by a thin silk shirt. His fingers glided slowly along a satiny thigh and then beneath her sweater, leaving a trembling warmth when they passed.

Both of them knew instinctively that they could go only so far on the hard, narrow ledge in the damp chill of the night, and perhaps that knowledge made them freer with each other. Graham knew the danger far more acutely than Teddy, but she, too, sensed that giving herself to this man entailed the risk that the gift could become permanent.

Neither of them was really conscious of a decision to bring the sweet torment to a halt—but that decision was made. There was a slow, regretful separation, interrupted by more caresses and soft sounds meaningful only to themselves.

Graham propped himself up on one elbow and stared down at her. "Last time I blamed it on the moonlight and the beach. This time I guess I'll blame it on the rain."

Teddy gestured to the roof, where silence reigned. "I think it stopped raining some time ago."

"I didn't notice."

"*I* noticed that you didn't notice," she replied with a satisfied smile as she traced the mustache that had left its tickly imprint on her skin.

He returned the smile as he took her hand and pressed his lips against her sensitive palm. The warmth that poured forth from his dark eyes engulfed them both in a silence. Thoughts trembled on the very brink of speech.

Graham was wondering if it was really true that it was better to have loved and lost than never to have loved at all. It was a question he'd never expected to confront.

Teddy wondered what it was in Graham's past that was making him so very wary of involvement and how she could pry that information from him. Not once did it occur to her that he was thinking of the future, not the past.

They left the boathouse and went out into a night fragrant with the cleansing rain and enveloped in a fine mist. Graham was still holding her hand when they entered the house and immediately became aware of its empty silence. Their separate thoughts converged on two empty beds upstairs, and they paused just inside the terrace doors.

Graham stared down at her as he traced one long finger over the line of her jaw and then threaded all of them through the tangle of curls that glowed in the lamplight.

"Teddy," he murmured, trying to put into that one word all that he was feeling, but couldn't say.

In response, she moved closer to him, fitting her soft curves against the hard angles of his body and fanning still further the flames that were burning away all reason. In his mind, they were already upstairs in his bed and she was welcoming him with her warm, moist womanhood.

Then, just as the last shreds of reason began to evaporate in the all consuming heat of desire, there was a sound at the door.

His instincts told him to cling to her, to make it clear that this was his woman. But Teddy herself broke off the contact by taking a backward step. He wanted to tell her that it was useless to pretend nothing had happened, that the very atmosphere vibrated with their combined need, but he let her go—and then knew a moment of pure hatred for Ted Sothern as the man walked in.

For a brief moment, as he stood framed in the open doorway, both Teddy and Graham saw a haunted look on his face. But almost before the impression could register, it was gone—replaced by a smile that included them both.

"You're home early," Teddy said brightly. "Wasn't your luck running good tonight?"

The older man advanced into the room and Graham's readjustment to cold reality was completed when he realized how wet Ted was. It hadn't been raining that hard for some time, and there was no reason he should have been any wetter than they were. No good reason, that is.

"I'm afraid not," Ted replied in answer to his daughter's question. Then he gave them a knowing smile. "I'm sorry that I can't volunteer to go for a walk on the beach to leave you two alone, but it's not exactly a good night for a stroll."

Graham thought that it wasn't a good night to be hanging around deserted docks either, and knew that he had to find a way to make a call first thing in the morning.

Teddy laughed. "I wouldn't send a dog out on a night like this, let alone a father. Why doesn't someone build a fire and I'll make us some hot chocolate? I think Mrs. Watson must have gone to her room already."

She hurried off to the kitchen and Graham's eyes followed her. Her innocence in all this—like everything else about her—had a bittersweetness that he knew he would carry with him forever. After suggesting somewhat curtly that Ted get out of his wet clothes, Graham went to build a fire.

In the kitchen, Teddy put on the milk and then stared out the window. Her father's expression those first few seconds was worrying at her. He'd looked so...bleak. She could find no better word for it. And she couldn't quite believe that poker losses could be the reason, either.

Through the window, she could see that nothing more than a fine mist was falling now, certainly not enough to have soaked him so thoroughly.

She stood there with the imprint of Graham McKinsey still clinging to her—and knew that something was terribly wrong.

Chapter Six

Teddy's worries rode alongside her as she pedaled around the island this bright morning. They were like a yappy little dog, nipping at her heels as she pedaled ever faster, trying to outdistance them. Where, she wondered, was the peace and serenity for which she had always prized this place? It certainly wasn't much in evidence this summer.

On the one hand there was her father; on the other, Graham. She didn't know what to do about either of them, but clearly, something had to be done. Teddy wasn't one to sit around waiting for events to shape themselves without her assistance.

Last night, for the second night in a row, she'd heard her father prowling about the house late at night. He continued to deny that anything was troubling him and Graham brushed it off, too. But Teddy knew better.

Her best opportunity to get some answers from her father would come in the next two days. Graham was making a short trip to campaign headquarters, and with him out of the way Teddy felt sure she could wear her father down. Sometimes it seemed to her that the two of them used each other as a shield in order to avoid her.

Then, of course, there was Graham himself. Teddy was growing very tired of the ever-changing nature of their relationship. Since the night of the boathouse, he had reverted to his other persona: friendly, teasing—and nothing else. She did note with some satisfaction, however, that after each of the times he'd let loose his emotions, he didn't recede quite so far into polite formality. Perhaps she was already wearing him down.

The reasons for Graham's behavior remained as elusive as ever. Her best guess was that he'd been burned at some time in the recent past. Still, Graham seemed so very sure of himself in every way that it was nearly impossible for her to see him suffering from some past love affair.

She had briefly wondered if she might be coming on too strong, but that seemed as unlikely as the other explanation and for the same reason. No man who was that sure of himself could feel threatened by an assertive woman.

With those vexing problems still nipping at her heels, she rode hard for the final quarter mile to the house, then parked the bike and went in to get a well deserved cup of coffee and one of the housekeeper's luscious sticky buns. Through the window, she saw Graham down on the beach, doing pushups at the moment, so she gathered up coffee and bun and decided to join him.

She knew perfectly well that she distracted him, so she made certain that she perched in a prominent spot on a small dune, then proceeded to devour her breakfast as she watched him finish his routine. He gave her a quick glance before turning to his labors and she wondered wickedly whether his passion for exercise might not be a way of sublimating other passions.

The truth was that she did find it rather enjoyable to torment him a bit, although she suspected that if he was to rise to the bait, *she* might well be the one to back off. Hovering in the very back of her mind was a fear that that passion could prove to be uncontrollable.

He finally finished his routine and came up to her just as she was licking the remnants of the sticky bun from her fingers. She paused with her forefinger at her lips as she became achingly aware of his attention to that gesture.

Beads of sweat glistened on his face, his unruly hair was plastered damply to his brow and he needed a shave. A spreading heat inside her told her that she found this all very appealing. He sat down beside her and opened a small thermos of orange juice.

"Why are you so obsessive about your exercise?" she asked, hearkening back to her own explanation.

"I'm not obsessive about it," he protested mildly. "I just like to keep in shape. I'm not a kid anymore, and it's easy to slide into middle-aged flabbiness."

"Anyone who goes running even in the rain is obsessive, Graham."

"So is anyone who can't do more than grunt until she has her first cup of coffee."

"That's self-preservation, not obsession."

"Exactly what I said about myself."

They sat there companionably, staring out at the sparkling water. Teddy smiled to herself. The intimacy of their living situation, while in some ways very frustrating, was also very pleasurable. She enjoyed seeing him unshaven and rumpled in the mornings, and suspected that he found her waking grumpiness and dishabille rather appealing, too. In moments such as this, it was all too easy to think of Graham as a permanent part of her life.

"Dad was up prowling around the house again last night," she said in what must have sounded like a non sequitur to him, but was in fact merely a switch from one of her problems to the other.

Graham gave her a sidelong glance, then tipped up the thermos to finish his orange juice. "Now, *that's* an obsession. He's fine, Teddy. Everyone suffers from insomnia from time to time."

"He never did before."

"And how long has it been since you lived with him for any length of time?"

"We were here last summer," she pointed out. "Sometimes he didn't sleep well then, either, but that was right after Mom's death."

Graham covered the thermos and got up. "Stop worrying about him, Teddy," he said with mild annoyance.

She was taken aback by his tone. "He's my father, Graham, and I love him. If something's bothering him, then it affects me, too."

She felt, rather than saw his sidelong glance, but he kept his silence all the way back to the house.

Teddy was with her father in his den an hour later, when Graham appeared in the doorway, clad in a business suit and carrying an attaché case. He was, she thought, one of those rare men whose appearance didn't change at all, regardless of what he wore. In sweats or in a vested suit, he exuded the same rugged appeal. They exchanged glances just as a car horn sounded outside, announcing the neighbor who was giving Graham a lift to the mainland.

He said goodbye to her father, then seemed to hesitate momentarily as he turned to her. Teddy got up to follow him to the front door, where they both paused rather self-consciously. For a moment, his expression was disturbingly grim, but then he dropped his attaché case and reached out to cup her face between his palms as the grimness gave way to a gentle smile.

"I think I miss you already," he said simply.

"What a coincidence," she said wryly. "I was thinking the very same thing myself."

"On the other hand," he went on, still holding her face, "it might be pleasant to boss people around without an argument for a change."

"Well, enjoy it while you can. I'll be waiting right here to take up where I left off."

"In more ways than one, I suspect," he said as his eyes roved over her face with undisguised hunger.

She was about to respond to that when he stopped her with a soft kiss. Certain that he intended for it to go no further, Teddy grasped his head before he could pull away. He tensed for one brief second, then groaned and wrapped his arms tightly about her, surrounding her with himself as he unleashed his need.

"Teddy," he groaned against her neck, "what the hell am I going to do about you?"

Even given the huskiness in his voice, Teddy sensed that this was no rhetorical question. It seemed to spring from a deep well of pathos that she couldn't begin to understand. But she had no opportunity to ask questions, because he released her quickly, picked up his bags and was gone without a backward glance. She stood there in the doorway, staring at his back and wondering what it was she didn't know and how she could go about learning it.

"DAD, I'M TIRED of beating around the bush. I want to know what's bothering you and I don't want another of your vague answers. You're not sleeping well, and when you're not working, you're lost in a fog."

Teddy worked to keep pace with her father as they rode their bikes along the deserted road. She'd already tried twice before to get him to open up, but to no avail. When he said nothing, she forged on.

"As I see it, there could be only two things wrong: business problems or a change of heart about the race. So which is it?"

"The business is doing fine, which you'd already know if you ever read the reports I send to you. And I haven't changed my mind about the race."

She was not about to let that end-of-discussion tone stop her this time, although she was well aware of the source of her own stubbornness.

"Then what is it? Because you sure aren't yourself these days."

"Teddy," he said in a tone that was half-annoyed and half-placating, "you've always been too imaginative for your own good. If I seem distracted at times, it's because I've got a lot riding on this race."

"What's riding on it?" she asked with a frown. "I mean, I know you want to win, but if you lose you've always got the company to go back to."

He shot her a quick glance and, for just an instant, Teddy saw that same haunted look she'd seen on his face the night he'd returned early from his poker game, dripping wet.

"I want out of the company, Teddy, and this is the way out."

"But why?" She persisted, hurrying to keep up with him as he accelerated still more. "You've always loved your work."

"I'd think that you'd be pleased to see me wanting to get out of what you refer to as the death-and-destruction business."

"Well, I'm not, because I can't believe that you want to give it up."

He said nothing at all in reply, and in that silence Teddy became certain that he didn't want to give up the company, but was somehow being forced to do so. That would even explain his sudden, unlikely decision to enter politics. She knew she had absolutely nothing but gut instincts going for her but she believed it completely.

Still, how could anyone be forcing him out of the company, since he was still the majority stockholder? She didn't know much about business, but given his controlling interest, she couldn't believe anyone could oust him. Besides, it wasn't like the father she knew to be giving up without a fight.

Having seized upon this as an answer, Teddy was like a terrier worrying a bone. She made no further attempts to drag information out of him because she was now certain that she had at least grasped the dimensions of the problem, if not the exact cause. It was time to pursue this matter on her own, and she began to mull over how she could do that.

She was at work with her father in his study when Graham called from New Haven. As the two men talked, Teddy began to wonder if Graham could be of some assistance in solving this puzzle. She doubted very much that he already knew the answer, since she didn't think he would be capable of deceiving her. And yet, he'd already told her she was obsessed, and nothing she could say would be likely to change his mind. It was better that she pursue this on her own for the time being.

She left off her thoughts when her father hung up the phone, and her expression must have mirrored her disappointment that Graham hadn't asked to speak with her because her father smiled at her understandingly.

"You really like him, don't you, honey?"

She returned the smile and nodded. "I'm sure you must find that surprising, since we argue all the time, and you yourself said that he isn't the type women usually go for."

"That's true," Ted agreed with a chuckle. "But then, I never expected to see you end up with an ordinary man."

"It isn't very likely that I'm going to end up with Graham, either," she said with a sudden burst of frustration. "He's fighting it. And in any event, I don't want a man who's going to be running all over the country managing campaigns."

"I don't see him doing that indefinitely," her father replied thoughtfully, "in spite of what he says."

"Then what do you see him doing?" Teddy asked. She was glad to see that his thoughts agreed with hers on that subject.

"I'm not sure," he replied slowly. "But I pride myself on being a pretty fair judge of men, and I just don't see Graham staying in this business. In fact, I'm surprised that he's been in it this long." He paused, then added, "Or at all, for that matter."

Teddy found that very interesting, in view of her own initial reservations about Graham, but before she could pursue it, the phone rang again. Her father said hello, and then, after a brief pause, asked his caller to wait.

"Honey, would you mind going up to my room for that printout of opinion surveys? I left them there last night and I want another look at them."

Teddy obediently got up and left the room, but as soon as she was out of his sight, she stopped. It sounded to her as though he had wanted to get rid of her. The memory of those other calls propelled her to the screened porch. Feeling guilty but nonetheless determined, Teddy crept quietly over to the side closest to her father's window. This time, his voice came to her clearly.

" . . . said I'd get in touch with you when I've decided," he was saying in a low tone.

"Don't threaten me," he went on after a short pause. "I told you before that I could—" The rest was cut off abruptly, as though the caller had interrupted him.

"No, no more meetings. I won't take that chance again."

After another, longer pause, he said belligerently, "What makes you think I'd believe you? You told me that before. This time, I'm making damned sure—by getting out."

Then, a moment later: "You gave me two weeks and I'm taking them. You'll hear from me then. I can't get to the office before that."

Teddy jumped nervously as the receiver was slammed into its cradle, followed by total silence. She bolted from the room and ran for the kitchen, not wanting to risk being seen by her father as she headed for the front staircase. After a mad dash up the narrow back stairs, she returned to the study, clutching the sheaf of papers he had requested.

She found him standing at the window, staring out. Such was her state of mind at that moment that she feared he might know that she had eavesdropped on his conversation. It was a heart-wrenching moment for Teddy, who hated deception at all times and most certainly with the father she so loved.

"Was that Graham again?" she inquired brightly, hating her falseness.

He turned around very slowly, but when he did his expression was bland and seemingly untroubled. "No, it was Elizabeth. She's having trouble with my personal filing system."

Teddy felt a shard of ice lodge in her chest. Elizabeth was her father's long-time secretary, and Teddy knew that of all the people it might have been, it could not possibly have been her. Her father was lying to her. He was definitely in trouble.

For the remainder of the day, Teddy replayed that over-heard conversation endlessly in her mind. It made no more sense to her after the fiftieth time than it had after the first—but she now knew that the trouble *did* involve the company, since he'd made a reference to getting to the office.

The lies between father and daughter hung over her, a heavy, ugly cloud much like the ones that were pushing across the late afternoon sky when she went across to pick up Graham.

GRAHAM PACED THE DOCK restlessly, his eyes searching the horizon for her. He was a bit early, and he knew from ex-perience that she wouldn't be. Teddy was one of those peo-ple whose personal clocks always ran from ten to twenty minutes late.

His trip to New Haven had accomplished only one of its two purposes: the one he hadn't admitted to Teddy and her father. He had met with his support group and satisfied himself that all was proceeding as he had believed.

His stated purpose—to check on progress at campaign headquarters—had masked a hidden desire to find things gone awry. If that had been the case, he could have per-suaded Teddy to leave Matiscotta to take charge of the op-eration. Unfortunately, the staff at work there were functioning very well, just as Teddy had said.

The result was that Teddy would remain on Matiscotta through it all, and he had gotten to know some very good and dedicated people who were working hard for nothing.

There were moments when he truly hated Ted Sothern, with an anger that was far too personal. Hadn't the man ever considered the others whose lives he was affecting?

Then he would veer off into a deep, aching regret. He liked Ted as a person and could empathize, if not sympa-thize, with his motives. Graham had long ago learned that anyone was capable of anything, given the right set of circumstances: the tragic flaw theory dramatized so eloquently by Shakespeare.

He scanned the horizon again and this time saw a boat streaking for the harbor, churning up froth behind it as it knifed through the gray-green waters. In spite of his dark mood, he smiled. In the boat was the one good—and ultimately, the worst—thing that had come from this mission.

TEDDY STREAKED INTO THE HARBOR, where she could already see Graham awaiting her. A small thrill of pleasure rippled through her, but it failed to drive out the chill that had penetrated to her very soul. She shivered despite the warmth of her suede jacket.

That overheard conversation continued to replay itself, like an unending tape recording. And the more she listened to it, the more ominous it became. What could he have meant when he said that he couldn't take a chance on another meeting? It conjured up images of trenchcoat-clad figures skulking around in dark corners: the material of overblown thrillers and not of reality. Or at least not the reality of a father who had always been a straightforward, honest man.

She throttled back and approached the pier, where Graham stood waiting. For a moment she let her fears slip away. A part of her wanted very badly to leap out of the boat and grab him and never let go. But she was held back by his unwillingness to commit himself and a question about whether she would be content without it.

He reached out to take the line she tossed to him. They had planned to have dinner at the pound again before returning to Matiscotta. And until this day's revelations she had been looking forward to spending time alone with him.

Now, however, she knew that she was far too preoccupied to enjoy their evening together.

She took the hand he extended to her and let him help her out of the boat. They exchanged greetings, and then he circled her waist and stared down at her with that unique intensity that often made Teddy think he was committing her every feature to memory. At other times, she had merely found this curious; now, in her present state, she found it frightening.

She lowered her gaze, not wanting to see that look, but he cupped her chin and drew her face back up again, then paused for only a second before claiming her mouth in a softly persuasive kiss.

Too much was swirling about in her mind at the moment: thoughts of her father, thoughts of Graham. His kiss felt somehow wrong, even as it aroused in her all that nameless, fathomless yearning. And then, suddenly, all those thoughts coalesced into one devastating question: what if Graham was somehow involved in all this?

Later, when reason had returned, she would blame that absurd thought on her initial doubts about him, brought back to life by her father's concurrence in her opinion, and then blown completely out of proportion by the subsequent events of the day. But for now, the question had a horrifying, paralyzing validity. She stiffened involuntarily and pushed at his chest. He loosened his hold on her, but did not let her go entirely and gave her a puzzled look.

"What's wrong, honey?"

His gently concerned tone and the term of endearment partially restored her rationality. She lowered her head, flushing with embarrassment for having harbored such ridiculous suspicions. But once again, he hooked a finger beneath her chin and forced her to look at him.

"Teddy, what's happened?" His mind began to race through the possibilities. Had Ted drawn her into this? Surely he wouldn't do such a thing. Or had Teddy somehow found it out for herself? That, too, seemed unlikely but not impossible.

She managed a smile that she hoped looked genuine. "Nothing happened. You just surprise me sometimes, that's all. I never know how you're going to react." For the first time she was actually glad about his changeable attitude toward her.

She took his hand and started toward the rental car he had waiting for them. "Are you hungry?"

Under normal circumstances, Graham would have told her just what it was that he was hungry for—and it wasn't lobster. But he heard the false brightness in her voice and contented himself with a nod.

Teddy began to chatter away, barely pausing for breath and giving him no indication at all about what was really on her mind. He was a patient man—the perfect counterpoint to her more impetuous nature—but his patience began to wear thin as they sat down to dinner without her having yet told him what was troubling her.

Through dinner he continued to wait, prodding her whenever the opportunity presented itself. But she ignored his thinly disguised attempts and countered with alternating silences or trivial conversation.

After an uneventful and mostly silent crossing, they reached the Sothern dock, and Graham immediately suggested a stroll on the beach, knowing that he'd get nothing out of her if they returned to the house. She agreed to the walk on the beach, although with a notable lack of enthusiasm. Finally having exhausted his patience, Graham seized upon a silence to confront the issue.

"Are you still worrying about your father?"

He was holding her hand at the moment, and immediately felt a brief tension run through her at the question. His fears loomed ever larger as he awaited her response.

"Yes, but I suppose I'm being foolish. He says everything is fine so I have to accept that. I guess he must be feeling more pressure than I'd expected him to feel."

Teddy knew that she was unnecessarily belaboring the point, but Graham's question had caught her unprepared. She'd thought she'd done a good job of avoiding the issue.

"Did you talk with him about it while I was gone?" he asked, certain that she had.

"Yes, but I didn't get anywhere." Having reached a sudden decision, Teddy came to a halt, forcing Graham to do likewise. She faced him squarely and gave him that level look she could use so effectively.

"Do you know anything about him that I don't know, Graham?"

The most difficult thing Graham McKinsey had ever been forced to do in his life was what he now did. He looked straight into those striking blue eyes and shook his head.

"No, of course not. I'm the one who's been telling you there's nothing to worry about, remember?"

Teddy continued to stare at him for long, agonizing seconds and he tensed inwardly, half-expecting her to call him a liar. Later, he'd wonder what he would have done if she'd accused him. Fortunately, she didn't. After searching his face carefully, she made a dismissive gesture.

"Well, I didn't really think you did, but you two have gotten to be awfully close, and I thought Dad might have confided in you when he wouldn't in me."

"You two are about as close as any father and daughter I've ever seen."

"Oh, I know we are, but it's possible he would keep something from me. Out of love, you know."

Graham knew, and he hoped desperately that was the case. It now seemed increasingly unlikely that Ted had told her anything, which meant that she had somehow picked up something on her own.

They continued to stroll slowly along the beach hand in hand, alone in a salt-scented world of pale moonlight and the susurrous sounds of the sea. Even though they were both locked in their private fears, they were not immune to the sensuality of the night and the setting.

They reached the end of the strip of sand and paused in the dark shadows of a rock jetty. Both of them were temporarily paralyzed, caught between the dark world of their minds and their suddenly escalating awareness of each other.

Graham whispered her name hoarsely and gathered her to him. He felt a tremor run through her and encircled her more tightly, as though by so doing he could protect her somehow from fears he knew could be close to the truth. He was not a religious man, but he sent up a prayer now: that all he loved about her would not be destroyed by what was to come.

She was clinging to him, seeking his strength, and he well knew how unusual that was for her. But still, she said nothing and that silence told him that she couldn't bring herself to trust him completely. Had his anguish and his doubts somehow communicated themselves to her? She couldn't have learned anything of his role in this, but when he felt as close to her as he did now, he was almost ready to believe that she had read his mind.

He buried his face in her soft curls, then lifted her face to his with a groan. Her mouth was soft and pliant and seeking as he covered it with his own. He knew it was time to back off, but instead, his hands found their way beneath her jacket, then under the thin silk of her shirt to soft, warm skin.

She returned his kisses hungrily as she wound her hands around his neck. Her nails pricked skin that had already become almost unbearably sensitive. He slid his hands slowly down along taut curves until he was cupping her rounded bottom and pressing her against his growing hardness.

She was his. She belonged to him. That certainty roared through his brain, burning away reason. He lifted his head briefly and saw behind them a stretch of long beach grass that waved slightly in the evening breeze. Without conscious intent, but with an all consuming need, he swept her up into his arms, startling her into a gasp of surprise. Before she could ask what he was doing, he had laid her down in the makeshift bed.

Then he knelt beside her and pushed the suede jacket off her shoulders. Her sweater came next. Then, when he began to fumble at her back for the bra clasp, she gave a nervous little laugh and opened the front clasp herself, letting the bra fall away.

Graham tore off his own jacket and struggled with his shirt buttons as he kept his eyes riveted to her. Moonbeams and starlight played over her bare skin, giving it an ivory sheen. Darkened by the pale light, her coppery curls tumbled about her face and touched her bare shoulders. He started to reach for her, then hesitated as rationality began a final, deadly war with passion.

She frowned slightly and then wrapped her arms about herself. It was a uniquely vulnerable gesture, and in that instant, Graham knew that the need to protect her had won out over the need to possess her. That it was himself he had to protect her against was an irony that was not lost on him as he moved forward and enfolded her into his arms.

Because he knew that he would have this and no more, Graham began to stroke her carefully, letting his fingers learn the feel of her, letting his brain fill up with memories he knew would last a lifetime.

But then, when that final moment came, when he knew that he must stop, he moved abruptly, setting her aside even as his eyes continued to devour her.

"Graham! What is it?" Her voice was both harsh and husky.

He reached shakily for her clothes and almost thrust them at her.

"Get dressed, Teddy."

Their eyes met in the dim light, and for a moment he was sure she would refuse, that she would reach out to him and bring them both to ultimate disaster. But perhaps she saw the fear in his eyes, because, without a word, she picked up her bra and put it on, then followed it with the shirt and jacket. He put on his own shirt and jacket as he tried to formulate an excuse that would work. She stood up, brushed the sand from her skirt and stared down at him in the semidarkness.

"You owe me an explanation, Graham, and I want it now!" Her voice had a tremulous quality, but was nonetheless very firm.

He said nothing as he got clumsily to his feet, discovering to his shock that his legs were rather shaky. He was still seeking some magic words that could be a middle ground between the lies he couldn't tell and the truth he mustn't divulge.

"Teddy, we have time. It isn't necessary for us to rush into anything."

She stared at him long and hard, her expression unreadable. "Do we have time, Graham?"

Then, while he was desperately seeking an answer to her startling question, she took a few steps away from him, turning her back on him as she stared out to sea.

"You're right. There's no need to rush into an affair. But I do want you, Graham."

Her voice broke a little on the last words, and that brought him to her. He circled her from behind and felt her yield, but only partway. The pliant woman who had flowed beneath his touch was gone now, and he mourned her loss even as he gave an inward sigh of relief.

"Do you trust me, Teddy?" he asked huskily.

There was a heart-stopping moment of hesitation, but then she nodded slowly. He felt both triumphant and anguished at having gained from her that to which he had no right.

"Then you'll just have to accept that I have my reasons for letting things stay as they are for now." The ugly, mocking echo of his last, lying words hung there in the night breeze.

She turned around in the circle of his arms and scrutinized him once again, before nodding a second time. He took her hand and led her back to the house, alternately congratulating himself and cursing himself for a fool.

FROM HIS CIGAR SMOKE-HAZED CORNER, Graham watched Teddy. On either side of him, Ted Sothern and Senator Oldham held forth on the state of the economy. He interjected the occasional comment, but the future of the economy held far less interest to him than the vibrant woman on the other side of the room.

She was exceptionally colorful this night in a gauzy blue dress with a ragged hem that was a near-perfect match for her eyes and a startling contrast to her hair, swept back from her face by a matching blue scarf. Even in the midst of

George's exotic household, Teddy stood out. Perhaps, he thought wryly, she had even planned it that way.

George's mother, who was part of the group surrounding Teddy, reminded Graham of a sleek blackbird, with close-cropped black hair that might have been natural at one time and huge, green-painted black eyes set in a small, sharp featured face. Even her movements were nervous and bird-like, in contrast to Teddy's fluid motions.

Off in another part of the room, George's father held forth in a powerful bass voice that matched his bear-like physique. He was, Graham had learned, a constructor. He created gigantic outdoor art, generally in iron or steel, working in the summers in a dilapidated old barn behind their house.

There was also, lost somewhere in the cavernous living room, a sister who appeared to be a leftover from the sixties, and Teddy had told him there was yet another sister who was an acknowledged lesbian and activist for the gay community.

Teddy glanced his way and smiled before turning her attention back to her companions. Graham wondered what would happen if they didn't already know each other. He wasn't by nature an extroverted, party-loving type, although he found this eclectic group very interesting. But it was generally his style to remain unobtrusive at large parties, and neither was he usually the target of feminine flirtations.

Perhaps because of his reserved nature, he'd often found himself attracted to women of Teddy's type. But he'd never carried it beyond a brief flirtation because he was convinced that whoever had declared that opposites attract had written a prescription for disaster. He was sure that such an attraction had to be short-lived, leaving only the glaring differences when it departed.

But Teddy was different. Although she was obviously enjoying herself in this noisy gathering, she seemed to derive equal pleasure from their quiet walks on the beach and the hikes through the forest. Splashes of gaiety and oases of quiet calm. Sparkling wit and moments of introspection. These were the contrasts that had attracted him from the beginning and still held him in thrall.

He left off his thoughts as Ted Sothern drew him into the conversation, but he noticed Teddy slipping out the door with her old friend, Alex Johns, whom Graham had met the day he'd first met Teddy herself. He hadn't missed that serious, purposeful look on Teddy's face and wondered what the two of them might have to discuss.

Teddy led Alex to a quiet spot just off the terrace, rather nervous now that she was taking her first concrete step toward learning about the source of her father's problems.

"Alex," she began, "I need your advice about something. Something confidential."

Alex grinned at her. "My lips are sealed, you know that, Teddy. And my advice, admittedly on very brief acquaintance, is to marry him and put the poor guy out of his misery."

Teddy was momentarily surprised before she grasped his meaning and laughed rather self-consciously. She hadn't realized that others were aware of that electricity between her and Graham. Especially, she thought, since he had returned to his friendly, but not *too* friendly mode once again.

"It has nothing to do with Graham," she said, hoping desperately that that was true. "It's about Dad."

At his questioning look, she forged ahead. "Since you're a big deal corporate type, you must know all about boards of directors and such."

"I'm afraid I haven't yet reached the point where I've had any actual dealings with them," Alex replied dryly. "What's going on? Is your father still giving you grief about your refusal to take an active role in the company?"

"No, he's long since given up on that, but it does concern the company. You see, between the two of us, we control a majority of the stock—or rather, he controls it, since I gave him my proxy to vote my stock as he pleases. As I recall, the two of us together have some sixty percent of the stock.

"I think someone is trying to force him out of the company, Alex, and what I wanted to ask you is whether or not that's possible."

Alex frowned. "Why would anyone want to do that?"

"I don't know why." Teddy shrugged. "Dad won't talk about it. All I know is what I overheard of a phone conversation. But the point is: could someone do it?"

"Short of bringing suit against him, claiming that he was destroying the company, there isn't a damned thing they could do, Teddy. And that would be absurd, because the company is doing very well. I know because I keep tabs on it. If there's another stock issue, I'd like to buy some myself."

He stared at her thoughtfully. "Tell me about this phone conversation you overheard. Maybe you just misinterpreted it."

Teddy hesitated, then realized that if she had come this far, she might as well unburden herself of the whole story. Alex was an old and trusted friend, and she knew he liked her father as well. That word "trust" nagged at her briefly as she recalled Graham's asking for that from her and her less than honest reply.

"Well, there were two telephone calls, actually, or maybe three." She went on to repeat to Alex all she could remember, which was almost verbatim in the case of the last call.

Alex listened in silence and didn't speak even when she had finished. He was still mulling it over uneasily when he saw, over Teddy's shoulder, a figure approaching from out of the darkness.

"Hello, Graham. I was planning to rescue you from the cigar smoke when Teddy grabbed me. I guess you can understand that I might prefer her company to yours."

Teddy whirled around just as she heard Graham's low, distinctive chuckle and felt his arms slide possessively about her waist. Annoyance at the untimely interruption vied with pleasure at this apparent change of mood.

"Am I interrupting anything?" Graham asked, knowing full well that he was, and possibly just in the nick of time, too.

"Nothing more than reminiscences that would bore anyone but us," Alex replied equably, after shooting Teddy a quick glance.

There was a split-second shifting of conversational gears, and then they began to talk about their party hosts. Graham kept his arm about Teddy's waist, but he couldn't help noticing a certain rigidity on her part.

He'd overheard enough of the conversation to know now what it was that Teddy had learned and how she had interpreted it. Then he'd interrupted them before Alex could ply her with more questions and possibly suggest a more dangerous explanation.

Graham was very much relieved, because if Teddy persisted in believing that someone was trying to force Ted out of the company, it would keep her out of trouble, for a while anyway. There was no way to keep her out of this indefinitely, but he desperately wanted to protect her for as long as he could.

Teddy was not exactly displeased by Graham's display of jealousy, but she was still annoyed at the interruption. Although there was no denying that his touch had the power to excite her, her main concern at the moment was her father.

She was glad now that Graham had backed off that night on the beach. Now was not the time for them. Still, she couldn't help wondering what *his* reason was—and hoping fervently that it wasn't the same as hers.

Chapter Seven

"I'm going home for a few days." Teddy made her carefully casual announcement to Graham as they both lay on the beach, soaking up the bright sunshine.

He propped himself up on one elbow and stared down at her. "Why?"

"I have some grad students to supervise. If I don't keep an eye on them, they'll just laze away the summer. Besides, they do require guidance from time to time." The lie tripped off her tongue with ease, the result of much practice beforehand.

"I see." Graham lay back down again. He didn't believe her, but he had no intention of confronting her on the matter. She'd told him before that she had a temporary replacement and it stood to reason that the guest professor would be dealing with her students at this point.

He was sure she was planning to pursue her theory regarding her father's problems with the company, and he wondered just what she intended to do. Since she had kept her distance from the company, it wasn't likely that she had any sources of information there. Still, if she chose to exercise her very potent charm...

She stirred restlessly beside him, jolting his awareness of that charm, very nicely displayed at the moment in a bright green bikini. He opened his eyes just as she flopped over onto her stomach and was rewarded—or punished—by the sight of smooth full breasts nearly spilling from the scanty top as she moved.

"Would you mind putting this on my back?" she asked, holding out the tube of suntan cream.

He minded, all right, and he suspected she knew that. She was driving him damned near crazy as it was, lying there half-naked, giving life to all his fantasies. He uncapped the tube, all the while staring at that sleek body covered by only a triangle and a thin strap.

He was sure she knew exactly what she was doing to him, and furthermore, was probably enjoying it. Far from being hurt by his rejection the other night, she seemed almost pleased by it, as though she had been saved from making a mistake herself. Now, he suspected, she felt perfectly safe.

She made a soft contented sound as he massaged her shoulders and back. By the time he finished this chore, she'd be safe only if he threw himself into that forty-five degree water out there.

Very slowly, so as to torment himself for as long as possible, Graham worked his way down her back, sliding greased fingers caressingly along the hollows of her waist and the rise of her lower back. She was lying still, but it was the stillness of rising tension. That made him feel much better. Sadomasochism was definitely preferable to straight masochism.

When he paused at the top of the triangle of cloth, she murmured, "The legs, too, please."

He looked down their long, lightly muscled length and then out to the water, wondering if even it would be cold enough. After squeezing more cream into his hand, he began at her ankles, then slowly worked his way up to the tautness of her thighs. She shifted slightly, spreading her legs a bit, and desire roared through him with all the subtlety of a runaway freight train. There was a split second when it all came apart, when he saw himself reaching for that bright green triangle and ripping it away, shredding it with his bare hands in a frenzied effort to reach the womanly heat beneath. He took a deep, quavering breath and forced the image away.

His fingers hovered tantalizingly along the edges of her inner thighs, and he could feel through their tips the powerful tension in her. He hurried to finish the job, then abruptly got up and headed at a trot for the water.

He was tempted to fling himself headlong into the surf, but instead strode into it stoically. After the warmth of the sun and the far more intense heat of desire, the water felt more like twenty degrees than forty-five. Although he stopped when the water had reached his knees, the icy sensation traveled all the way through him. It did the trick, all right, but just to be sure, he stooped and gathered water to toss over the rest of him. Then he turned and started back toward her.

"If you're that desperate to go swimming," Teddy said with studied casualness, "I'm sure there must be a wet suit at the house that would fit you."

Graham dropped down beside her, intensely aware of his coldness and her heat and a desire to mingle the two. She turned her head to look at him and they exchanged glances that moved slowly to smiles, and then to outright laughter.

Teddy wondered if he knew that his behavior had created a depth of feeling in her that was perhaps even stronger than his lovemaking might have accomplished. She still didn't understand his reasons, but she accepted them because she knew instinctively that they sprang from his feelings for her. No man would reject what he wanted, what was clearly being offered, unless he cared very much.

They continued to lie there in the sun, side by side, with the electric traces of eroticism thrumming just below the surface, sparking fantasies that both soothed and discomfited them. Teddy felt a great temptation to level with Graham, but despite the closeness she felt toward him at moments like this, she kept her silence. She would follow through on her plans, and then perhaps when she returned, she would discuss it with him.

So there she was, two days later, pursuing that plan by poring over company reports in the spare bedroom of her townhouse that she used as a study. From downstairs came the mournful sounds of a cello, played, she supposed, with some skill. She felt jumpy enough without being forced to listen to unfamiliar sounds in her home. The visiting professor's wife was a cellist. She was also something less than a good housekeeper. Teddy was vaguely irritated with herself for having let them use her home, and that did little to improve her state of mind.

The board minutes yielded nothing, except for the information that she had been wise to have avoided the meetings. If there was any disharmony on the board, it had been covered up in the minutes. She tossed them back into the box she had brought down from her attic, then leaned back with a sigh, still annoyed by the sounds from below. She had been so sure that she'd uncover some clue, at least as to who might be threatening her father and why.

She cast a baleful glance at the financial reports that were part of the regular correspondence she received and ignored. With little or no hope, she turned to them, and they confirmed only what she'd already known: the company was in superb financial shape. How could it be otherwise, with all that defense department largess?

There was, she recalled, only one time when the company had been in difficult financial straits: some five or six years ago, just before the current onslaught of Pentagon contracts. And she had learned of it only because she'd happened to overhear part of an argument between her parents. Her mother had been begging her father to accept a loan from her trust fund to see him through the crisis, and he had flatly refused to consider it.

Teddy remembered that incident for two reasons: first, because arguments between her parents had been very rare, and secondly, because for the first time, she had learned of her father's sensitivity toward her mother's wealth.

Later she had privately questioned her mother about it and had found out that Ted Sothern had always been particularly sensitive to that issue. Matters hadn't been helped at all, her mother had told her, by her family's initial disapproval of him, based solely on his lack of personal wealth.

Rather shamefully, Teddy realized now that she had let the whole matter slip from her mind. She hadn't been living at home by then, and her own life had been busy, with a heavy grad school schedule and her first serious romance. She supposed that she'd been unable to take the situation too seriously because she'd assumed her father would eventually give in and accept her mother's help. Probably he had, because the company had survived and then prospered once more.

Sighing, she replaced the reports and then carried the boxes back to the attic. After bidding the cellist goodbye and apologizing once more for her intrusion, Teddy returned to the apartment she had borrowed from a travelling colleague.

That evening, she had dinner with another fellow professor whom she'd been dating casually for several months. Simple curiosity had been responsible for her calling him upon her arrival. She had given some thought to the possibility of inviting him up to Matiscotta when his summer classes ended, but that had been before Graham McKinsey entered her life.

Even before their entrées had been served, Teddy had learned what she'd suspected: that spark of romantic interest was gone. He was as interesting as ever and even better looking, with a tan to complement his blondness, but she might as well have shared her dinner with a female friend for all the interest he sparked in her. The invitation to visit Matiscotta was not extended, and she fell asleep later with Graham's rugged visage swimming in her mind.

Her last conscious thought was that when she had finally solved the mystery of her father's behavior, she would have to face up to the fact that Graham McKinsey had staked out a very large claim to her.

The next noon found Teddy waiting impatiently at a restaurant for the arrival of her father's secretary. By now she was less hopeful for some enlightenment from this source, although Elizabeth had been with her father for many years and knew him well. Her failure to uncover any clues thus far had put her into a pessimistic mood.

But at least her earlier visit to campaign headquarters had buoyed her spirits. It was filled with busy, enthusiastic people who were eager for the summer to be ended so that the real campaign could begin. There were, of course, events scheduled for the summer, but the real crunch didn't come until Labor Day and the weeks immediately following.

The offices had been plastered with campaign posters, most of them showing her father's smiling countenance. Surrounded thusly, Teddy had begun to wonder again if she might be worrying unnecessarily. Even if her father had lied to her, he might have had good reason to keep a business problem to himself, especially in view of her opinions on that business. And maybe even Graham was partly responsible for her getting carried away. Her life had been topsy-turvy ever since his arrival.

It was difficult, she thought, for her to see beyond the campaign to a time when her life would return to normal. A chill ran through her at that thought, the kind of chill her mother would have referred to as "someone walking on my grave." She deliberately conjured up images of her classes and of office sessions with students, but the unsettling thought persisted until, at last, she saw Elizabeth enter the restaurant.

Teddy had always liked Elizabeth and greeted her enthusiastically. As she looked at the handsome woman with her slim figure and stylish salt-and-pepper hair, Teddy was shocked to find herself considering Elizabeth and her father. Elizabeth's husband had died a few years ago, so she too was free. Teddy told herself that she wasn't really being traitorous to her mother's memory with such thoughts, but the whole issue was still very disturbing.

As soon as the conversation permitted, Teddy inquired about Elizabeth's future plans.

"Will you be staying on at the company if Dad wins the election?"

"I'm not sure," the older woman replied. "I could, of course, but your father has asked me to consider coming to Washington with him."

"He'd be lost without you," Teddy said encouragingly, even as that twinge of guilt returned. "Do you think you'd like Washington?"

"Well, it might be interesting. A fresh start, you know. There's really nothing to hold me here, other than friends, of course. Rob is in California and Jennifer is down in North Carolina. I've just found out that I'm going to become a grandmother next winter, and it would be nice to be closer to her."

Teddy said that she hoped Elizabeth would decide to stay with her father, and the two women broke off conversation for a few moments to peruse the menu. Teddy made her selection quickly and cast a few surreptitious glances around them. Normally, this quiet restaurant, away from both campus and the downtown business district, would have been perfect for a private discussion. But as luck would have it, two men had come in just after her own arrival and with dozens of tables to choose from, had managed to take the only one close to hers. Furthermore, they didn't seem to have much to talk about between themselves, either. Even before Elizabeth's arrival, Teddy had heard only sporadic conversation from them.

As soon as they had ordered, Elizabeth inquired about Ted. "I hope he's not having second thoughts about his decision to run."

"Strange that you should mention that," Teddy said, glad for the opening. "I've been wondering the same thing myself lately."

"Oh?" Elizabeth asked.

Teddy affected a careless shrug, uncertain about how much to divulge to Elizabeth. "Well, he just seems...not quite himself lately. He claims that he's fine and that he doesn't regret his decision at all, but I don't know."

"Frankly, Teddy, his decision nearly bowled me over. He'd never been that interested in politics that I knew of."

"I thought that maybe it was because he just didn't feel the same about the company after he took it public," Teddy suggested.

Elizabeth shook her head emphatically. "Oh, he was a bit upset about it at the time, but he got over it quickly. And that's another decision of his that I never understood, although I'll be the first to admit that corporate finance is all Greek to me."

"It is to me, too," Teddy agreed. "But I never understood that, either, and neither did Mom, actually. It seems that there's a lot I don't understand about him anymore."

The older woman nodded. "He seemed to be handling the loss of your mother about as well as could be expected and had just about returned to normal when he suddenly made his decision to run for the senate. I knew that something was on his mind just before that, because he became so distracted. He'd forget things that he'd never forgotten before—not even when he returned after your mother's death. And he was even a bit short with me and some of the others once or twice, although he always apologized later."

Teddy considered her next words carefully and leaned forward, lowering her voice because she had the strange impression that the silent occupants of the next table were eavesdropping.

"Elizabeth, do you have any reason to think that someone might be trying to cause trouble for Dad?"

Elizabeth frowned uncomprehendingly, then shook her head. "I don't understand what you mean, Teddy. Who could possibly want to do such a thing?"

"Well, I overheard part of a telephone conversation of his recently that made me wonder." She shrugged and leaned back in her chair again. "Of course, it was one-sided, so it's possible that I just misinterpreted it."

She didn't tell Elizabeth about her father's subsequent lie that it had been her he'd been talking to. She could see that Elizabeth was already upset.

"If you're worried that it could be someone at the company who's causing problems, you can forget it. Everyone misses him like crazy. He certainly has no enemies there."

"What about the board?' Teddy asked.

The secretary shook her head emphatically. "They're all just as upset about his departure as the staff is. I know them all, since I attend the meetings, and believe me, if begging on their hands and knees would have kept him there, they'd have done it. Every one of them. He's the heart and soul of the company.''

Teddy didn't know whether to be gratified or disappointed to hear all of this. There seemed to be nothing left to say on the subject and she didn't want to trouble Elizabeth any further, so she let the matter drop after a rueful reference to her own overactive imagination and they moved on to other topics as they enjoyed their lunch.

As she talked, though, Teddy was facing up to the fact that she had drawn a great big blank in her first stint at detective work. What could she do now? She had pretty much decided to lay it all out to Graham when she returned to Matiscotta, but what point was there to that now? She knew nothing more and he might think that she was some sort of neurotic fool if she persisted in believing her father was in trouble.

Teddy said goodbye to Elizabeth outside the restaurant and headed for her car, already dreading the long trip ahead that would mean too much time alone with her murky thoughts. She had flown to Maine last time, but had decided this time to take her car with her. It was a classic Jag, one of the models with a twelve-cylinder engine that required the almost full-time services of a mechanic. Thanks to its latest trip to the garage, it was running smoothly, but it wasn't a very comfortable car in which to make such a long trip. Nevertheless, Teddy loved the car and was prepared to overlook its many faults. She was also eager to show it off to Graham, who had already expressed an interest in it.

As she started the engine and then listened with satisfaction to the low growl, she saw the two men who had been at the next table emerge from the restaurant and head for their car, which was parked across from hers. After waiting until they were out of her path, she put the Jag into reverse and roared out of the parking lot.

Just as she had suspected, the monotony of the trip gave her far too much time to think. By the time she crossed into Massachusetts, she knew that she had reached the point where further rehashing of the scanty information she possessed was becoming counterproductive. She had chosen to take back roads rather than the interstates in order to put the Jag through its paces, but not even the car's exceptional road-handling capabilities could relieve either her boredom or her depression over her failure to get any answers.

She attempted to console herself with the thought that the trip hadn't been a complete waste of time. As a result of her lunch with Elizabeth, she had learned two things: that she was not alone in having found her father's recent behavior to be unusual, and secondly, whatever was wrong wasn't likely to have anything to do with the company. She felt sure that Elizabeth would have known of any problems there and would have told her.

Beyond that, all was speculation, and Teddy was tired of speculating, especially since it had gotten her nowhere. So she thought instead about Elizabeth and her father. The idea of a romance between them still disturbed her, but she forced herself to remember that her mother had been gone for over a year, and that she herself had hoped her father had now put it behind him. Should she drop some encouraging hints? It might not be a bad idea, since her father might be reluctant to bring a new woman into his life if he thought she would disapprove.

The parent-child relationship had never before seemed so fragile and so fraught with tensions. Her father was hiding something from her and behaving strangely, and she was uncertain about encouraging him to consider a replacement for her mother. A life that had always been so simple and straightforward had suddenly become tortuous and unclear.

And then there was Graham, who seemed to be looming ever larger in her life, and whose behavior was also baffling—not to mention frustrating.

As she mulled all this over, she slowed the car slightly, having belatedly noticed that the road was wet and the sky ahead was ominously dark. She was traveling along a deserted stretch of rural road in New Hampshire, not far from the Maine border. When she'd last checked her rearview mirror, there hadn't been a car in sight, but now she saw that a dark van was behind her. She had only a scant second to think that he was tailing her far too closely before he pulled out to pass and she automatically slowed down a bit to allow him to get back in safely.

The next few moments would remain forever a blur to Teddy. Instead of passing her, the van stayed alongside, scant inches away. She started to brake, but at that moment, he shot forward and then cut in so sharply that he could not have missed her by much more than a coat of paint.

With her foot already on the brake, Teddy now swerved sharply, certain the Jag could handle it. But as she swerved, the right wheels of the car left the pavement and dropped onto the spongy berm. In one sickening second Teddy knew that she had lost control.

The Jag shot down an embankment, lurching wildly. It flipped over onto its roof, then flopped back again, finally coming to rest in a field with a groan and shriek of protesting metal and springs. The engine coughed twice and died.

All of this had happened so fast that Teddy barely had time to let out a startled cry. The lap and shoulder belts had held her securely in place through the wild ride, but at some point, her forehead and shoulder had struck something.

She sat there, stunned and still unable to accept what had happened. Finally, she looked out through the rain-spattered windshield that had miraculously remained intact, and saw that the van had stopped a short distance beyond where she had left the road. The passenger door hung open as a man scrambled down the steep embankment toward her.

Teddy watched his approach and anger began to drive out the shock. She had plenty to say to him, that was for sure. What kind of game had that driver been playing? If she didn't know better, she would think that it had been deliberate.

The man had reached the bottom of the bank and was now crossing the rutted field toward her, not yet clearly visible in the waning light of the approaching storm. But he became more distinct with every hurried step—until he was close enough for her to see the gun in his hand.

The horrifying image had just begun to register in her bruised mind when the man stopped, brought to a halt by a sudden blaring of the van's horn. He whirled around to look back at the van, then turned again to stare at something behind Teddy's range of vision. She turned, too, ignoring a spasm of protest from her injured shoulder.

Another car had stopped alongside the road, at about the point where Teddy had left it. It had barely skidded to a halt when the passenger door was flung open and a man appeared. He, too, started toward her.

She swiveled back to see the reaction of the first man and saw that he was already at the foot of the bank, headed toward the van. It took off before he was completely inside and was gone in a screech of tires.

The second man reached her just as the heavens opened up and a crack of thunder split the silence. Thoroughly confused now, Teddy didn't move, except to check that her doors were still locked.

The man's face appeared at her window, distorted by some cracks. "Are you all right?" he shouted above the storm.

Teddy nodded, straining to see his face more clearly.

"We've already called the police," he went on, seemingly oblivious of the drenching he was getting. "We have a phone in the car."

By now, Teddy was beginning to feel sorry for the man, standing out there in the rain and so obviously concerned about her. She hesitated, then tried to open her door, but found that it wouldn't budge. The man backed off and looked down at the side of the car.

"I think it's sprung. Try the other side."

He disappeared from her view, then reappeared at the passenger side. She reached over to flip the door lock and he opened it without difficulty. Just as he leaned in to extend a hand to her, she heard the distant sound of a siren. Reassured, Teddy accepted the man's help in crawling out of the car.

Ignoring both the rain and the questions of the man, Teddy circled the car. She very nearly started to cry when she saw the dents and scratches on its formerly pristine body. Her rescuer trailed along after her, still inquiring about possible injuries, while up on the road the police car screeched to a halt and the other man from the car went toward them.

"Look at it," she said in a choked voice to the man beside her. "There wasn't a mark on it. Why did they do that?"

As she spoke, she turned toward the man and in a flash of lightning, got her first good look at him. She frowned and swiped at her wet face.

"Haven't I seen you somewhere before?" Then, as soon as the question was out of her mouth, she had the answer. "You were at the next table in the restaurant."

She had only a moment to notice that he looked both surprised and uncomfortable, before a police officer came hurrying up to them and hustled them back to the road, saying that they made too good a target for the lightning in the middle of an open field.

They reached the road when an ambulance arrived, and in the midst of the police officers' questions and the paramedics' inquiries about her condition, Teddy didn't notice the two men leaving.

The paramedics insisted that she accompany them to the local hospital emergency room, and Teddy finally acquiesced, more to get out of the rain than because she felt the need of medical care. One of the police officers went along to question her more about the accident. And it was during the ride to the hospital that she remembered the gun and realized that her rescuers were gone.

X rays and an examination revealed nothing more than bruises and a small cut, and Teddy returned to the waiting room to find the police officer still there.

After many more questions, Teddy was left with the impression that her story about the gun was not believed. Her rescuer hadn't mentioned seeing it, although the officer assured her that he would check with the man, who had left his name and a phone number. His companion had given the police the make and license number of the van and they were checking that out, but it was a New York license and could take a while.

Wet and hungry and somewhat dazed, Teddy didn't press the issue. Perhaps she hadn't seen a gun, after all. It had been dark and stormy and she hadn't exactly been at her most observant. Or, as the officer suggested, the man might have been carrying a screwdriver or something to pry her out of the car. Then, when he'd seen help at hand, he had taken off to avoid being implicated in the accident.

The officer told her that arrangements had already been made to have her car towed to a local garage, then asked her what she planned to do. It was growing late and there was no car rental agency in the small town, so he recommended that she consider staying the night and then seeing to her car in the morning.

"There's an inn at the edge of town," he told her. "It's a nice place, one of those places city folks come to to get the flavor of New England. Good food, too."

Teddy sighed. "You're right. I'm really in no shape to drive anymore tonight, anyway. It's a two-hour trip. And I'll have to see to the car in the morning."

The officer drove her over to pick up her things from the Jag, which had by now reached the garage. She stared at it disconsolately, wondering if it could ever be put right again. The police officer saw her expression.

"We've got a good body man here in town. His hobby is restoring antique and classic cars. You might want to check him out."

She thanked him, then accepted his offer to a lift to the inn, which was as promised: one of those quintessentially New England inns that drew city people in droves. Fortunately, since this was the middle of the week, she had no problem renting a room.

A short time later, she was sinking gratefully onto a big bed covered with an antique quilted spread in a large room filled with antique furniture and papered in a charming floral print. The aromas that had drifted out from the small dining room downstairs had even awakened her appetite.

She continued to sit on the bed, staring at the phone. She had to call because they were expecting her tonight. But what should she tell her father, or Graham?

No sooner had the thought of Graham entered her mind than she began to miss him with an ache that was almost physical and far worse than her bruises. It would feel so good to have his comforting arms around her just now. Even the cozy, romantic atmosphere of the inn conspired to keep her thoughts on him. With a ragged sigh, she picked up the phone.

GRAHAM REPLACED THE RECEIVER with a grim expression. Teddy's call had not come as a surprise, since he'd already received a report on the "accident." But her brave attempt to make light of what had been a very close brush with death had shaken him almost as much as the earlier phone call.

He picked up the phone again to call Ted at Senator Oldham's and inform him of the situation. Taking his cue from Teddy, he downplayed the seriousness of the incident, but it was obvious that Ted was badly shaken, too.

As well he should be, Graham thought angrily after he'd hung up. Hadn't the man ever considered the possibility that his daughter could be dragged into this? Did he think he was dealing with Boy Scouts? Graham had no doubt that Ted had immediately guessed that it was no accident.

He paced the small study for a few minutes, debating with himself over what course of action to pursue, then let his heart make the decision for him.

BY THE TIME SHE HAD EATEN and returned to her room, the blessed numbness that had kept her calm had given way to a nervousness on its way to panic.

It was still too early to go to bed, and she wasn't really tired. There was nothing of interest on TV and she had brought no books with her. She considered going for a walk, but found that she was afraid to leave the inn. Despite her earlier dismissal of the gun, deep down inside, fear had taken hold. Suppose those men from the van were still lurking about somewhere, waiting to finish the job?

She paced back and forth in the room, unable to focus for any length of time on anything. Her thoughts swirled and then finally coalesced in one horrifying question: could her accident have had anything to do with her father's problems?

On the face of it, it sounded absurd. But then, everything was absurd at this point. If her father had been threatened, wasn't it possible that she, too, was being threatened, for reasons she couldn't even understand?

The police officer had suggested that the accident was the result of some beered-up wiseguys, trying to get the attention of an attractive woman in a flashy sports car. He ventured the opinion that they hadn't really intended to run her off the road, but the wet conditions had resulted in an unforeseen accident.

It *did* make sense. From what she had seen of the one man from the van, he had been young—perhaps in his early twenties—and the van itself had been decorated with stenciling.

But there had been one piece of information that she had withheld from the police, perhaps out of fear of being thought crazy. She hadn't told them that her rescuer had been a man she recognized. A man who had sat near her in a restaurant hundreds of miles away. A man she had briefly thought might have been eavesdropping on her conversation at lunch.

She simply could not accept coincidence as an explanation for his sudden—and timely—reappearance. The route she had been taking was hardly a direct route to anywhere; it was a series of scenic back roads she had mapped out herself several years ago when she had first acquired the Jag and had wanted to enjoy both the car and the New England countryside. How could they possibly have chosen that same circuitous route—unless they too had been following her?

And she also recalled very clearly the look on the man's face when she had recognized him.

But are you so very sure that you did *recognize him?* a small voice whispered. *You were probably in a state of shock. He was soaking wet and in semidarkness. And there'd been nothing at all distinctive about his appearance, either.*

Teddy, quite simply, did not know what to think or what to do. She did stop her pacing and sank down into a chintz-covered chair, but that was the extent of her willful action. Her spine felt as though it were made of cold steel and the sharp, metallic taste of fear remained in her mouth.

She told herself firmly that now was the worst possible time to be trying to evaluate all of this. Adrenaline was still being pumped through her system in large quantities, and it was interfering with her thought processes. Tomorrow morning, after a good night's sleep, would be time enough to think about all this.

Having reached that decision, she picked up the current issue of *Time* magazine that the desk clerk had lent her and looked through the table of contents for something to put her to sleep. The latest crisis in Central America was accomplishing just that when a sound in the hallway outside her room made her start nervously.

The inn was very quiet and consequently, the footsteps sounded very loud and close. Panic gripped her when she heard the unmistakable sound of a key being inserted into a lock. Instantly, Teddy became convinced that someone was trying to get into her room. She had noted earlier that the door had no inside chain lock. She was out of her chair and looking about wildly for a hiding place when she realized with a sigh of relief that someone had entered the room next to hers.

But that relief was very short-lived as she remembered the connecting door between the two rooms. Tiptoeing—and already feeling foolish—she crept over to the door and cautiously tried the knob, prepared for instant flight if it was unlocked. But it was reassuringly rigid and she returned to her chair at last, cursing her paranoia as she picked up the magazine again.

She was trying to renew her interest in the article when a loud, peremptory knock at her door sent reason skittering away into panic once again.

Chapter Eight

Panic jumbled her thoughts. Who could be out there? Could it be those men from the van? Surely it was possible. This was a small town and she'd seen no other inns or motels. Would they dare such a thing? If that had been a gun she'd seen, could they fire it through the door or blast away the lock? She'd seen such things in movies and every one of those scenes now ran through her mind at lightning speed. Finally, she remembered the phone and rushed toward it. But at that moment there was another knock—and this time, it was accompanied by a voice.

"Teddy! Open up!"

Her legs would barely support her as she ran headlong for the door, then fumbled with the lock for so long that he called her name again before she got it open. Deeply embarrassed now at her panic-stricken behavior, she forced herself not to rush into his arms.

But after a long, silent look at her, Graham reached out to pull her roughly into his arms as he kicked the door shut behind him.

"Dammit, why didn't you ask me to come?" he rasped as he stroked her soft curls and kneaded her rigid spine.

"I . . . I'm glad you came anyway," she admitted, feeling relief and embarrassment and happiness in roughly equal measure. She did want him here, although she was already wondering what to tell him. Making light of the accident on the phone was one thing; doing so face-to-face was quite another.

He continued to hold her and stroke her, then finally held her off at arm's length and peered at her intently.

"I saw the car, Teddy," he said with gentle accusation. "That was no little accident."

"It wasn't as bad as it looks," she hastened to explain. "I'm not hurt, except for a cut and some bruises."

"You could have been killed," he stated bluntly in a voice that shook with emotion.

Teddy nodded, then quickly lowered her face to keep him from seeing the tears that were threatening. But Graham lifted her chin, and then brushed away the tears with a gentle touch.

"There's a quiet bar downstairs. Let's go have a drink while you tell me all about what happened."

Teddy nodded her agreement and let him lead her downstairs. As soon as their drinks arrived, Graham leaned back against the high wooden booth and gave her that level look that told her clearly that the time for equivocating had just run out.

"Okay, Teddy, the truth."

"I told you the truth," she responded, knowing only then that she couldn't bring herself to divulge her fears to him, but not really understanding why.

"You told me on the phone that you had a 'little accident' and you wouldn't be back until tomorrow. From what I've seen of the car, it looks like you rolled it over. That's not 'little.'"

She said nothing. He said nothing. She chewed on her lower lip nervously. He watched her and waited.

"The road was wet. The car skidded and rolled down over an embankment." She stopped, wondering if he would let it go at that.

"My guess is that you're a good driver and that the Jag handles well. The tires are good; I checked them. Now tell me the rest of it."

There was another silence as she met his determined gaze, then let her eyes slide away. Could she tell him the truth about the accident without divulging her fear that it could somehow be connected to her father's trouble? She decided to give it a try, since it was obvious he was going to drag the truth out of her. Besides, he could easily go to the police and learn the truth.

"Two men in a van forced me off the road," she admitted. "One of them started down toward me, then took off when another car stopped, too."

She went on to tell him the police theory and ended with a shrug. "They're probably right. I know that kind of thing happens."

"I've no doubt that it does," Graham agreed. "But that isn't the point. Do *you* believe that's what happened?"

"What do you mean?" she asked reluctantly.

Graham lifted his shoulders in a broad shrug. "Just a gut feeling that there's something you haven't told me."

Once again she met his steady gaze, then lowered her own. Graham, she decided, was very good at cross-examination.

"There is something else," she admitted finally, feeling a strange wave of relief sweep over her as she spoke. "Two things, actually."

But then the hesitation was back again: a fear of sounding foolish, she supposed. She drew a shaky breath and went on.

"I think that the man who came down after me had a gun. The police officer thought it was probably a screwdriver or something he might have brought to help me get out of the car. It was very dark because of the storm, but I still think it was a gun."

Graham's only reaction to that was a stare that went on for so long she became convinced that he had decided she was an overly imaginative, foolish female.

"You said there were two things," he prompted her finally.

She wished she hadn't, since the other thing sounded even more ludicrous. Unfortunately, she had no choice now but to continue.

"The other man—the one from the car that stopped—was the same man who had sat at a nearby table where I had lunch in New Haven. I'd met Dad's secretary for lunch after I stopped at campaign headquarters."

Graham just frowned, and she thought he looked somewhat irritated. Certain he was thinking just what she'd feared, she hurried on in a defensive tone.

"New Haven is hundreds of miles from here, Graham, and the route I took was all back roads. He couldn't have been there unless he was following me."

He said nothing and Teddy became agitated. Knowing that she was probably just digging herself in deeper, she continued. "I remembered him and his companion because they were so quiet at lunch. A couple of times it really seemed to me that they were eavesdropping on my conversation with Elizabeth."

"Teddy," he said placatingly, "did it ever occur to you that they might just have been interested in *you*, just like the guys in the van?"

"Of course it occurred to me," she said angrily. "But how do you explain their showing up at the accident like that? They surely weren't interested enough to trail after me for hundreds of miles. And they left in a big hurry, too, as soon as the police got there.''

Faced with her righteous wrath, Graham just gave her that uncomfortably direct stare. ''And do you have an explanation for all this?''

Now Teddy knew she had boxed herself in. Either she told him the whole truth or she admitted to being a fool. Once again it occurred to her that this was a man who was very adept at getting at the truth. She took a deep breath, then returned his stare measure for measure. In for a penny, in for a pound, she quoted to herself nervously.

''I think all this—the men in the restaurant and the men in the van—could have something to do with the trouble Dad's in.''

He showed absolutely no surprise, and Teddy was reminded again about his poker playing skills. Or was he not surprised because he'd already guessed she'd blame it on this, a concern he'd insisted was groundless?

''Is that why you were having lunch with his secretary? Were you on a fishing expedition?''

''Yes,'' she said defensively. ''In spite of what you think, I know something's wrong. And I thought Elizabeth would know, if it had anything to do with the company.''

Then she abruptly recalled that she hadn't told him about the phone calls, so she told him now, watching his face carefully as she spoke. By the time she had finished, she'd decided that this man could take the news of the end of the world without betraying any emotion.

''You really think I'm imagining all this, don't you?'' she challenged angrily. ''Just because you've heard all those stories about me as a kid—''

''I don't think that at all, Teddy. But why didn't you tell me before about the phone calls?''

That was one question she hadn't considered and didn't want to answer. She struggled silently for some acceptable lie, and finding none, prepared to tell the truth.

"Partly it was because I thought you'd just laugh at me and partly it was because I was afraid that you might be mixed up in all this yourself."

The silence that followed that admission was deafening. Teddy cringed inwardly as she recalled his having asked for her trust and her giving it.

"But you've decided to trust me now?" he asked with a surprising gentleness.

She nodded, greatly relieved.

Graham leaned forward and picked up her hand that had been toying nervously with the cocktail napkin. "Teddy, I want you to promise me something. I want you to promise that from now on you'll stay out of this. No more Teddy Sothern, Girl—excuse me, Woman—Detective. I'll look into it."

"Don't patronize me, Graham. I don't think you're taking this seriously at all."

"I'm not patronizing you," he said, continuing to hold the hand that she had halfheartedly tried to wrench free. "And I am taking it seriously. But I want you to let me take it from here. You've just admitted that you'd come to a dead end."

She nodded reluctantly. "But what are you going to do?"

"I don't know yet. I have to think it over. But in the meantime, I want to know that you're safe. You're going to stay on the island unless I'm with you, agreed?"

She nodded, then gave him a considering look. "Dad might talk to you, you know. He likes you and trusts you and he might not keep it from you the way he has from me."

Graham said nothing, and for some unaccountable reason Teddy's mind spun back to that night on the beach when she had first referred to the friendship between her father and Graham. Then and now, he seemed disturbed or even embarrassed by it.

Teddy didn't dwell on this, however, because she was far too worried about the connection between her accident and the trouble her father might be in. It had taken a while for the full impact of all this to sink in, but now that the shock had subsided a bit, the possibility that the accident could be connected to her father's problems very nearly overwhelmed her with fear.

"Graham," she said in a voice thinned with worry, "what could have happened? What could these people want?"

Her fear tore at Graham's heart. He came within one heartbeat of a decision that would have destroyed all he had worked for. But after that brief hesitation, he squeezed her hand that he still held and forced himself to speak reassuringly, hating himself with each word.

"You don't know that this had anything at all to do with Ted's troubles. You're only guessing."

She nodded reluctantly and said nothing. But the tension in her continued, and Graham had an overwhelming urge to hold her and shelter her from the storm that was gathering around them.

"Let's go back upstairs," he said in a voice made thick with a desire to give her what he knew he had no right to give.

She merely nodded and he sensed the terrible struggle within her to maintain her self-control. He got up and helped her to her feet, then kept an arm protectively about her waist as they left the bar.

The trip up the staircase to their rooms lasted forever. In his mind, he held her in his arms to soothe her but he never lost sight of the ultimate outcome of such a scene. Even if he had been able to overcome his scruples, this was not the time and he knew it. As he walked in the present, with his arm encircling her waist, Graham saw far too clearly into the future, a future in which she could never forgive him and would most certainly hate him.

They passed his room in silence and went on to her room, where she fumbled with the key, then abruptly handed it to him. Even that small insignificant gesture seemed fraught with great importance. Teddy was a strong woman, and her vulnerability at this moment touched him deeply.

He took the key and opened her door, then hesitated. The bed seemed to fill the room and the need to close the space between them beckoned.

She went into the room, then stopped and turned to him. Graham stared at her, then stepped forward into the room and drew her into his arms. He felt her soft pliancy, her need to be held, and then his own surprising need to reassure himself that she was real and that she needed him—not just someone to hold her and soothe her, but him.

They stood there in the center of the room for a long while, not speaking because speech was unnecessary. What passed between them required no words at all.

Teddy wanted him to stay to hold her and to drive out the fears and to be with her in the morning. But the request stuck in her throat as somewhere in the depths of her need, she too recognized that this was not the time.

Graham released her slowly and took a few steps backward, until he was in the open doorway of her room. He knew that if she asked him to stay, he wouldn't be able to refuse and he also knew that he wouldn't be staying just to comfort her. He backed through the doorway, reached for the door to pull it shut behind him, then hesitated.

"I want you more than I've ever wanted any woman," he blurted out suddenly in a low, husky voice. "I . . ."

He hesitated again, then quickly pulled the door shut behind him, leaving her standing there staring at the space he had occupied as his parting words echoed through her brain.

"You what?" she finally asked aloud of the closed door. "What were you going to say to me, Graham?"

But there was no response, and she heard him go into his own room next door. Frightened and confused, Teddy crawled into her lonely bed and spent a night in the throes of ugly, terrifying nightmares.

TRUE TO HER WORST EXPECTATIONS, the day after the accident proved to be far more painful than the immediate aftermath. Graham appeared at her door just as she had completed the difficult task of dressing a body that protested every movement. She complained to him that she didn't understand how she could have bumped herself in so many places, and he replied dryly that doing somersaults in a car did tend to produce some strain on the human body.

They had breakfast in the dining room, then went to see to the car. In the cold light of day, Teddy realized for the first time just how close she had come to serious injury, or even death. She was so stunned that she let Graham make the arrangements for repairs, merely nodding her agreement that the local body man seemed to be quite good.

Before they left town, Graham suggested that they stop by the police station to see if the van had been traced. However, once she had managed to maneuver her aching body into his rental car, she was reluctant to get out again, so he went in alone.

He was gone for only a few moments and returned to tell her that they still hadn't traced the owner of the van, but expected to have the information soon. He remarked that the chief seemed to agree with the officer who had suggested that the occupants of the van had merely been trying to gain her attention.

"Is that what you believe?" she asked irritably. "What about the gun I saw, and the other man?"

Graham glanced at her briefly as he started the car. "Teddy, you admitted that it was dark and raining and you were almost certainly in a state of shock. That other man could well have been on your mind subconsciously because of his behavior at lunch."

"Then you don't believe any of it, do you?"

"I don't know, but I promised you that I'd look into it and I will," he said gently. "Are you planning to tell your father about your suspicions?"

"No," she replied shortly. "Not because I doubt what I saw, but because I don't want to worry him still more. Like you said, I'll be safe enough on Matiscotta until you find out what's bothering him."

Graham merely nodded his agreement and said nothing more. Teddy remained silent, lost in confused thoughts about her father, the accident and finally, about Graham. Neither of them had made any reference to that abruptly ended statement of his last night. Furthermore, he hadn't so much as kissed her good morning, although she had to admit that she hadn't exactly been pleasant, thanks to her preoccupation with her aches and pains.

During one long, uncomfortable silence, Teddy was tempted to ask him what he had been about to say to her last night, but before the question could be formed, she thought better of it. She sensed now that he had spoken in a moment of weakness, no doubt brought on by his concern for her, and it seemed likely to her that whatever he had intended to say then, he wasn't going to say it now.

It's better to wait, she thought. *There will be time enough for us when all of this is over.*

By the time they finally reached Matiscotta, Teddy had become very apprehensive about confronting her father. What if he had already guessed that her accident was in some way related to his problems? If he began to ask too many questions, could she continue to pretend that it had been nothing more than what the police were suggesting?

Ted Sothern appeared immediately when they entered the house, and Teddy thought that he looked even worse than she felt. His normally pleasant features had a tight, drawn appearance and there were dark circles under his eyes. Father and daughter embraced carefully, and Teddy could detect an abnormal tension in him.

Then he held her off at arm's length and peered closely at her. His tone was anguished. "Thank God you're safe. If anything had happened to you . . ."

He let his voice trail away as he continued to grip her arms and stare at her, almost as though he expected her to disappear if he should so much as blink.

There was a moment when both of them seemed on the verge of saying something, but it passed and he then asked about whether or not the police had caught the driver of the van. Graham explained what the police had told him that morning, while Teddy remained silent, fighting an urge to tell her father about her suspicions. But half-truths wouldn't do, and she could not bring herself to tell him she knew he had lied about that phone call.

Another silence followed Graham's explanation, and then he suggested in a matter-of-fact tone that they get to work. The brief tension lifted, and the threesome went off to the study to discuss the black-tie fund-raiser being held in New Haven in five days' time.

Teddy announced proudly that it had been sold out, and they began to discuss changes in the speech she had already written for him. After that, they took turns bombarding him with questions likely to be asked during a pre-dinner session with the press.

Teddy moved uncomfortably through the day, suffering from the aches of a battered body and the anguish of an equally battered mind. She tried hard to hide all this from her father, but when she and Graham were alone, the mask slipped.

It surprised her to see that the tender concern he had shown for her the night before was still there; somehow she'd expected it to vanish when they returned to business. But his warm, dark gaze followed her all day, and when she sat on the terrace, unconsciously rubbing at aching neck muscles, he came up behind her and began to massage the soreness with strong, sure fingers.

After dinner, when she was hobbling about like a ninety-year-old, Graham slid his arms about her waist and suggested that she take a long, hot bath to ease her misery. She smiled at him, gave him an appreciative kiss on the cheek, then started upstairs. She felt his warmth follow her all the way up.

After filling the big old tub with steaming water, Teddy lowered herself into it gingerly, then relaxed with a deep sigh. Leaning her head back against a folded towel, she let her thoughts drift through the events of the past twenty-four hours.

Now that she was back in the tranquillity of Matiscotta, it was becoming difficult to sustain the sense of imminent danger that had tormented her earlier. Her father seemed pleased about the fund-raiser and eager to plunge into the campaign. She wondered if that tense, drawn look she had seen on his face this morning had been nothing more than concern for her.

Except, she told herself with a heavy sigh, he had lied to her about that phone call. And she was absolutely positive about the identity of the man who had rescued her. As far as the gun went, she was now willing to admit the possibility that she had been mistaken.

But lying here in the warm water, in a place she loved, Teddy found it difficult to believe that her fears were justified. There had to be an explanation and Graham would find it for her.

Graham. Now there was a subject that seemed appropriate for her sensual surroundings. Teddy smiled. Did he love her? Surely it was far too soon for such feelings. And yet they'd been spending every waking moment together for more than six weeks now, certainly an unusual situation.

What about her own feelings? She wasn't yet willing to use the word "love," but there was no doubting the fact that Graham McKinsey was a very major figure in her life. A past in which he'd played no part was only dimly remembered, and a future without him seemed, well, incomprehensible.

She gnawed nervously at her lower lip. If that wasn't love, it was awfully close to it, wasn't it?

Both of them, she knew, were decisive people not generally given to hesitation and "what ifs" or "well, maybes." And yet they were both hesitating now, weren't they? Didn't that fact alone suggest that something unusual was afoot here?

Perhaps she'd been mistaken to have sought some deeper explanation for Graham's behavior. It might well be that he, too, was hesitating because he knew this was serious business. And yet, she had to admit that there was something about him that continued to elude her, no matter how well she thought she knew him in many ways.

She drifted off into a series of erotic fantasies in which she learned every inch of that lean, hard body, and then shivered with the imagined touch of his mustache on sensitive skin. Graham would be a gentle and considerate lover. And a very passionate one, she decided as she recalled the emotion in that declaration last night.

The water had grown rather cool by the time she finally climbed out of the tub, feeling far less achy than before and wonderfully voluptuous as a result of her fantasies. Even her fears for her father had retreated to a back corner of her mind, not really gone, but not truly menacing, either.

She dressed and went downstairs to find the two men still seated on the terrace, talking in low voices that reached her only as murmurs. She stopped in the middle of the living room to watch them: shadowy figures lit only by the light spilling out from the house.

Ted Sothern was sprawled in his favorite chaise, with only the top of his silvered head visible to her. Graham sat in a nearby chair, leaning slightly forward, legs apart and one hand braced against a muscular thigh in a thoroughly masculine pose she had often seen.

There was really nothing unusual about the tableau, but Teddy remained where she was, watching them. It came to her slowly that there sat the two people who meant the most to her in all the world, and here they were, in the place she loved best. For a moment, she felt as though she were seeing into the future, a future that certainly had to include Graham McKinsey.

Was she falling in love with him? Was this how it happened? One strange moment when the veil was lifted from the future?

Graham turned then and saw her, and even in his shadowed face, she could see the warmth. She went out to join them, feeling almost giddy with happiness.

GRAHAM STOOD IN A CORNER of the club's large ballroom, surrounded by a group of Ted's supporters. It was difficult indeed for him to be around these people, but the evening was made bearable by watching Teddy as she played the role of hostess with great aplomb and in her own inimitable way.

Even though she was constantly in motion, he had no trouble spotting her amidst the crowd. To him, she seemed to move always in a pool of light that eclipsed those around her. She was wearing a long, floral-printed gown and her copper curls had been tamed into an elegant chignon that his fingers ached to pull free.

He watched as she danced with someone and felt an irrational sting of jealousy that it was not his own arms around her. But he couldn't risk that this evening because his attention to her was more than personal. Perhaps he was overreacting, but he didn't intend to let her out of his sight until they were safely back to Ted's house. A crowd like this could be the perfect opportunity for— His thoughts broke off abruptly as she was whirled past him and met his gaze over the shoulder of her partner. The poignancy of the moment tore at his very soul. Was this how he would always remember her—in the arms of another man? He could barely return her smile.

When the dance ended, Teddy made her way determinedly across the floor. As soon as she reached Graham, she linked her arm through his and gave the others a charming smile.

"You gentlemen will have to excuse us for a few minutes. We have some very important campaign matters to discuss." Teddy put just the faintest mocking emphasis on her words.

Graham seemed to hesitate and Teddy slid her hand along his arm, then stopped suddenly with a sharp intake of breath. He immediately made his excuse to the group and circled her waist to lead her away to the terrace.

Teddy said nothing because she was too numb with shock. But as soon as they were outside and away from the guests, she let out her pent-up breath in an explosion of words.

"You're wearing a gun! I felt it!"

Graham looked uncomfortable, but nodded slowly. "I have a license for it, Teddy."

"I assume you do, but that's not the point. Why are you wearing it? What's wrong?"

"Nothing's wrong," he said soothingly, taking her hand and rubbing the pad of his thumb along the inside of her palm. "It's just a precaution, that's all."

"But there are security people here. Why should you need to carry a gun?" All her fears that had lain dormant for the past five days now sprang back to life.

"Those security people are nothing but rent-a-cops," he said disdainfully, then realized how he'd sounded when he saw the look on her face. He drew her hand up to his lips.

"I told you," he said gently. "It's just a precaution."

But she pulled her hand away, still shocked at the contempt in his tone a moment ago and fearing there was something he hadn't told her.

"Do you really think something could happen? Has Dad told you something?"

"No, he's told me nothing. I haven't really pushed him. I thought it could wait until we get back to Matiscotta."

He reached for her, but she backed away a few steps. An icy fear was coursing through her veins now and she was half-convinced that there was indeed something he hadn't told her.

"You tried to convince me that I just imagined that other gun, but I didn't, did I?"

"I don't know, but I'm not taking any chances, not where you're concerned."

Teddy heard and felt the emotion in his voice and when he reached for her again, she went into his arms, letting him surround her with reassuring warmth. But her hands kept fluttering about nervously, trying to find a resting place that wouldn't remind her of that gun strapped beneath his arm.

Graham, too, felt the ugliness of that weapon and hated himself for exposing her to it. He wondered uneasily what she would think if she knew that he had spent the better part of his adult life carrying a gun, a gun that had been used on more than one occasion.

He had a powerful urge to shut out all the ugliness, past and present, for just these few moments when she was his. He slid his hands along her silken curves and lowered his mouth to hers with an all-consuming need. Lost in her softness, feeling her hunger that matched his, Graham could forget about the harsh reality of the present and the even harsher future.

She trembled slightly under his touch, but he sensed that it was now from rising desire, not from fear. Their bodies clung together as that desire flowed from one to the other, and Graham knew that no matter what the future might hold for him, he would never know the equal of this feeling. No mere need to possess this woman could account for the surge of tenderness that flooded through him.

He drew slightly away from her, then laid his fingers against the warm smoothness of her cheek. Her lips were slightly parted and those remarkable blue eyes were dark with passion and almost unfocused. She felt what he felt and it had to be said.

"I love you, Teddy, and I'll love you as long as I draw breath. Whatever happens, I want you to remember that and believe it."

Then, without giving her any time to respond, he took her hand and led her back inside. He just couldn't stand to hear her return that declaration, but he needed desperately to believe that he would have heard it.

As soon as they stepped back inside, Teddy was forced to return to her role as hostess. She managed, but anyone observing her closely, as Graham was, would have noticed that her smile wasn't quite natural and her normally direct gaze had a tendency to stray off to some distant point.

She moved through the crowd, barely conscious of the presence of others, her mind whirling with echoes of his declaration and of the frightening qualification he had added.

It should have been a supremely happy moment for her, and a part of her was happy, but his final words denied her that greatest of pleasures. Had she read too much into that? Was he saying only that he wasn't yet sure what the future held for them? If so, she could understand that: her own feelings seemed to have outrun more practical considerations, too. But deep down inside, she feared that wasn't what he had meant.

They had no time alone until they had returned to her father's house in suburban New Haven and Ted had gone off to bed, declaring himself well pleased with the evening. Although Teddy was pleased to see her father so happy, her attention was focused on Graham. She thought that he seemed nervous, but even so, there was no doubt in her mind that he had meant what he'd said. Graham McKinsey was not a man for flowery speeches, and those words he'd spoken had come from the very depths of his soul.

When Ted got up to leave them, Graham got up too, and for a moment, Teddy feared that he was also going to go to bed. But he stopped before her as he undid his formal bow-tie and opened the stiff collar of the pleated shirt. She sat on the sofa and looked up at him, and in that moment had no doubt at all about their future together. She thought about the day she'd first met him, at the Rockland docks, and wondered if there really was such a thing as love at first sight. Perhaps only her resentment at his intrusion into her plans had kept her from recognizing it then. Certainly, something in him had reached into her that very first moment.

He sat down beside her and brushed away the lacy shawl she wore around her shoulders, then bent to kiss the smooth skin he'd exposed. Teddy murmured with pleasure at the touch of his lips and mustache, then lifted his head until their faces were scant inches apart.

"I love you, too, Graham, and I think I have from the very first." She spoke the words as though no time at all had elapsed between his declaration and this moment—because for her, none had.

He smiled at her gently. "You had a strange way of showing it, Theodora Sothern. I would have sworn you were trying to capsize the boat and drown me on the way over."

She laughed. "I was, actually. I guess I don't give in to my fate too easily."

He threaded his fingers through her curls and then began to pull loose the pins that held it captive. "I never thought that I had any image of the ideal woman for me—until I met you."

Graham took her into his arms and felt her own certainty that this was right. Their time would come. It had to.

Chapter Nine

Teddy propped her elbows on the typewriter and stared at the speech she was composing. It was the morning after the fund-raiser and she was alone in her father's house at the moment. The two men had gone off to campaign head-quarters for the morning, and they all planned to return to Matiscotta that afternoon.

There was no real urgency to this speech, since it wouldn't be delivered for several weeks, but Teddy had decided to work on it anyway. She'd discovered that whenever she had any idle time, her thoughts turned immediately to her twin problems: her father and Graham. For the moment, she chose to ignore them both.

She reread what she had written and thought that it sounded too much like the one he had given the evening be-fore. Graham had stressed that although the basic themes must remain the same in order to avoid charges of waffling on the issues, there should, nevertheless, be some differ-ences. Both speeches stressed economic issues because of the audiences involved.

She looked around on her father's desk for a copy of last night's speech and couldn't find it. Then she noticed his at-taché case sitting on the floor beside the desk. No doubt it was in there. She reached down and picked it up, then laid it on the desk. To her surprise, she discovered that it was locked.

She frowned at it. The darned thing must have locked itself; her own had done the same thing a few times. Such locks were never very good to begin with, and they had a tendency to slip into place as a result of the bouncing around such a case normally received. She checked the desk drawers for a key and couldn't find one. He probably didn't even know where it was; she'd had the same problem. But she was sure it could be opened with her nail file, which she happened to have in her purse.

She paused for just a second to consider whether she should call him to ask for permission to open it. But that seemed ridiculous; why should he care? When he discovered that it had locked itself, he'd be asking her for a file to open it, anyway.

The nail file took a few seconds to accomplish its task, and Teddy opened the case. The copy of the speech was there, right on top. She took it out and then noticed that the papers beneath it were the company's monthly financial reports. She knew that he had spent part of the previous day at his office, and wondered what else he might have brought home. Despite his secretary's assurances to the contrary, Teddy was still half-convinced that the root of his problems lay within the company.

So she riffled through the remaining papers, noting that they all appeared to be financial data, and then came at last to a thick sheaf of papers in the bottom of the case. Her heart stopped as she stared at them.

Heading each page were bold red letters: TOP SECRET. Teddy's neck became clammy and prickly and her hands trembled slightly as she started to lift them out, then paused to look quickly about the room, half-expecting to see some military types waiting to take aim at her.

What were they doing there? Teddy knew full well that such materials weren't supposed to leave the security of company safes. Her father had told her that once long ago, when some minor breach of security had brought him home in a rage.

With her unsteady hands, she lifted the papers out, then leafed quickly through them. They were filled with incomprehensible charts and diagrams, and even where there was writing, she could understand no more than a few words. But understanding the contents and understanding their importance were two different things—and those big red letters said it all.

She quickly replaced them in the bottom of the case, put the financial papers back on top and after a moment's hesitation, also replaced the speech. Then she hurriedly closed and locked the case and set it down on the floor where she had found it.

Only after all this had been accomplished did the significance of her actions strike her. Without thought, she had decided to deceive her father into believing that she hadn't opened the case.

A terrible, ugly coldness engulfed her, and she hugged herself in horror. Did she actually believe that her father was capable of...? She simply could not finish the thought. There had to be another explanation. Perhaps as head of the company, he had privileges that the others didn't have. But no sooner had she begun to accept this than she recalled quite clearly that he had said that no one—not even himself—could remove classified materials from the premises. His uncommon anger at the time of that incident had impressed it clearly into her memory.

She got up quickly and left the room, wanting nothing more at the moment than to get away from that damning evidence. But not even that was enough, so, propelled by pure terror, she left the house.

Behind the house was a stretch of woods her parents had bought years ago to prevent another house from being built too close to their property. When she was a child, her father had built her a tree house there, and she had spent many happy hours in her private little hideaway. The tree house was long gone; her father had pulled it down after a storm had damaged it. But the memory of those happy times drew her there now, and she sank down at the base of the huge old oak, where the wounds from the nails that had secured the ladder were still evident.

It seemed like a very long time before the horror diminished, leaving only that ugly coldness. Slowly, she began to think rationally once more. Those phone calls were beginning to make a terrible kind of sense. Could someone be threatening him in order to gain classified information? She now recalled his having said something about "getting to the office."

But if such was the case, why hadn't he gone immediately to the FBI or whoever dealt with such things? And what threat could they possibly be using to have persuaded him to do this?

And then more of that overheard conversation came back to her. Something about having been "told that before" and about "making sure this time by getting out."

The horror washed over her anew. Did that mean that he had done this kind of thing in the past? She desperately wanted to find another explanation but his words fit her ugly thoughts all too well.

She looked down at her watch. He and Graham would be returning any moment. She had no time now to speculate further on this. Instead, she had to decide what to do. The first thing that came to her mind was that she would simply admit the truth: that she had opened his case to get the speech and had found the papers there. That way, she'd know immediately if her terrible suspicions were correct, because he'd never be able to conceal his reaction from her.

But even as she considered it, she knew she couldn't do it. She couldn't do it simply because she couldn't face the possibility that her suspicions could be true. Ignorance wasn't necessarily bliss, but in this case, it was far better than knowledge.

Teddy drew up her knees and hugged them to her chest. Her eyes had begun to burn, and that was followed quickly by a torrent of tears. She *had* to be wrong. There had to be another explanation. She would just keep quiet until she found it.

"Teddy!"

She lifted her head, and through a haze of tears saw Graham approaching. He'd already caught sight of her, since her bright-red T-shirt stood out against the leafy greenness. For one brief moment, she was overjoyed to see him and wanted nothing more than to throw herself into his arms. Perhaps he could find the explanation that eluded her.

But even as she swiped hastily at her tears, she knew she couldn't tell him. If she was wrong—and surely she was— what would he think of her for having suspected her own father of such a thing? And if she was right, how could she even consider dragging him into this?

He came up to her before she could get to her feet, then frowned with concern and squatted down beside her.

"What's wrong?" he asked, gently rubbing away the last of the tears with his thumb.

"Nothing," she said hastily. "I just came out here to think."

Then, with a quick inspiration born of desperation, she gestured up at the tree. "I had a tree-house up there when I was a kid."

Graham followed the direction of her gesture, but only briefly. "What were you thinking about?" he asked, letting her know by his tone that he wasn't buying her explanation.

She could think of nothing to say, so she got up quickly. "Let's go. We have a long trip ahead of us."

Without waiting for a response from him, she started back toward the house, wracking her brain for an explanation he'd accept if he insisted upon pursuing the matter. She'd gotten only a few feet before his hand closed about her arm and drew her to a halt.

"Teddy, I want to know why you were crying."

She could not bring herself to meet his gaze, but just then she thought of an excuse he might accept.

"It's, uh, that time of the month and sometimes I get this way."

He said nothing, but he didn't release her, either, so she gave him a defiant look. "It's called PMS—Pre-Menstrual Syndrome. Surely you've heard of it."

"I've heard of it. And I still don't believe you."

"Well, that's your problem." She jerked her arm from his grasp and began to walk rapidly toward the house before she could give in to the temptation to throw herself into his arms.

He caught up with her a few seconds later, but he didn't pursue the issue, and she breathed a sigh of relief. They walked into the house together and found her father in his study, talking on the telephone. The attaché case still sat in the same spot on the floor. He hung up shortly after they entered and smiled at the two of them.

Teddy hesitated just a fraction of a second before returning the smile, and behind her, Graham sensed a fleeting tension in her.

"I see you were working on my next speech," Ted said, gesturing to the paper she'd left in the typewriter.

Teddy nodded. Here was her chance. She made a quick compromise with herself. "I quit because I wanted to review last night's speech and I didn't have a copy of it. I thought you might have it in your attaché case, but it's locked."

He bent over quickly to pick up the case, thereby preventing Teddy from seeing his expression. By the time he had put it on the desk and tried unsuccessfully to open it, his expression was neutral.

"You're right. It must have locked itself. I don't even have the key with me."

"I have a nail file," Teddy said quickly. "That will probably do it. I've opened mine with one."

She moved quickly toward her purse, but her father made a dismissive gesture.

"Never mind. You won't be working on the speech until we get back to Matiscotta, and I have a key there."

He got up and picked up the case and Teddy retrieved her purse and the speech from his desk. When she turned around, she saw Graham's gaze fall very briefly on the attaché case. Her breath caught in her throat as their glances met. She could read nothing at all in his face, but she wasn't so sure that he hadn't seen something in hers. After a brief surge of panic, she calmed down again. He couldn't possibly have guessed what the case contained.

GRAHAM HAD LONG SINCE LEARNED to trust his instincts, but this time, he didn't want to listen to them. The state in which he'd found Teddy and that little scene between father and daughter over the locked attaché case had led him to the inescapable conclusion that Teddy had in fact opened the case and had seen what Graham knew it contained.

There was no doubt in his mind that she had put that discovery together with the phone conversation she'd overheard and come up with something very close to the truth. He could all too well imagine the anguish such a conclusion had caused.

He slanted her a glance as she sat curled up in a chair on the terrace, contributing little to the conversation. She'd been unnaturally silent all the way back to Matiscotta. They had stopped to pick up her Jag en route, and despite the fact that the garage had done a superb job in restoring it, she had shown little enthusiasm.

Ted had gone on, leaving the two of them to return in the Jag, and Graham had hoped that she would confide her fears to him. But even after they were alone, she had remained uncommunicative. He could understand her silence, since the ugly reality was a far cry from her earlier, vague fears.

The truth was that if she *had* confided in him, he would have been in a terrible quandary. But that hadn't prevented him from wanting her trust, however much he didn't deserve it and would have to betray it. Graham knew that he was sinking ever more deeply into a miasma of ambivalence and contradictions from which there was no escape.

Even his feelings toward Ted Sothern remained just as they had been almost from the beginning: an uneasy melange of anger and regret and a dangerous empathy. He would do what he had to do because he was what he was, but he knew that he would spend the rest of his life wondering if he'd chosen the wrong course.

He looked again at Teddy, who was still lost in her own world, paying neither of them any attention as she stared out into the darkness beyond the terrace. The light from the house bathed her curls in a coppery sheen as the rest of her remained in shadow.

What would she do? he wondered. Was she sure enough of her suspicions to confront her father? He doubted it, and unless she was very sure, she certainly wouldn't confront him. And what would happen if she did? Could Ted convince her that he'd made the only choice possible? Graham guessed that he would convince her of that, because her love for her father would win out over all other considerations. He wasn't at all sure that he wouldn't do the same in her situation—and the thought dismayed him.

Lost in his bleak thoughts, he barely noticed as Teddy got up and started off the terrace in the direction of the beach. As she disappeared into the darkness, Ted turned to Graham.

"What's wrong with Teddy? She's been awfully quiet."

What Graham wanted to say was: *what's wrong with her is that she knows what you're doing, you bastard, and it's tearing her apart.*

But he didn't say it, of course. He still couldn't hate this man and he couldn't jeopardize his mission here. So he shrugged instead.

"It's that time of the month, and she's not feeling well."

The older man just nodded and didn't inquire just how it was that Graham happened to know this. Considering Ted's own distraction this evening, Graham was surprised that he'd even noticed Teddy's state of mind.

Then Ted got up and announced his intention to go to bed. Graham got up, too, and as Ted walked past him, he laid a hand briefly on Graham's shoulder in a gesture of affection. Graham stood there long after Ted had gone upstairs, still feeling the weight of that hand. Then he started off toward the beach.

Teddy walked slowly along the beach, staying in the packed, wet sand just beyond the high tide line. A sense of impending doom hung heavily over her and she was gripped in an icy knot of fear.

Inaction certainly did not come naturally to Teddy and she chafed against it. But the consequences of any action at all seemed so dire that she was rendered helpless. There was still too much that didn't make sense—and there remained the hope that she was wrong.

She was tired and her head throbbed and she wanted only to go to sleep and awaken in the morning to find that this had been nothing more than a particularly vivid nightmare.

Having reached the end of the long strip of sand, she turned wearily back toward the house and immediately saw Graham's shadowy figure striding toward her. Once again, she struggled against the nearly overwhelming impulse to run to him and fling herself into his comforting arms. It was an unsettling thought for someone who had always been almost fiercely independent.

They met near the center of the beach and Teddy briefly recalled that night when Graham had conjured up that wonderful old love scene. The beach and the moon and the water lapping at the store were the same, and she knew that they'd found the love they had so tentatively explored that night . . . but the magic was gone.

She stopped a few yards from him and he took the final steps to her, then reached out to brush away the curls that the sea breeze had blown across her face. After searching her face with a gentle, silent inquiry, he drew her into his arms and surrounded her with a warmth that began to penetrate her bone-deep chill.

"Have I ever told you about Rusty?" he asked as he continued to hold her gently.

She drew back slightly to frown up at him. "Who's Rusty?"

"Rusty was my cat. He died about six months ago, at the age of sixteen. He had fur about the color of your hair. Most of the time he was very warm and affectionate, but once in a while, for reasons known only to him, he withdrew. He'd let me hold him and pet him, but he still managed to pull into himself and shut me out. Right now, you're reminding me of Rusty."

In spite of herself, Teddy laughed. "I'm not sure that I appreciate being likened to a cat."

"Why not? Don't you like cats?" he asked with mock innocence.

"I love them. I had a Manx until about three years ago. He was fourteen when he died, and he used to come up here with me every summer."

Graham told her that he had heard of Manx cats, but knew little about them. Teddy needed no further prompting to begin singing the praises of the unusual tailless cats. She recognized his conversation for what it was—a diversion—and was grateful to him for his understanding of her needs, if not the reason for it.

They continued to talk about the particular foibles of their respective former pets, with one story leading to another in the manner of all pet owners. Graham drew her down onto the sand, settling her against his chest, his legs propped up on either side of her and his arms circling her loosely.

There was a hauntingly fragile beauty to the scene. Teddy gradually relaxed against him as the conversation died out. Graham knew how very precious and temporary this beauty was—and Teddy would remember it and understand that much later.

OUTWARDLY, THE NEXT DAY PASSED uneventfully, but there was an atmosphere of tension in the house that seemed to grow with every hour. A chain of storms pelted the island for most of the day, keeping them all indoors and contributing to the charged atmosphere.

From their falsely hearty morning greetings to each other to their mutual decision to pursue largely solitary tasks that day, the trio engaged in charades. Ted paced about the house, pausing often to peer out at the dreary day. Graham, while managing to preserve an outward appearance of calm, nevertheless betrayed his emotions by following Teddy's movements with even more than his usual interest.

Teddy spent the day ostensibly working on campaign speeches and her own paper, but in reality, she was trying desperately to find a way to confront her father with her knowledge and suspicions. Hour after hour, imaginary dialogues took shape, only to be rejected. Having initially hidden her discovery of the papers, she now knew no way to admit that she had seen them. A casual "Oh, by the way, I just happened to see..." simply wouldn't work now. And there was always the possibility—and the fervent hope—that she was wrong.

What it came down to was that, unless she had incontrovertible proof that her suspicions were accurate, she could not risk making an accusation, no matter how carefully worded. Such words could never be taken back and would never be forgotten. She now felt trapped by her own deception.

So, lost in their own thoughts, the trio carved out their individual spheres of tension and largely avoided conversation. Some of the tension must have communicated itself to the housekeeper, too, since she made no comment when all three failed to do justice to the meals she prepared. They ate their breakfasts and lunches separately, and when they were forced to come together at dinnertime, conversation was largely limited to the campaign and the rotten weather, which they all hurried to blame for their dreary moods.

Then, just about dusk, the weather cleared and there was a brief, glorious sunset. The rainwashed heavens sparkled with stars and a sliver of moon, promising fair weather the following day. Graham suggested a stroll on the beach, but Teddy declined the invitation, stating that she was too deeply engrossed in her novel.

The truth was that she didn't want to let her father out of her sight. Sometime during the course of the day, she had gone from questioning her suspicions to a consideration of how the documents would reach the unknown people who were threatening him. The result of that was that she no longer believed they were safe on Matiscotta.

She had at first assumed that no strangers bent on evil deeds would allow themselves to be seen on such a small island. But then two incidents had returned unbidden to cast doubt upon that assumption. The first was the time she and Graham had seen her father at the deserted dock below her lookout, and the second was the night she had thought she'd seen lights at that dock during their stormy crossing after dinner at the pound. When she finally recalled that her father had returned early that night dripping wet, Teddy thought she might have her answer. The dock was possibly the only place on the island where an arriving boat could be virtually guaranteed of secrecy. It was invisible from the road and in the middle of the longest strip of deserted land on the island.

Now, finally, as darkness settled in around them, Teddy thought she knew what would happen. Her father would meet with the unknown people at that dock and hand over the papers. The meeting could even take place this night, since the weather had finally cleared.

A part of her wanted it to be over and done with, even if her father was committing a crime. Whatever his reasons for doing such a thing were, they must indeed be compelling, and she knew there would be no way she could stop him. So she just wanted it to be done and in the past.

But another part of her wanted to stop it—or to find out that she'd been wrong all along.

The thought of telling Graham continued to hover about the edges of her mind. He loved her and liked her father; surely he could help, even if she couldn't at the moment see how.

A few moments after he had left the house to go for a solitary stroll, Teddy got up to follow him, intending to pour out her fears. But her footsteps faltered before she had even reached the terrace door. She had no right to drag Graham into this. Despite his feelings for her and for her father, he was an outsider. She returned to her chair and her novel.

But the book was nothing more than a prop; she hadn't read more than a few pages. Until now, she had avoided thinking about the true implications of what her father was doing, other than that it was a crime. Now, it was staring her in the face in all its ugliness: her father was in all likelihood betraying his nation's secrets to the enemy.

Teddy had been involved in the disarmament movement for some time and had loudly decried the nation's recent weapons buildup. Few subjects could arouse her indignation more than the billions being spent on weapons systems, a small part of which came from her father's company. But no matter how loudly she protested defense policy, she simply could not justify betrayal of those secrets to the enemy.

Still, for Teddy the bottom line was the love and loyalty she bore her father. No matter what he was doing and why he was doing it, she loved him. She clung desperately to that love, and then, through an act of sheer determination forced herself to concentrate on the neglected novel.

"Teddy."

Her name, spoken softly by that familiar voice, nearly failed to arouse her from a confused dream that combined elements of her own fears and those of the mystery she had been reading. But when fingers touched her cheek softly, followed by the pleasant tickling of a mustache, she jerked awake quickly.

Graham was bent over her, his hands braced against the arms of her chair. He brought with him the smell of salt air and the faint odor of cigarette smoke. She frowned and wrinkled her nose.

"Were you smoking?"

He stood up and gave her a rather sheepish look as he nodded. "I gave it up a few years ago, but sometimes I backslide a bit."

She was disappointed at his withdrawal and smiled at him. "I don't mind. I'm not one of those people who's developed a sudden allergy to cigarette smoke."

But he remained where he was, apparently not understanding her subtle invitation. "It was a beautiful night for a walk," he said conversationally. "I'm sorry you didn't join me."

"I should have," she said with an attempt at lightness. "Obviously, I didn't find this book too exciting."

Teddy sensed that Graham was withdrawing from her in more than the physical sense, something he hadn't done for a while now. Or was she only imagining it? She hadn't exactly been affectionate toward him since her discovery of those papers.

A new terror filled her as she wondered if all of this could result in her losing Graham. She'd been so preoccupied that she hadn't really considered it before. And yet, not even that terror could stir her to action.

Finally she got up, stifling a yawn and wondering how she could manage to stay awake, or at least sleep lightly enough that she would hear her father if he left the house. Then she realized that she didn't know where he was at the moment, and looked around with alarm?

"Where's Dad?"

"Outside in the terrace. He said he was about ready to turn in."

As if on cue, her father appeared in the terrace doorway. They both turned to him, but he avoided their gazes and went to the liquor cabinet, where he poured himself a cognac. Carrying it with him, he said his good-nights and went up the stairs. Both Graham and Teddy stared after him.

"I'm going to bed, too," said Teddy, fighting off another yawn.

She said good-night and started toward the stairs, then stopped and turned around to look at Graham. He hadn't moved, and was watching her with that intensity that never failed to send little curls of heat through her. There was a tension in his stillness, as though some sort of inner battle were being waged. After a moment's hesitation, she went to him and wrapped her arms about him, burying her face in the rough weave of his sweater.

Not one word passed between them as they stood there holding each other. Finally, it was Graham who ended it with a slow, soft kiss, before releasing her. She left him there and walked slowly up the stairs.

Despite her determination to remain vigilant, Teddy was very nearly asleep when something jolted her back to full wakefulness. She sat up quickly, ears straining, but no sound broke the stillness of the house. Still, something had aroused her; she was sure of that.

She debated with herself very briefly, then got out of bed and listened at the door for a moment before opening it quietly and creeping out into the hallway on bare feet. Across the hall, Graham's door was closed and no light was showing.

She padded softly along the hallway until she had reached her father's door. Still there was only silence in the house. Finally, she put out a hand nervously and touched the cool metal of the doorknob. He was a sound sleeper, so it wasn't likely that she would disturb him if he was in there asleep. Nevertheless, she couldn't bring herself to open it without knocking first, so, with a furtive glance back toward Graham's door, she raised her hand and tapped lightly. At the same time she held her breath, wondering how on earth she could explain herself to either man if she should waken one of them.

There was no response to her quiet knock, so she took a deep breath, uttered a silent prayer and opened the door. The bed and the room were empty. In fact, the bedcovers hadn't been turned down, proving that he had never even gone to bed.

He could be downstairs, she thought with increasing desperation. On other nights he had prowled about the house late at night. But she'd always heard him before, since her bedroom was directly above his study.

Still barefoot and clad only in her nightshirt, Teddy hurried downstairs. All was darkness, but she took precious moments to check his study and then the kitchen. Then she thought to check the garage and opened the connecting door to find both the Volvo and his bike still there. But of course he couldn't have taken either one without disturbing them by opening the garage door.

Teddy stood there in the darkness for a moment, her heart pounding and her mind racing, seeking another explanation for his disappearance. He could simply have gone for a walk on the beach.

She dismissed the thought abruptly and dashed back through the house and up the stairs, then dressed hurriedly and left the house without giving herself any more time to consider her course of action. She had reached the beach and set off at a brisk trot before it occurred to her that if she was wrong about his meeting place, she would never know what happened.

Was that what she really wanted, she wondered as her feet struck the sand with soft, rhythmic thuds? Did she want to leave room for hope that she might have been wrong?

No, that was not what she wanted. She wanted this to end and she wanted to know that it had indeed ended, even if that ending left wounds that would never really heal. No matter what he might be doing, he was still a good man. She would cling to that and to her lifelong love for him. Besides, if he won his race for the senate, he would have the opportunity to make up for this mistake by serving his country, and that, she now realized, was probably just what he had in mind.

She reached the end of the strip of beach and had to slow her pace to clamber over some rocks and dunes, then wade through a patch of coarse beach grass. After that came another strip of sand, so narrow that now, at high tide, a thin sheen of water had nearly overrun it. She saw the footprints then, etched into bold relief by the pale moonlight. Even as she stared at them, the water crept higher and washed them away.

Certain now that he had come this way and was headed for the abandoned dock, Teddy was momentarily paralyzed by a stab of icy dread. The explanations had run out, washed away just like those telltale footprints in the sand. She had to push herself on.

Another half mile of increasingly rugged terrain lay between her and the old abandoned dock. Obviously, he had taken this route rather than using the road because there were several houses close to the road along that route and he had wanted to avoid the possibility of being spotted. The deserted rocky beach wasn't even visible from those homes.

She made her way quickly but cautiously, forced to slow down considerably as the hill rose beyond the beach and blocked the pale light of the moon. It was easier going somewhat inland from the beach and she chose that route, thereby cutting off her view of the sea.

Cold with fear despite her exertions, Teddy climbed slowly up a dune that she thought would afford her a glimpse of the old dock. The grass here was several feet high and as she reached the top, she dropped into a crouch that she hoped would keep her invisible to anyone out there. Then, parting the grass carefully, she peered out.

Her pounding heart thudded to the pit of her stomach as she saw her father standing there on the dock with his back to her as he stared out to sea. In his hand was what looked like a large envelope.

She squeezed her eyes shut and felt the tears begin to leak out anyway. When she forced herself to open them again, he was an indistinct blur but still very much there.

There was still time, she told herself. She could run out there and persuade him not to do this. Her body jerked forward, then sank back again as the tears streamed down her cheeks into the grass. She couldn't do it. She couldn't bring herself to confront her father. If there had been any other way out of this, he would surely have taken it. In spite of the horror of this scene, Teddy knew that there must be other, perhaps even worse, things she didn't know. And didn't want to know.

It would be over with this. He would leave the company and whatever hold these people had over him would end. She told herself this over and over as she lay there, cold and miserable in the quiet stillness of the night.

Then a sound grew slowly, gradually becoming recognizable as the whine of a boat's engine. Cautiously, Teddy lifted her head once more and saw the lights headed toward the dock. Just ahead of her and still closer to the dock were two large boulders that would provide adequate cover. She slithered forward, half crawling on her stomach, until she had reached them. It wasn't curiosity that urged her closer; rather, it was an innate need to be as close as possible to her father, perhaps to lend him her silent understanding.

Then a new fear gripped her, causing her to shudder violently. If these were the same people who had run her off the road, they were dangerous. Could they mean to harm her father, especially now that they must know he could be of no further use to them? Her father couldn't possibly protect himself from them; he'd never even owned a gun of any kind.

"Graham!" She whispered his name involuntarily as she hugged herself in terror. She should have awakened him. He had a gun, a gun she'd seen only once. That evening flashed through her mind, drawing along behind it a newly aroused suspicion. But she let it go as the lights from the boat grew brighter and the engine was throttled back for the approach to the dock.

The boat eased its way up to the dock and she could see two occupants, although they were nothing more than shadowy figures beneath the canopy. Her father reached out to take the line one of them threw to him, and Teddy held her breath as a man jumped from the boat to the dock.

But there was no sign of a weapon, and it was over very quickly. She could hear the low murmur of voices but could not distinguish any words. Her father handed the man on the dock the envelope, then backed away and held his hands up, palms outward, in a gesture that seemed to indicate that he was washing his hands of the matter. The man got back into the boat, clutching the envelope, and the boat immediately backed away from the dock, trailing behind it the line her father had cast off quickly. A few seconds later, it was swallowed by the dark sea, with only a distant whine to prove it had ever been there.

Teddy watched as her father continued to stand there, still facing the sea, his stance a heart-wrenching picture of defeat and dejection. She swallowed a strangled cry and had to look away from him.

And that was how she saw the other figure—high above them on the ledge of her lookout.

Chapter Ten

The figure on the ledge was indistinct, but someone was definitely there. Teddy opened her mouth to scream, but the paralysis of terror had overtaken her and all that came out was a low whimper.

He had something in each hand—dark shapes she could barely make out—but the one in his right hand was long and slender. A rifle. She was sure of it. The scream began to work its way out again, but at that moment, the figure backed away and disappeared into the darkness. A few more seconds ticked by as she peered up at the empty ledge, and then she finally drew a ragged breath. She'd never really gotten more than a fleeting, shadowy glimpse of him, but she was still convinced that he'd been carrying a rifle.

She turned to look toward the dock again just as her father stepped off it and started back down the beach in her direction. With one final glance up to the empty ledge, Teddy scrambled from her hiding place between the rocks to the greater cover of the tall beach grass. Then she waited for her father to pass by as she tried to fathom that other man's purpose, and what she should do now.

Had he been up there as some sort of insurance policy, to guarantee that her father didn't back out at the last moment? If Ted Sothern had refused to hand over the documents, would the man on the ledge have shot him? Teddy shivered uncontrollably and flattened herself against the sandy soil. A moment later her father passed by, walking slowly, his head down. She held her breath again as he passed within twenty feet of her, then let it out as he continued on his way.

As soon as he had disappeared around the end of the rocks, she stood up with yet another glance up at the ledge. Had that man seen her? It was difficult to tell. The ledge afforded an excellent view of the dock, but she might have been back far enough to have avoided his scrutiny.

Teddy continued to stare up at the ledge, wondering what the man intended to do now. Whoever he was, he had to get off the island before morning. Strangers were entirely too obvious on Matiscotta. Perhaps he was even now making his way down here, to be picked up by the boat that might be merely circling about off the island.

Or perhaps he still intended to harm her father. She drew in a sharp breath, then took off like a frightened deer. The man posed no immediate threat. Teddy knew how long it would take him to reach the road, especially with the added difficulty of traveling over unfamiliar terrain in the darkness. If he intended to attack her father, it would have to be back at the house. That meant that she had to get back to the house—and to Graham—as quickly as possible.

The fastest way back to the house was the more visible route both she and her father had avoided: along the road. Although it was by now rather overgrown, there was a gravel driveway that led from the burned-out house to the main road, and it was this road that she took, stumbling along in the darkness as best she could.

She felt highly vulnerable as she ran out onto the moon-washed road a few minutes later. Even though the most agile of men could not possibly have reached the road before she did, she still paused long enough to peer in that direction before she set out at a jogger's pace for home.

Turning every few minutes to glance behind her, Teddy ran back toward her house. If the man came out onto the road behind her, she would make a perfect target, but there was simply no help for it. She had to get back to the house as quickly as possible and rouse Graham, in case that man intended to come after her father. It no longer mattered to her that she would be dragging Graham into this; her concern was for her father's life.

The chilled night air rasped through her overworked lungs and there was a painful stitch in her side, but she kept on. When she came at last to her driveway, she turned around one last time, then exhaled audibly in relief when she saw that the road behind her was still blessedly empty.

Slowing to a walk in the driveway, Teddy started for the front door, then deviated from her course at the last minute and went around the side of the house. There was no way that her father could be there yet, even if he had begun to run, but she wanted to be sure.

The beach was empty and Teddy finally went into the house, her thoughts turning to Graham and how she was going to explain all this to him. Shivering from fear and trembling from overexertion, she came to a stop outside his door and knocked sharply before turning the knob.

The room was empty. Teddy stared at the still made-up bed in disbelief. Where on earth was he? For just a moment, she forgot all about the possible danger to her father as she assimilated this new development. Then, belatedly remembering her purpose here, she went to his closet, hoping to find the gun.

It hung there in its holster, concealed beneath a sports jacket. Nervously, she lifted it out of the holster, stared at it, then quickly put it back. She didn't know a thing about guns and wouldn't even know if it was loaded.

Teddy stood there, gnawing at her lip as she considered the situation. If that man on the ledge had intended to attack her father, wouldn't he have done so when Ted Sothern had made a perfect target on the moonlit dock? Why come back here, where there would be others about? She backed away from the gun and the closet, feeling somewhat better.

But the empty room reminded her again of Graham's absence, and a slowly dawning horror struck her anew. Could Graham himself have been the man on the ledge? She shut her eyes and conjured up that briefly seen image. The man had been wearing something dark, like a Windbreaker. Graham owned one in navy blue. She went back to his closet again and pawed frantically through it, searching for the garment. It was nowhere to be found, just like its owner.

Unable to think anymore about this latest discovery, Teddy fled from his room and crossed to her own room, then went immediately to her window and peered out toward the beach. A moment later, her father came into view, walking more briskly now as he often did when he was out for a constitutional on the beach. Clearly visible in the moonlight, he once again made a perfect target. But this time, Teddy's fear was lessened. If Graham had been the man on the ledge, she was certain that he would never have harmed her father.

Ted Sothern came up the path toward the terrace and then disappeared from her view as he strode toward the house. A moment later she heard a soft sound and knew he was safely inside the house.

She sagged with relief against the window, then abruptly remembered Graham's open door and the light she'd left on there. So she ran back across the hall, closed the door behind her and switched off the light as she heard her father's furtive footsteps on the stairs. That was followed in a few seconds by the sound of his door closing. Teddy sank into the bedroom chair, bone weary and emotionally drained.

GRAHAM MOVED UP to the house through the short coarse grass rather than along the driveway, to avoid making any sound. Neither Ted nor Teddy had bedrooms that faced the front of the house, but he was taking no chances. He paused to check the luminous face of his watch. Even if Ted hadn't hurried home, he would have arrived some time ago.

He made a cautious circle of the house, peering in darkened windows on the first floor, then checking for light upstairs. All was silence and darkness. After setting down one of his burdens, he slid open the terrace door, then stopped to listen once more to the silence. With a sigh of relief, he picked up the small, strangely shaped suitcase and entered the house, heading directly for Ted's study.

Dropping the items again, he closed the door behind him and picked up the phone. His call was answered on the first ring, indicating that all had gone as planned.

"You've got them?"

He waited impatiently through the detailed description, then, keeping his voice low, said, "I'll see you in the morning, then." There was a brief silence on his end of the line, then more words in a low, annoyed tone: "Yes, I still want it that way."

He hung up in a sudden burst of anger. It was none of their damned business why he'd chosen to handle it this way. They had their orders.

But as the anger subsided, he knew it had been directed more at himself than at them. He didn't care what they thought about him, but he did care what he was thinking about himself. And at the moment, the word coward was looming large and ugly in his mind. It wasn't a word he would ever have associated with himself, and it left a bitter taste in his mouth.

He considered having a drink, then shrugged off the need and went instead to pick up the gun case and the camera. Inside that camera was the irrefutable evidence, caught in the lens of the high tech infrared mechanism that could probably have recorded the words TOP SECRET on those papers if they'd been taken out of the envelope. And inside the strange suitcase was the broken-down high-powered rifle he hadn't had to use.

This should have been a moment of triumph for him, like many others he'd known over the years. But the emotions that swirled about inside him as he left the study did not include exhilaration.

He stole quietly up the stairs, already feeling like a stranger in this house. As he passed Ted Sothern's closed door, powerful emotions nearly brought him to a halt. There was pain and anger and regret, followed by a brief glimpse of a bleak future.

Lost in this unhealthy melange, he didn't notice Teddy's open door until he was nearly to his own room. The unanticipated could produce panic or even a temporary paralysis in most people, but in Graham it brought just the opposite: a rational calmness that allowed for split-second decision making.

He reversed his steps and slipped into an unused bedroom, where he deposited his burdens in the back of a closet. After allowing himself a few moments to collect his thoughts, he returned to the hallway. He confirmed that Teddy's room was empty, then opened his own door with an icy certainty about what awaited him there.

Teddy was jolted awake by the sound of the doorknob turning and had only a second to wonder how on earth she could possibly have dozed off. Then the door opened and Graham appeared.

Her startled and then fearful expression tore at his heart, but his mind was already working on a way out of this confrontation he had taken such care to avoid.

"You followed Ted, didn't you?" he asked, having already guessed that was what had happened.

She nodded, sensing that the question had been rhetorical. She felt drained of all emotion and incapable of deception now. Then, as her dozing brain began to awaken, she remembered the man on the ledge and stared at Graham's empty hands. Had she been wrong, after all?

"Where were you?"

Once again Graham thought about concocting a plausible lie. But he too was drained and empty and incapable of deceit.

"Following him, too," he said, stalling for time.

"Then it was you up at the lookout," she stated in a voice devoid of emotion.

It was that tone of voice that dragged Graham out of his own misery. He thought about what she must have been through this night. No matter what she had suspected, the bald truth would have been devastating to her.

He literally ached to hold her and comfort her, but he knew that would be the ultimate blasphemy. In desperation he clung to the hope that she wouldn't hate him, and was determined to take every precaution to guarantee that fantasy.

"Yes, it was me," he replied quietly as he stepped into the room and closed the door behind him.

"Were you there to protect Dad?" she asked, still sitting in the chair and staring at him intently.

Graham heard the desperation in her voice and knew that's what she wanted to believe, what she needed to believe.

"Yes," he responded, knowing that it was at least a half-truth.

She got up then and turned her back on him as she wrapped her arms about herself. "Wh—what is your role in all this, Graham?"

Then, before he could reply, she whirled around with a surprising speed. But her face showed the tiredness that he, too, felt: a bone-deep mental weariness and soul draining pathos. She made a small, dismissive gesture.

"No, don't answer that. I don't want to know now. I can't face... any more."

Impelled by emotions that drove away all reason, Graham moved toward her, his hands reaching for her. But she eluded him and opened the door, then paused briefly in the hallway without turning. As he started to move again, she almost ran for her own room and closed the door quickly behind her.

Graham stared at that closed door for a long while. Then he finally closed his own door and sank down into the chair. Tears he hadn't shed since childhood stung his eyes.

TEDDY AWOKE VERY SLOWLY, and even as her brain struggled to rouse itself, she knew that she wanted to remain asleep. For a few moments she succeeded in holding off the day by staying in that in-between state, but with each breath, more of the past night's events intruded. Then, when it had all returned, she was stunned to believe that she had actually been able to sleep.

Finally, she pulled herself out of bed with nothing more in mind than a trip to the bathroom. Even so, she opened her door cautiously, as though expecting some new and terrible discovery to be lurking just outside her room.

Across the hall, Graham's door was open and his room was empty. He was generally up before her and this sameness to the morning routine was vaguely reassuring.

After she had dressed, she went downstairs, taking the back staircase in the hope that she could avoid seeing either Graham or her father until she'd had a restorative cup of coffee.

"Good morning, Mrs. Watson," she greeted the housekeeper with forced cheerfulness, briefly envying the woman her ignorance of the past night's events. "Where are Dad and Graham?"

"Your father left just a few minutes ago for his bike ride," the housekeeper responded, "But I haven't seen Mr. McKinsey this morning. He's probably out on the beach."

Teddy nodded, thinking that both men seemed to be going about their lives as though nothing out of the ordinary had occurred. Was she the only one who was suffering in all this? The thought made her angry.

After pouring herself a cup of coffee, Teddy left the house to find Graham. She was trying to quell the foolish hope that he would tell her her assumptions had been wrong, that her father had done nothing illegal. In the bright sunlight of a morning in her favorite place in the world, Teddy Sothern could almost believe that.

She searched the strip of beach for him in vain, and then began to pace back and forth as she drank her coffee. Through her mind in kaleidoscopic fashion ran various conversations with Graham. She refused to examine any of them carefully, lest her imagination take her even deeper into horror. But still, there remained one throbbing question: was his refusal to become involved with her somehow connected with her father's deed?

As she thought about this, she had continued to walk along the beach and she stopped now in front of the boathouse at the one end. Still, it took several seconds before something registered on her agitated brain: the boathouse was empty.

Teddy whirled around and stared back at the house. Only one person could have taken the boat. Dropping her mug and its contents onto the sand, she ran headlong toward the house, not stopping until she had run up the stairs and into Graham's room.

Her suspicions were confirmed very quickly: nothing of Graham remained in the room. The closet was empty and so were the dresser drawers. For a wild, irrational moment, she was sure there would be a note: surely he wouldn't have gone without a message for her. But then reason reasserted itself and she sank down onto his bed.

He had gone because his job here was ended. Whatever his reason for being here, it hadn't been to act as campaign manager. She felt a bitterness as she recalled how she'd questioned that role at the very beginning.

She felt darkness closing in on her, but she pushed it away angrily and concentrated instead on the immediate future. Her father would be returning soon. Did he knew that Graham was gone? Did he knew who Graham really was? What kind of excuse could he possibly offer for Graham's abrupt departure?

Teddy didn't even know what she hoped would happen. She didn't want to believe that Graham had been one of those who was threatening her father. But then what had been his role?

She closed her eyes and willed him into her mind, peering into every memory of their time together, examining every shred of evidence: his failed attempt to play the role of cynical political pro, his approach-withdrawal behavior toward her, and small, insignificant things she had ignored previously—like his obsession with fitness, the reason she had never learned for his possession of a gun and even that rather strange remark he'd made during that stormy boat ride about machismo being an "occupational hazard."

Then, into this simmering stew she threw the qualities she so admired in him: his quiet competence, his rigid self-discipline that even she hadn't been able to crack, and beneath that sometimes cynical exterior, a hint of the true man—one of strong principles and unshakable beliefs.

All of this coalesced, finally, into something as close to certainty as she had felt in a long while. And that certainty left her with such sharply divided feelings that it would be a long time before she could face them.

She went back downstairs to find her father just returning from his bike ride. Ted greeted his daughter and met her gaze with outward calm, but with a suggestion of deep pain lingering just behind his dark eyes. She saw that suffering and hoped for a moment that she was wrong. But a different kind of pain lay in that direction.

"Did you know that Graham is gone?" she asked in a deliberately flat tone.

There was a brief but unmistakable flare of concern in her father's eyes. "You mean he's out exercising?"

"No, Dad. He's gone." Teddy was certain now that he hadn't known. "He took the boat and all his things."

Ted stared at her in silence and as Teddy watched, a variety of emotions flitted across his features. She couldn't read any of them clearly, but she guessed that he might now be reaching the same conclusion she herself had reached. A charged silence held them both motionless until Teddy took a deep breath and forged ahead.

"I followed you last night, and so did he—separately, I mean."

She had to force herself to look at her father as she spoke, and as her words came out haltingly, she saw him seem to crumple into himself. His normally straight shoulders sagged and his eyes became shadowed and haunted. He raised a shaky hand to run it distractedly through his hair.

With a cry of anguish, Teddy ran to him and wrapped her arms about him. "I love you, Dad. I don't understand why you did what you did, but I still love you."

She held on tightly as he wrapped his arms around her and heaved a heavy, ragged sigh. They remained that way for a long while, clinging to each other and drawing on a lifetime of love. Then Ted set her away from him, and she could see the moisture glistening in the corners of his eyes.

"Thank you, honey," he said as he bent to press a kiss against her brow. "You've no idea what that means to me now, even if I don't deserve it." Then, when he saw that she was about to protest, he turned his face away and in a hoarse voice asked her to go get him a cup of coffee.

Teddy didn't want to leave him for even a moment, but she knew that he wanted a few minutes to collect himself, and so forced herself to do his bidding. She wondered when this nightmare would end and the new one would begin, but in a very strange sort of way, she felt calm and more clear-headed than she had in a long while.

When she returned with coffee for them both, she found him in his study, slumped into his big desk chair as he stared at the photo of her mother he still kept there. She immediately guessed the direction of his thoughts.

"Mom would still have loved you, Dad. She always said that love wasn't just for the good times."

He looked from the photo to her and then back again, then nodded. "There's a lot of your mother in you, Teddy. I've always been very grateful for that."

Teddy managed a brave smile. "There's also a lot of you in me, and I've always been grateful for that, Dad."

Once more, he nodded, then dragged his gaze away from the photo and stared at her bleakly. "How much do you know?"

"Most of it, I think," she said in a voice she had willed to remain matter-of-fact. Then she went on to tell him all she knew, in a voice that seemed to her at times to be coming from someone else.

When she had finally finished, she asked the question that had been plaguing her ever since she had pieced it all together.

"But why didn't you go to the FBI, or whoever it is who deals with such things?"

He met her gaze briefly, then looked away. "I couldn't, honey, because I had dealt with these people before."

At some deep inner level, Teddy had been prepared to hear this, but she still stammered in her shock. "B—before?"

Ted winced as though in physical pain at the shock his words had caused, but then he nodded. "Yes, about six years ago, when the company was in trouble."

He paused, looking off into some place Teddy couldn't see. She waited in silence as an anguished love flowed through her and tears blurred the sight of this man she so admired and loved. When he spoke again, his voice was low and lost in that past.

"The seventies were lean years for the business, but I'd managed to squeak through. By the time it seemed likely that there was going to be a defense buildup, the company was nearly bankrupt. I was sure I'd get some good contracts, but I was also sure that it was going to be too late.

"The banks wouldn't lend me any more, and with interest rates as high as they were then, I couldn't have met the payments anyway. Your mother wanted to lend me the money from her trust fund, but I just couldn't face that. The fund was controlled by her family, as you know, and they would have found out."

He paused to give Teddy a look that was a quiet plea for understanding. "They were against our marriage, Teddy. In those days, class was all-important. She had it and I didn't. Furthermore, they were sure that I'd never be able to support her in the style she was used to.

"But she loved me and married me anyway, and other than using some of her money to get the company started, we never touched it. I repaid that loan with a check that I all but threw in your grandfather's face." He actually smiled for a moment, recalling a moment he had obviously very much enjoyed.

"So you see, I just couldn't touch that money again, despite your mother's pleas. I was about to file for bankruptcy when some men approached me. I think they must have spent all their time seeking out companies like mine—and there were a lot of them then.

"What they wanted to buy wasn't really strictly defense-related. It was state-of-the-art technology that was on the restricted list, meaning that it couldn't be exported. They assured me that the information wasn't going to our enemies, and I let myself believe that. After all, some of our allies wanted that technology, too. For all I know, it might well have gone to an ally. I suppose they sold it to the highest bidder.

"I demanded a high enough price to keep the company going, and then the defense contracts began to come in. I didn't hear from them again, and foolishly believed that I never would. But about two years ago they contacted me again. I refused to deal with them and they began to make threats. I knew that one phone call to the right place and I could lose my defense contracts. So I took the company public, because making myself an employee, rather than the owner, seemed safer. I wouldn't have been able to cover things as easily, and they would know that.

"It worked, for a while. Or maybe they just had other, more willing, prospects and just put me on hold. In any event, they didn't come to me again until just after your mother had died." He paused briefly and his gaze fell on her mother's photograph with a deep sadness.

"That's when I knew they'd never leave me alone as long as I had the company. Your Uncle John had been suggesting that I run for the senate, because he knew I hadn't really felt the same about the company since I'd taken it public. And I suppose he also thought that a new challenge would help me get over your mother's death.

"Anyway, getting into politics seemed like a good idea. I'd be of no further use to them, and besides, public service seemed like a good way to repay the debt I owed for having sold that technology.

"So I thought I was off the hook, but they still kept after me. They threatened to expose me and ruin my chances for the senate, and when I still kept putting them off, they threatened to harm you. I didn't believe them, but after that accident of yours, I knew they meant business. So I gave them what they wanted, knowing it would be the last time. I couldn't go to the authorities, because they would have found out about the other time, and they might even have gotten to you again in revenge."

Father and daughter sat in silence for a few moments, both of them lost in a sad maze of "what ifs" and "if onlys." Teddy thought about the sin of pride and wondered what she might have done in his place. Her own proud independence was a direct inheritance from her father.

Finally, Ted looked at his daughter with a sad smile. "I still like him, you know. I liked him from the beginning. If I hadn't, I might have been more suspicious, despite Jack Oldham's recommendation."

Teddy snapped out of her reverie. The other portion of this painful voyage of discovery had gotten lost temporarily. Her father's words confirmed her own conclusions about Graham.

"But how could Senator Oldham have betrayed you like that? He must have been lying about Graham's having worked for him."

Ted shrugged. "I suspect he was forced into cooperating. Few people in politics have completely clean records, and knowing Jack as I do, I suspect that he has a few skeletons in his personal closet."

"I told you that Graham followed you last night, too. I saw him up on the lookout, and he admitted that he was there. He was carrying a rifle, although I didn't see it later when he came back. But he said that he was up there to protect you." Teddy spoke the last words with bitter mockery.

"He probably was, honey," her father said gently. "He wouldn't have been the only one worried that they might decide to get rid of me."

At the moment Teddy just didn't believe that, but if her father wanted to, she wasn't about to deny him that now.

"But he had something else in his other hand. I couldn't see it clearly. Something fairly large and strangely shaped."

Ted Sothern thought for a moment, then nodded. "An infrared camera, I imagine. That would have provided the proof they'd need."

Teddy was amazed at his calm acceptance and his lack of fear. She'd still entertained faint hopes that her father could get out of this, and that Graham wasn't what she'd suspected.

"Then he really is . . ." She faltered, unable to get out the words.

"FBI, I suppose," her father finished for her. "This would fall under their jurisdiction, and it seems a far more likely career for Graham than politics."

He watched his daughter, and his anguish grew when he saw the expression on her face. "Teddy, I know how you feel about him, and I—"

His words were cut off abruptly as they both heard a loud knock at the front door. Father and daughter stood quickly. Teddy looked wildly about the room, as though seeking a place to hide. Her father came around his desk and put his arm around her shoulders.

"Somehow, honey, I don't think it'll be Graham. My guess is that he left to avoid this, for all our sakes."

Teddy wasn't quite so sure, but she prayed that he was right. She knew she could not face Graham McKinsey, now or ever again.

They went to the door together, and Teddy was overwhelmed with relief when she saw the two men. She recognized them immediately: they were the two men who had sat across from her in the restaurant, and then rescued her after the van had run her off the road. At last, a small part of the story fell into place.

Lines from every cops and robbers film she'd ever seen were actually being spoken, and Teddy had the surrealistic feeling that cameras were grinding away somewhere just beyond her vision. She held tightly to her father's hand until one of the men asked if he wanted to call his attorney. He let go of her hand and went back to the study, trailed by the two agents.

At that moment the housekeeper appeared, wearing a puzzled frown. Teddy shooed the woman back to the kitchen with a promise to explain later, then followed the others into the study, where her father was already on the phone with his attorney. The conversation was brief, and thereafter, one of the men suggested that he pack a bag, then followed him upstairs. Teddy was left alone with the other agent, the one who had come to her rescue after the accident.

She made a feeble attempt at a smile. "I never had a chance to thank you for your help after the accident."

The man looked chagrined. "I'm sorry it happened, Ms Sothern. We were following you to prevent something like that, but we had a flat and had to stop."

He seemed as uneasy as she herself was, and hurried on to ask her about her car after expressing admiration for it. Teddy told him that it was fine, thanks to an expert body man, and wondered how they could be standing here exchanging pleasantries at such a time.

"Will he be able to get out on bail?" she asked suddenly into a small silence, as her mind at last turned to consideration of the immediate future.

"I don't know, ma'am," the agent answered in his soft southern drawl. "That'll be up to the judge."

Teddy merely nodded, then before she could lose her courage, asked the other question on her mind at the moment. "Where is he?"

"Who's that, ma'am?"

"Graham," she managed as she wondered if that was even his real name.

The agent was silent for a moment, staring at her as though he was just beginning to figure something out. Teddy felt embarrassed by his scrutiny, as though all her confused feelings were being laid bare.

"He's on his way to Washington by now," the man said finally. Teddy breathed a ragged sigh of relief that drew yet another sharp look from the agent. She prayed that he was telling her the truth, since it had just occurred to her that Graham might be waiting somewhere nearby, planning to come to her when the others had left.

Her father and the other agent returned and the two men withdrew slightly as Ted Sothern gathered his daughter into his arms. Teddy hugged him tightly and struggled to retain her tenuous hold on her self-control.

"I'm sorry, honey, for what this must be doing to you," he said in a voice choked with emotion.

Teddy shook her head and managed to smile bravely at him. "I love you, Dad. Nothing can change that."

And then he was gone, walking between the two men as they left by the terrace door to head for a boat tied up at their dock. She stood in the doorway and watched until the boat had become nothing more than a tiny speck, far out in the gray sea.

The housekeeper reappeared, still wearing her anxious frown, and Teddy was forced to explain who the men were. The woman immediately asserted that it must be a mistake, and Teddy began for the first time to grasp the full dimensions of what lay ahead for her.

She was alone on the sunny terrace a while later, trying to force some warmth into the coldness that had settled into her very bones when she heard the sound of a boat approaching. As it grew even louder, she focused her attention on it and saw with a jolt of awareness that it was their own boat.

By this time the boat was pulling up to the dock, and Teddy looked about wildly for a place to hide. She could not face him. She wanted neither his pity nor his explanations. But as she stood there, half-paralyzed by fear, a young man she recognized as being an employee of the Rockland marina jumped out of the boat and waved at her. Then she saw a second boat pulling in behind him. She breathed an audible sigh of relief and went down to meet him.

"Do you want me to put it in the boathouse, Ms Sothern?" the youth asked.

Teddy shook her head. She would be taking it back to the mainland soon herself. She asked him to wait until she went up to get some money to pay him, but he shook his head.

"He already paid me, and there's a full tank of gas, too."

They left and Teddy remained on the empty beach for a while, trying to recapture some of the happy memories of this place. But Matiscotta held too many memories now— and the good ones seemed very far in the past.

GRAHAM PUT DOWN THE PHONE and looked around his new office. The walls were still bare and some of his things remained in boxes stacked against one wall. A corner office and a private secretary: all the trappings of success. Not even the FBI was immune from those little touches.

So Ted Sothern was pleading guilty and cooperating in the investigation. Graham was grateful for that, because Teddy would now be spared the horrors of a long trial with all the attendant publicity.

Absently he rubbed his still-throbbing temples. He'd forgotten just how bad a hangover could be. He probably should have gone out with some of his friends who had wanted to celebrate his promotion. But instead, he'd gone home and deliberately tried to drink himself into oblivion. It hadn't worked.

He stared balefully at the boxes of files, the result of nearly a year's work. Graham had been put in charge of a special task force set up to gather evidence against a group of American and foreign dealers who acted as brokers for illegal weapons and technology exports. At the time he'd been very pleased at being given the highly coveted assignment. He'd never been particularly driven by ambition, but he did have his goals, and the leadership of an important investigation had been a definite step in the right direction.

Ted Sothern had been only one of a half-dozen people they were watching closely, people with high tech secrets who had possibly sold out before. Plodding, patient investigation would probably have brought results sooner or later, but when Ted's campaign manager had been killed, they had seen an opportunity to get someone close to him.

The only one among the group with any political expertise was Graham himself, and since the outline of the investigation had already been put in place, he had jumped at the chance to get out of the office and back into the field again.

He mused sadly about it now. He'd been so damned eager because he'd always enjoyed the excitement and maybe even the danger of undercover work, and it had been several years since he'd had the opportunity. But it seemed to him now that it had gone bad from the very beginning.

First, there'd been the object of the investigation himself: Ted Sothern. From the beginning, Ted had reminded Graham of his own father: a self-made man who'd never quite forgotten his struggle and his humble beginnings. Graham had liked him immediately.

And then, of course, there had been Teddy. He'd felt that first little twinge of interest before he'd even met her, when he'd seen her prominently displayed photograph in her father's office. But the photo, good as it had been, hadn't come close to doing justice to the living, breathing woman. Graham suspected sadly that the die had been cast from the first moment she had snapped those outrageously blue eyes at him.

He wondered—and he guessed he'd always wonder—just how it was that she'd seen through his disguise almost from the beginning. Graham knew he was good; he'd had a long, successful career in undercover work, persuading people to accept him for what he said he was. But Teddy hadn't bought it, and the more he was attracted to her, the less he'd wanted her to buy it. It was some kind of miracle that he hadn't managed to sabotage his own operation.

What did she think of him now? The question had been nagging at him incessantly for the past two weeks. Her emotions could be volatile at the best of times, and she was going through hell right now. He wanted so desperately to go to her and give her comfort, but he knew that was out of the question.

Perhaps he'd made a mistake by running out at the end. Maybe he should have stayed to face her certain wrath, hoping to salvage something by reminding her of his restraint and his love for her. But he'd run because he just couldn't face the hatred he knew he would have seen in those blue eyes. Now he wondered if seeing that hatred might not have been the only way he could have begun the process of putting her out of his mind.

There was a knock at the door and his new secretary came in. She was a very attractive woman, perhaps even beautiful, and she had already signaled her interest in him. He wondered if he should have insisted upon one of the older, married women, thereby releasing this one to pursue a more appreciative boss.

As she sent a few more discreet signals, Graham sent one of his own: not interested. Not now—and maybe not ever.

Chapter Eleven

Teddy's days passed in a blur of pain and anguish. There were many times when she was certain that she could not survive another day, but then she would fortify herself with the thought that her father needed her. And however bad it was for her, it was far worse for him.

She left Matiscotta to be with him in New Haven. He had been allowed out on bail, but was not permitted to return to Matiscotta for reasons that were never made clear to them. They supposed that it had to do with the island's remoteness and the possibility that he might disappear by boat. Teddy was secretly glad about this restriction, because Matiscotta held too many painful memories for her now. She wasn't sure she would ever be able to return.

But however unpleasant it was, her life was indeed busy. She sat in on all her father's many sessions with his attorneys, more to be a comfort to him than to be of any assistance. It was during the first of these sessions that she learned that Graham had been in charge of a large operation, of which her father was only one small part. Sometime later she learned how he himself had come to be involved personally in an undercover capacity. It was a tragic irony that her uncle's death had been responsible for bringing into their life the man who had destroyed her father.

When Teddy wasn't busy with the attorneys, she was even busier dismantling the campaign. There were contributions to be returned, since very little of the money had actually been spent. Along with the refunds went a letter Teddy herself had written, thanking contributors and apologizing for a failure to live up to their expectations. It was altogether a sad and difficult chore.

She also attended her first—and last—company board meeting. Despite her dislike of the company's business, Teddy had hoped that she could retain her own stock in it. It meant nothing to her, but she had thought that her father would be pleased to know that a part of her company remained in the family.

His own stock had been sold almost immediately to avoid any damage to the company. But when she met with the board, she was politely but firmly told that her stock should be sold, too, since it was tainted by association. The stock brought a very good price, proving that public confidence in the company hadn't suffered, and Teddy found herself with far more money than she either needed or wanted. This then necessitated several sessions with an investment counselor to decide where to put the money.

In the meantime, the word prison hung over every conversation. The more blunt of the two attorneys stated that he very much doubted that Ted Sothern would be let off with a fine and probation, despite his willingness to cooperate. The other lawyer, however, continued to hold out that hope, and both Teddy and her father clung tightly to it.

Friends and relatives called, assuming that he was innocent. But then, two weeks later, when he pleaded guilty, all but a few stopped calling. Her mother's family dissociated themselves completely from their son-in-law, while letting Teddy know that they still considered her to be a member of the family. She managed to bite back some very ugly words, but never forgave them.

Her father's family, who still lived on their rural Vermont farm where their son's success had made their lives more comfortable, gave him their unquestioned love and support amidst their own quiet suffering. Teddy took a few days off from her depressing work to visit them and came away with a vastly greater love and appreciation for them than she'd ever had before.

She stayed away from her college, except for a few phone conversations with old faculty friends, and she had already begun to think that she might never return. All of her past life seemed to have come to an end, or rather, to have been reduced to living a single day at a time.

Before her father, she managed to keep up a determined cheerfulness that vanished as soon as she was alone. She also kept a careful watch over him, fearing that the ordeal would destroy his health. But to her surprise, once the initial shock had worn off, he appeared to be coping better than she was. A psychologist friend in whom she confided explained that he probably felt relieved of a terrible burden of guilt in the face of certain punishment. She, on the other hand, could feel no such relief, since she was being punished without having been guilty.

The subject of Graham McKinsey was held at bay by dint of sheer determination. Teddy was vaguely aware of the fact that she would have to face her feelings about him at some point, but this was not the time. Late at night, though, when she lay in bed awaiting the temporary bliss of sleep, he hovered there in the darkness, demanding that consideration. Then, if she succeeded in ignoring that phantom intrusion, he followed her down into her dreams, proclaiming his love for her, while at the same time retreating into an ugly darkness.

Occasionally in the morning after these dreams, Teddy would wonder if he, too, was suffering. But here, his strength became his undoing in her mind. He might be feel-

ing some pain and regret, but there was, in her opinion, a
stoicism about Graham that would prevent its wreaking the
havoc upon him that she was suffering. She became very
sure that, in short order, she would be reduced to a mere
footnote in his mental case files, while he was destined to
play a major role in her memories for the rest of her life.

Finally came the day of the court appearance at which her
father was to be sentenced. Her fears that he would have to
go to prison had grown steadily with the approach of this
day, and she hadn't slept at all the previous night. A generous application of makeup hid the worst of the evidence,
but nothing could mask her nervous exhaustion as she entered the courtroom. And then she saw Graham.

No one had warned her that he would be there, presum-
ably because no one had known it would matter, except for
her father, and he was as surprised as she was. She walked
in with her father and his attorneys and collapsed into a seat
directly behind them. He was on the far side of the crowded
courtroom and had his back to them. She willed her eyes to
remain on her father or on the judge, but they kept dis-
obeying her and sliding off to rest on that broad back clad
in a tawny-beige suit. She willed him to turn around, then
didn't think she could stand it if he did. As prosecutors,
attorneys and the judge droned on, Teddy knew that she was
close to collapsing.

At one point, the judge called Graham by name and he
got up with the prosecutor to approach the bench. Still, he
didn't turn in their direction, and it became very apparent
to Teddy that he was deliberately ignoring them. Even when
he returned to his seat, he angled in such a way that he was
able to keep his face averted from them.

Teddy's first thought was that he must be suffering as
much as she herself was, and that he wouldn't be here if it
hadn't been mandatory. But then, probably because of her

exhaustion, her emotions veered sharply in the other direction.

Was it possible that she had been no more than part of the plan to him, that he had dangled love before her eyes in case he had needed to use her? The notion, thus planted, began to take root, and the fact that he had showed restraint she quickly wrote off to an attack of conscience and nothing more. Or perhaps there was already someone in his life, a wife even. How could she know truth from lies where he was concerned? The man had been an actor, after all, playing a role.

Such were Teddy's thoughts when a sudden hush in the courtroom jolted her back to the present. Her father and his attorneys were standing before the judge.

"I sentence you to a term of five years in a federal prison and a fine of..."

Teddy never heard the rest of it. Five years! She went rigid with shock and remained in her seat as everyone else got up and the judge left the courtroom. Five years in prison! People began to talk and mill about and still she sat there, struggling to face that horrible reality. Her father and the one attorney were talking to a federal marshal, but the other attorney came over to her.

"Teddy, it's not as bad as it sounds. That means parole in just a little more than a year. And it's Lewisburg, in Pennsylvania. It's not the kind of prison you're thinking of."

She stared at him dumbly as images of cells and bars and gray ugliness engulfed her. What other kind of prison was there? A prison was a prison—and five years were being taken from her father. She didn't yet believe the attorney about the parole; he was the one who had doubted there would even be a prison sentence. And she had let herself believe him then, too.

Wild thoughts ran through her brain. They could leave the country, go to one of those places rich criminals were always escaping to. There was plenty of money; they could live comfortably. Why hadn't she made some plans? Was there still time?

Then her father was there, drawing her to her feet and folding her into his arms. "Honey, it's over now. Please promise me that you'll get on with your life and stop worrying about me."

She clung to him tightly, saying nothing. How much time did they have? When would he have to go?

He held her away from him and stared at her, his face etched with concern. "It's best for us both that I go now, Teddy. But I want to know that you'll be all right."

She started to protest, then fell silent. He was right. Another few days would only be torture for them both, and she had very little strength left to keep up a brave front. But she used what did remain now, as she squared her shoulders and held back the tears.

"Don't worry about me, Dad. I'll be all right."

He stared at her with a mixture of tenderness and pride, then bent to kiss her. "I love you, honey, and knowing you'll be all right is all that matters to me now."

"I love you too, Dad, and I'll visit you as often as they'll let me." She clung to him one last time, then let him go and stood there with a brave smile on her face as he left with the marshals.

As soon as he was gone, she turned on her heels and fled the courtroom, not stopping until she had gained the privacy of a nearby restroom. After a long while, she managed to stop shaking long enough to splash some cold water on her face. Then she stared at herself in the mirror.

The face that stared back at her was pale and haunted, the result of too many long days and sleepless nights. No wonder he had worried so about her. She fumbled through her bag until she found her oversized sunglasses, then hid most of the ravages with them. Finally, she told herself firmly that the worst was over, and she had survived it. If her father could remain calm and in control, so too could she.

Eventually, her self-blandishments worked and she felt able to leave the restroom. The hallway was nearly empty and no one paid her any attention. There had been a sizable contingent of reporters in the courtroom, but they had apparently gone.

The case had drawn quite a bit of attention from the media because of her father's senate candidacy, and, according to one of the attorneys, possibly because of the presence of a very photogenic daughter. Teddy had seen herself once on the evening news, and thereafter had stopped watching it.

She hurried out of the building with no plan in mind other than to retrieve her car from a nearby parking garage—and then she saw why the hallways had been empty. On the sidewalk in front of the building was a cluster of reporters, immediately recognizable because of their cameras and cassette recorders. It was foolish to think they wouldn't recognize her, but she let herself think it anyway, right up to the moment when they converged upon her.

True terror gripped her as she became convinced that she would break down in front of their cameras. In that moment, she vowed that she would never again watch the news with its privacy-destroying ugliness. Surely the public's right to know did not extend to this.

The cameras began to whirr, but what the evening news would show that night was an unidentified man shoving aside the group of shouting reporters, seizing her arm and propelling her into a car parked at the curb. Then he paused for one moment to give them all a disgusted look before getting into the car himself. One or two of the reporters thought he looked like the FBI man in charge of the investigation, but the others thought they must be wrong.

Teddy was inside the car before she quite knew what had happened. The imprint of Graham's hand was still on her arm, leaving a spot of warmth on an otherwise chilled body.

"Where shall I take you?" he asked without preamble as he started the car.

Teddy stared at him, not yet certain that he was real. "My car is in the garage around the corner."

The street was one-way in the other direction, so he began to circle the block, having to pause twice for traffic lights. Neither of them said anything more, but Teddy was slowly regaining her self-control. She kept her eyes fixed firmly ahead of her, trying as best she could to ignore the man beside her.

He pulled into the garage, then followed her instructions to reach her car. As he came to a stop, they both began to talk at once.

"Thank you for—"

"Teddy, I—"

They both stopped, stared at each other for a long moment, then looked away as though they could bear it no longer.

"Will you be all right?" he asked her in a peculiarly tight voice.

She nodded, then realizing that he couldn't have seen it, she managed a husky "yes." She cleared her throat before continuing.

"Thank you for coming to my rescue, Graham. I—I don't think I could have handled that myself."

"They'll leave you alone now," he replied, still staring straight ahead. "By tomorrow you'll be old news."

It was time to get out of the car, to get away before either of them could say more. Teddy knew now what she'd really known all along: she'd never been a part of his plan and there wasn't anyone else. In those brief moments when they'd allowed themselves to stare into each other's eyes, she had seen all her own pain and anguish mirrored in his darker eyes.

She slanted him a glance and saw moisture gathering in the corners of his eyes as he continued to stare straight ahead. At the same time, she felt the tears begin to well up in her own eyes. She reached over in an involuntary gesture and touched his arm, withdrawing as soon as she felt the rigid tension. Then she opened her door. He turned her way then, and their eyes met very briefly before Teddy started to drag herself out of the car. Halfway out, she paused, but kept her face turned away from him.

"I don't hate you, Graham. I want you to know that. You were just doing your job. Dad understands that, too. But I can't . . . love you, either."

Then she leaped out of the car and ran the few steps to her Jag, where she got in without a backward glance. With shaking fingers, she fitted the key into the ignition, then held her breath as she wondered if he might follow her. Anxious seconds ticked away as his car remained there . . . and then he pulled out.

MAISON BLANCHE WAS ONE of the power lunch spots of the nation's capital and to be seen lunching there with a re-spected senator was a situation to be coveted, but Teddy would have preferred to share her lunch with her co-workers.

The maitre d' informed her that Senator Oldham had not yet arrived, then led her to a highly visible table. Teddy was not displeased; in fact, she would not have been displeased to find that the senator had been forced to cancel their lunch date. She'd successfully dodged this meeting for several months now, until her father had reminded her at the time of her last visit that the senator had been very kind to them both. So here she was.

She ordered a glass of wine, then sipped at it and ignored the looks of polite inquiry she was receiving from other patrons who were undoubtedly wondering why they didn't recognize her.

Teddy had been living and working in Washington for nearly six months now, and she still hadn't made up her mind about the place. She found the obsessive interest in politics very interesting, since it happened to coincide with her own interests. But the concomitant obsession with power and connections was another matter altogether.

On the other hand, she thought wryly, she herself hadn't exactly been above using connections. Although the decision to leave the academic world and seek employment with a public policy research institute had been hers, the fact that she had gotten a very good job with one of the leading institutes had stemmed at least in part from Senator Oldham's intervention on her behalf.

The senator had been noisily contrite about his role and had written to her father, who forgave him, and contacted Teddy, who hadn't been so generous. Nevertheless, when he'd asked about her plans and she had mentioned a research position, he had insisted upon helping her.

The senator arrived in the company of another well-known senator and a cabinet officer whose face Teddy recognized, even if she couldn't quite recall his name. He brought both men over to the table, and after greeting her in his usual effusive manner, he introduced her to the other men as the daughter of an old and dear friend. Teddy managed to refrain from mentioning his role in sending that "old and dear friend" to prison.

"Teddy, my dear," he exclaimed when the others had departed, "you look wonderful! Washington must agree with you."

Teddy smiled ruefully. "Thank you, but you won't be saying that if you see me a month from now." She wrinkled her nose distastefully. "I detest heat and humidity. It's already terrible and it's only May."

The senator nodded in commiseration. "Thank God for summer recesses. Will you be going up to Matiscotta?"

Teddy shook her head. She would have some vacation time coming, but she just couldn't face Matiscotta. All her many summers of happiness there had faded to a blur, overlaid now with the anguish of the past summer.

The senator gave her a look of understanding. "You'll go back, Teddy, and so will Ted. You both love that place too much to stay away forever. Have you seen him recently?"

"I'll be seeing him next weekend. He's allowed one weekend pass per month now, but he must stay in the immediate area of the prison. So we take motel rooms and just nose around the area."

"Has he made any plans yet?" the senator asked. "He hasn't mentioned anything in his letters to me, and he's due to be released in a few more months, isn't he?"

"About four months, if he's granted parole. And no, he hasn't said anything to me, either." The subject of her father's future was one that troubled Teddy greatly. Although he could certainly afford to retire, she knew he'd never be content to do so.

"Perhaps he could do some consulting work," Senator Oldham suggested. "He couldn't get a security clearance again, but there must be plenty of work he could do without it. Or maybe he should think about starting another company."

"I've already suggested that, but he says he's too old to go through all that again. I'll have to talk to him about it next weekend."

"You know that if there's anything at all I can do to help, I will," the senator said with obvious sincerity.

Teddy just nodded. She knew that her father bore the senator no ill will, but she just couldn't be so charitable. Her expression must have conveyed that to him, because he looked at her imploringly.

"Teddy, I know you don't want to talk about it, but you have to understand my position. Every politician who's been around as long as I have has done some things he isn't proud of. I had no choice but to go along with McKinsey's plan."

The mere mention of that name that she had not heard spoken aloud for months now sent shock waves through Teddy, which she attempted to cover with a rather sharp tone.

"What you're saying is that he blackmailed you."

"No, it wasn't as heavy-handed as that. He came to me and asked for my help. It's not easy to refuse to help the FBI, but I tried to think of a way out of it. He just sat there, giving me that damned look of his and I caved in."

Teddy wondered what that "damned look" was. The only look she could remember was one she had been trying desperately to forget—and she was sure that wasn't the one the senator meant.

She realized then that she'd given virtually no thought to Graham's profession. Her memories were far more personal.

"I understand that he's gotten himself a nice promotion out of it, too," the senator continued. "Not that there's anything wrong with that, of course," he added hastily when he saw the strange look on Teddy's face.

"Is he in Washington, then?" Teddy asked. She'd suspected that he probably was, but ignorance in this case was at least close to bliss.

"Yes. I forget his title now, but the Bureau views him as one of its rising stars. From what I've seen of him, it wouldn't surprise me to see him reach the top some day. As you probably know, he was in charge of the whole operation, which involved far more than just your father. The only reason that he took on your father's case personally was that he was the best man for the job. He actually had had some campaign experience years ago, and John's death provided them with a perfect opportunity to get someone close to your father.''

Teddy frowned. She'd already known about that, but his promotion was news to her. That bothered her, although rationally, she knew the senator was right. However, his mention of her late uncle provided an opportunity to ask about something that had been troubling her for months now, something she certainly couldn't discuss with her father.

"Senator, do you think that Uncle John's death could possibly have had anything to do with Dad's . . . mistake?''

Senator Oldham regarded her solemnly for a long moment and when he answered, it was with obvious reluctance. ''It could have, Teddy, although I hope that your father never makes that connection.

"I thought about it myself sometime after your father's arrest, and I contacted McKinsey. He was reluctant to discuss it and tried to brush me off, but I told him that John had been a good friend of mine and that in view of the help I'd given the investigation, I felt he owed me something.

"He finally admitted that although they haven't been able to pin it on that bunch, they do have their suspicions.''

"So do I,'' Teddy admitted uneasily. ''But I just can't see how there could be a connection.''

"Well, McKinsey hit on the possible explanation that I'd been considering myself. John was a very thorough man, and even though your father was both a close friend and a relative by marriage, he would have wanted to be sure there was nothing in Ted's background that could cause problems. He was certainly aware of the financial difficulty that had led to Ted's first dealings with them, and he would also have known that the money that had gotten him out of it couldn't have come from your mother's share of the family trust.

"My guess—and McKinsey's—is that John might have begun to nose into things and somehow they found out."

"I'm not sure that I want to know if they ever do make the connection," Teddy said in a choked voice. "And I certainly wouldn't want Dad to know."

"Neither of you will ever know—at least not if Mc-Kinsey can help it. He told me that there's no reason either of you would have to be told. In fact, he told me in no uncertain terms to keep my mouth shut about it. But you asked and I've told you."

Teddy carefully kept her face averted and feigned interest in her lunch. Graham's concern for them both had reopened that never-healed wound inside her, the fierce tug-of-war between pain and love. She wondered sadly if it would ever end.

They finished their lunch as they talked more about her father's future. But however pressing that issue might be, Teddy could barely focus on it. Once the subject of Graham McKinsey had been introduced, it simply refused to go away. Her father had attempted to bring Graham's name into their conversations several times, but Teddy had steadfastly refused to discuss the matter. She told herself that she simply could not consider her own future until her father's was settled, but deep down inside, she knew that she was very much afraid to face that future.

When she had settled down for the long drive to the prison a week later, she once more succeeded in pushing Graham into the dark corners of her mind by resuming her consideration of her father's future plans.

Ted Sothern had been reluctant to give up his precious Cadillac, so Teddy kept it for him and used it for her monthly trips to central Pennsylvania. It was, she admited, far more comfortable than her own Jag for long trips, but she felt as though she were driving a living room sofa.

Guilt always rode with her on these trips, a silent but accusing companion. The truth was that she hated it all: hated the long drive, hated seeing her father emerge from the ugly prison, then hated herself for her selfishness. But she always went, and he was always happy to see her and to be able to spend time outside the prison walls.

This time, however, she kept that guilt in abeyance by thinking of her father's future. She'd tried discreetly a few times to get him to discuss it, but without any success. This time, she decided, she'd confront him head-on. For her sake as well as his, she had to know what he planned to do.

Why for her sake? she wondered. Her father was certainly not going to be a burden to her, regardless of what he decided to do. And yet it seemed very important that she get it settled.

Teddy thought about it for a while and gradually reached the conclusion that she had been avoiding consideration of her own future until he settled his. In a sense she, too, had been in prison for nearly a year now, a prison not unlike his, actually. Every effort was made to create a nonprisonlike atmosphere, but the walls remained. Inside them she went about her daily routine and ignored what lay beyond.

Such were her thoughts as she drove on, barely conscious of the rolling hills and large dairy farms that were lush and green in late spring. Winter wheat crops were nearly ready for harvesting and pastures were dotted with placid black-and-white Holsteins who went about their business of turning grass into milk.

Then she was there, at the prison that made a semi-serious attempt to look like something else. It didn't succeed, because there were still armed guards and a metal detector and the obligatory search of her handbag.

As she surrendered her bag, Teddy thought wryly that she had never before kept it in such good order. The strangest things had been taken from her: a nail file and a clearly marked plastic container of breath mints. What did they think her father was going to do: cut his way out with a nail file or swallow an overdose of breath mints? She'd been tempted to ask but had kept quiet, fearing that her behavior could somehow cause problems for her father.

As always the wait was interminable, although she knew it wasn't her father's fault. The unattractive waiting room was empty this time, but it was often filled with others whose faces she surreptitiously searched, wondering what crimes their loved ones had committed, and then wondering if they wondered about her in her expensive clothes and luxurious car.

Then he came through the door and she jumped to her feet to hug and kiss him with all the love and pain she invariably felt at such moments. It seemed so wrong that this essentially good man should be here in this place, and at such moments she came very close to hating Graham McKinsey, despite her denial to him.

She noticed that his clothes seemed just a bit tight, and when she asked him, he admitted ruefully that despite his exercise in the prison's well-equipped gym, the diet had gotten the best of him. He'd had his clothes tailor-made for years, but he suggested that perhaps they could shop for a few things in local stores until he could once again visit his tailor.

He assured her that parole was a virtual certainty, since he'd done nothing to provoke its denial and he had assurances that the FBI would not intervene to keep him here.

Any reference, no matter how oblique, to Graham always affected Teddy, and so she missed the touch of dryness in his tone as she hurried on to ask for details about the parole process.

They drove away, and Teddy noticed once more how quickly her father changed when he had left the prison behind. He became more animated, more self-confident, in short, more like the father she had always known. Seeing this gave Teddy hope that he hadn't been permanently scarred by his ordeal.

After they had checked in at the motel where they always stayed, he suggested that they go for a walk on the campus of Bucknell University, a small college in Lewisburg. This was their standard routine, regardless of the weather, and Teddy knew that he took an almost embarrassing pleasure in being able to stroll about without being under the watchful eyes of guards.

"You know," her father said as they strolled about the nearly empty campus, "I've been thinking about the possibility of teaching when I get out. I don't have a doctorate, of course, but I think I still might be able to get a faculty position somewhere. What do you think of the idea?"

Teddy couldn't think at the moment; she was dumbfounded. She'd come up here prepared to force him to consider his future, and it now appeared that he'd already decided it. Furthermore, despite the fact that she knew he had been teaching a computer course in the prison, she'd just never considered that possibility.

"I've enjoyed the teaching I've done here," he went on, oblivious of her astonishment. "And I'm told that I'm good at it, too."

"I think it's a wonderful idea, Dad," she said with genuine enthusiasm. "And I'm sure you'd be good at it. You've always been so patient. I can remember when you explained microelectronics to me. I even understood most of it—and believe me, that's a tribute to your teaching talents."

"You're going to be surprised when I tell you who first suggested it to me," he said in an amused tone.

"Who?" Teddy asked, nonplussed both by the question and by his expression.

"Graham."

"G—Graham?" Teddy got the name out with difficulty as she stopped dead in her tracks and stared at her father incredulously.

Ted was clearly enjoying his daughter's shock. "He came to see me a few weeks ago."

Shock turned rapidly to fear as she recalled her conversation with the senator. Had they finally found evidence to link her uncle's murder with her father's activities, and Graham had changed his mind about keeping it from him? But her father didn't appear to be at all upset. Still, she asked, "Why?" with some trepidation.

"Well, at first he tried to convince me that he was up here on business and just thought he'd look me up to see how I was doing. I think he was half-convinced that I wouldn't talk to him. But then he admitted that he'd come just to see me."

Teddy could almost hear the wings of hope fluttering to life within her. This connection with Graham, however tenuous, had the most extraordinary effect upon her. There were suddenly tiny cracks appearing in the walls she'd built around her future.

"I'm glad he came," her father went on, still seeming to be oblivious to her emotions. "I'd intended to look him up when I get out. I liked him from the beginning and nothing that happened has made me change that opinion. In fact, his coming here only makes me think more of him."

Teddy was thinking about that, too. It must have taken some courage—and affection for her father—for Graham to have done such a thing. But the fact that he had done it didn't really surprise her. Graham McKinsey was a man of his convictions, and if those convictions dictated that he should seek forgiveness, he would have done just that, when lesser men might have let well enough alone.

Her father had gone on to talk about Graham's promotion, but Teddy was only barely listening. Another of the many things she'd been refusing to consider was the sincerity of Graham's affection for her father. Now she recalled, nearly a year later, those times when she'd mentioned that bond to Graham, and his reaction.

She winced with inner anguish as she thought about the price Graham had paid for his integrity. How had he survived these months? Had he, too, been living from day to day? Was he, too, ignoring a future too painful to contemplate?

"He asked about you, Teddy."

His too-casual words struck her with the impact of a bundle of dynamite. Teddy looked away, not quite knowing what to say. She was afraid to let that hope loose. After all, it would have been perfectly normal for him to have asked about her.

"Teddy," her father said patiently, "I tried to talk to you before about Graham."

"Don't, Dad," she pleaded, growing more and more fearful.

"Yes. This time we have to talk, because now I'm sure that he's in love with you. I thought it then and now I know it. He's been going through his own kind of hell."

"He told me he loved me," she admitted in a near whisper. "But it seems so long ago."

"Well, I'm convinced that he still feels that way and that you love him, too."

When she said nothing, he pressed on. "Graham is exactly the kind of man I'd like to have for a son-in-law. And he apparently doesn't have any objections to having me for a father-in-law, either."

"He told you that?" she asked incredulously.

"The very fact that he came all this way to see me tells me that."

"I just don't know what to do," Teddy said in a voice filled with anguish.

Ted broke into an unexpected grin, reminiscent of the older, better days. "I think that's the first time I've ever heard those words from you, but I'm not going to seize the opportunity to dispense some fatherly advice. That decision is yours."

When he saw that he had teased a smile from his daughter, he said, more seriously, "What I will tell you is that I think you'll have to be the one to make the first move. He knows how I feel, but he doesn't know how you feel. I have his address, by the way."

Teddy thought about that scene in the parking garage. She'd made her feelings all too plain then. And there were still so many things she just wasn't sure of. Was Graham really the man she believed him to be? Could she forgive and forget as her father had obviously been able to do?

In the end, she took Graham's address, reasoning that taking it didn't mean she had to get in touch with him. All the way back to Washington she wondered if it might not be better to cling to the memories of the happy times they'd shared, rather than risk finding out that it had all been false.

She put his address into her desk drawer and tried to forget about it for a while. But she'd discovered that he was living only a short distance from her, and that became an irresistible lure.

Teddy frequently went for walks in the evening because she enjoyed Georgetown's undeniable charms. She was sure that she must have passed his home at some point, and now she decided to do so deliberately. It was a small, hesitant step.

There were two cars in the driveway alongside the brick town house. One was a domestic station wagon, and the other was a dark-green Saab. Graham had told her that he owned a Saab, but who owned the station wagon? Or was this town house divided into apartments like the one she lived in? What was his home like? What if he passed by a window at this moment and saw her out there, standing on the street like an idiot? When she found herself actually beginning to hope that would happen, she hurried on.

A few days later, on a pleasant Sunday afternoon, she went for yet another walk past his house. By now, she admitted to herself that she wanted him to spot her and take the decision out of her hands. The thought was galling, to say the least. When had she become such a wimp?

Just as she came upon the house, the front door opened and an attractive dark-haired woman came out. Jealousy spread its dark, ugly tentacles over her as she slowed her pace to watch. A few seconds later, two young children came hurtling through the door, calling to their mother that they wanted to take the small dog that had followed them outside. Teddy moved on as an argument ensued and the dog began to show an interest in her. Belatedly, she noticed that the Saab was gone, and she wondered where he was on such a beautiful day.

She continued on her walk and finally started back, entering his block once more. Just at that moment the Saab came around the corner at the far end of the block. There were other people and cars on the street, so she felt reasonably sure that he wouldn't see her. But if she hurried across the street, she could probably manage to be in front of his house by the time he pulled into the driveway.

She didn't do it. Pretending that a shoelace had come untied, she stopped and bent down to retie it. She wouldn't even let herself look in his direction. Then she about-faced and went home by another route. It would be wrong, somehow, to arrange an "accidental" meeting. If she was going to see him, it should be with every intention of doing so.

That afternoon she began her letter to him. A letter, she decided, was definitely the best way to handle it. If he didn't want to see her, he could just ignore it. She was no longer certain that her father had assessed the situation correctly. He liked Graham, and he might well have allowed that affection to color his judgment.

The letter underwent six drafts over four days before it finally went into the mail. With each draft, it became more formal. What the final draft said, in essence, was that she was pleased that he had visited her father, that she herself bore him no ill will and that perhaps they might get together some time, since they were living so close to one another.

As soon as she dropped the letter into the mailbox, Teddy became certain that she'd made a mistake. Either she shouldn't have written him at all, or she should have admitted honestly that she wanted to see him.

Chapter Twelve

eaving a weary sigh, Graham dropped his bags just inside
e door and let his gaze rove longingly to the small bar
tup in one corner of his living room. Remy Martin beck-
ed, and he crossed the still sparsely furnished room to
ed its summons.

Two weeks in Paris at Interpol's headquarters might have
unded like a dream to his co-workers, but it hadn't been
at for Graham. The fabled City of Lights hadn't glowed
ry brightly for him.

He sniffed the cognac appreciatively and wondered why
didn't do what most men in his situation would have done
fore this: find another woman. God knows, there were
enty of them available in Washington. Hadn't he seen
atistics somewhere proving that there were more single
omen in the capital than in any other comparably sized
S. city?

He settled back in his leather lounger and sipped the co-
ac as his mind drifted back to his meeting more than six
eks ago with Ted Sothern. He still felt a surge of glad-
ss at the knowledge that Ted had been happy to see him
d willing to forgive him. He'd been flying high after that
sit, convinced that the one obstacle between him and
ddy had been cleared away. If her father forgave him,
rely Teddy would, too.

He'd known that Teddy would be visiting her father on two weeks after his own visit, and he'd foolishly expected call from her as soon as she returned from that weeken For days he waited eagerly for a call that never came.

He'd thought about sending her flowers, then had di missed that as being too close to making the call himsel something he'd vowed he wouldn't do. The first move ha to come from her, signaling a willingness to forgive ar forget.

If Teddy had been a less assertive woman than she wa he might have been able to justify making that call. B then, he thought ruefully, if she'd been anything other tha what she was, he wouldn't have cared.

Now, sitting in his lonely home with only a bottle fe company, he was trying halfheartedly to accept once aga the reality of a future without her. And once again, he ju couldn't do it. He loved her, he wanted her, and therefo he had to have her. Life, he decided, had been a hell of a lc simpler when a man just picked out his woman and dragge her back to his cave.

He got up to pour himself some more cognac, then p down the bottle in disgust. Getting drunk wouldn't hel he'd already tried that without success.

Instead, he picked up his bags and carried them to h bedroom. The king-sized bed mocked him silently and l tossed the bags onto it, then let his coat and tie follov Restless and still slightly disoriented from the long flight, l decided to check his mail.

For a while after he'd given up any hope of a call fro Teddy, he'd sorted through his mail eagerly, too, thinkir that she just might do something dumb like write to hir even though they lived only a few blocks apart. Teddy, l knew, was capable of such unpredictable behavior.

This evening, however, his mood was such that he kne he wouldn't be disappointed when there was no letter fro er. Because he'd been gone for two weeks, the pile left for im by his obliging neighbor was quite sizable. Along with ιe possession of every major credit card and subscriptions ） half-a-dozen magazines came the inalienable right to re-eive every catalog and piece of junk mail in existence.

He began to sort through it without interest, thinking that e probably should take his neighbor out to dinner to thank er. The problem with that was that one thing might lead to nother, and he just wasn't interested. That she was had al-ady been made rather clear to him.

On the other hand, maybe he should just let it happen. he was attractive and a very nice person and he even liked er kids, who obviously needed a daddy to replace the one vho had gotten himself killed on the beltway a year ago.

He was pawing through the mail and toying unenthu-iastically with the idea when he came to an expensive ream-colored envelope whose return address fairly leaped p at him.

All his senses went on red alert, just as they had always one over the years whenever he was in danger. But this vasn't danger, unless there was danger inherent in hope. He ached for his letter opener, dropped it and instead tore the nvelope open with shaking fingers. His eyes fell immedi-tely to the signature in her bold scrawl.

Then he sank into his desk chair and read the brief note. after that, he reread it. Then he read it for a third time. Fi-ally, he threw it onto the desk and glared at it, swearing nergetically and colorfully.

"Perhaps we could get together sometime, since we're ving so close to each other."

What the hell kind of statement was that? It sounded like ιe kind of polite, meaningless thing people said to end a onversation. Why was she writing such a thing to him? It as almost worse than not hearing from her at all. Almost, ut not quite. However tentatively, she had made that first move. And if dinner was all she had in mind, she had made a very big mistake.

He flipped through his Rolodex until he found the number he'd already recorded there, then dialed it as a surge of hope coursed through his body.

TEDDY HATED RINGING TELEPHONES; consequently, her bedside phone didn't ring. But the one in her guest room office did, and that was enough to awaken her. Bleary-eyed, she stared at her clock radio. One-fifteen. Who on earth could be calling her at such a ridiculous hour? A wrong number, no doubt. Then, with a sudden burst of panic, she thought about her father. Had something happened to him? She reached for the receiver with a trembling hand and managed a very shaky and husky hello.

There was a brief silence on the open line, followed by a muttered curse. "I'm sorry, Teddy. I forgot how late it is."

Instantly, Teddy was sitting upright in bed, clutching the receiver in a death grip. "Graham?" Her tone denied the possibility.

"I just got back from Paris," he blurted by way of explanation.

"Oh," was the best she could manage as she wondered what he'd been doing in Paris, and with whom he had done it.

"An Interpol seminar," he explained as though he'd tuned in on her thoughts.

Vastly relieved, Teddy struggled for something to say, something as far as possible from her thoughts at the moment.

"Congratulations on your promotion."

"Thanks, but I think that all I've been promoted to is an endless round of meetings."

She managed an almost normal laugh. "I know all about them. I spend a lot of time in them myself these days."

"Ted told me about your new job. Do you like it?" He was wondering when he'd find the courage to turn this absurd conversation to more important things.

"Yes, I do. In fact, I like it even better than teaching."

"So you don't regret giving that up, then?"

"No, not at all. Do you regret giving up fieldwork?" Was he waiting for her to reiterate her desire to see him, or were they going to have to spend the rest of the night in this stupid conversation?

"Oh, I'd already given up fieldwork a couple of years ago. That, uh, was just an exception." *Just an exception,* he thought mockingly. *An exception that brought you into my life. Nothing major, you understand. Dammit, this went beyond ridiculous.*

"Let's have dinner on Saturday," he blurted, thinking that surely he could regain his sanity in two days' time.

There was a brief hesitation, just long enough that he felt himself begin to sweat, and then she said yes.

They set a time, he told her that he already knew where she lived, and then they said goodbye rather hastily. Teddy lay back against her pillows and waited for her pulse to slow down to normal, and Graham decided to have that second cognac, after all.

TWO DAYS LATER, Teddy stood in the middle of a room that gave every indication of having been trashed by an expert. Drawers gaped open and the bed and floor were covered with the bright, bold clothing favored by their owner.

She stood there, hands on hips, chewing at her lower lip. Two hours. She had only two hours before he would be here. Hardly enough time for a shopping trip. Why hadn't she considered this problem before?

Teddy hardly ever paid much attention to her wardrobe. Oh, she chose her clothes with great care during periodic

whirlwind shopping trips, but once that had been accom
plished, she tended to grab the first thing that came to hand.

So why, she asked herself in exasperation, wasn't she
doing that now? What did it matter, anyway, when just
about all he'd ever seen her in had been jeans and sweats?

It mattered. Everything mattered. She was acutely con
scious of one broken fingernail. She was suddenly aware of
the need for a haircut. She'd let herself run out of her fa
vorite perfume. In short, nothing was right and she desper
ately wanted to have everything right. Ever since that late
night call, Teddy had been living with the certainty that this
date was one last chance for them both. Failure tonight
meant acceptance tomorrow of a future without Graham
McKinsey.

She'd relived that brief conversation many times in the
past two days and had groaned inwardly each time. How
stupid could two people get? He obviously hadn't called her
in the middle of the night just after his return from Paris to
talk about their jobs. And she, who had almost given up
hope of hearing from him, had acted as though he were
nothing more than an old acquaintance to whom she was
being forced to be pleasant.

Well, she thought, she'd brought it on herself with that
idiotic letter. She was probably lucky that he had called at
all.

She began to pick through the scattered clothing, putting
away the things that were obviously unsuitable. But that still
left far too much choice. What did she want to be: sexy, so
phisticated or subtle? The last was rather difficult, given her
predilection for bold styles and bright colors, but she did in
fact own one basic black silk dress and one cream-colored
linen and silk suit. She stared at them, then put them back
into the closet, too. "Subtle" had just been eliminated.

Then she rummaged through the remaining piles and fi
nally came to a bright-blue cotton-and-silk blend dress with

a deep V-neckline that stopped just short of indecency. It was the first thing she had taken out, and she knew now that it was the best choice. The color was a near-perfect match for her eyes, and the full skirt was designed to swirl gracefully when she walked.

Since the dress had been the first thing out of the closet, it had ended up on the very bottom of the pile. As a result, it was wrinkled. With a sigh, Teddy scooped it up and went off in search of her iron.

GRAHAM WALKED into the florist shop feeling slightly foolish. What had possessed him to think of taking her flowers? He hadn't bought flowers for a woman since his senior prom. He had a ludicrous vision of himself standing outside her door holding the flowers like a grinning fool and nearly left the shop.

Roses in every conceivable shade stood in vases behind glass doors. Along with them were spiky gladioli in even more colors. No wildflowers to be seen anywhere. Teddy liked wildflowers. He remembered how she'd rhapsodized over them during the walks they'd taken on Matiscotta. At the time, he'd been thinking that they would have made a lovely bed.

A gray-haired woman clerk approached, her expression clearly one of approval. No doubt any man who still bought flowers for a woman rated highly with her.

"Uh, I don't suppose you have any wildflowers?" he asked hopefully.

She shook her head, openly smiling now. "I'm afraid not. They're very perishable, you know."

That was right. He remembered now that Teddy hadn't picked any for that reason. He looked doubtfully at the roses. He'd wanted so badly for everything to be perfect and already it was going bad.

"Daylilies," the woman offered, apparently seeing his expression. "They look rather like wildflowers and they last quite well."

Graham thought that it might not matter, because if this evening didn't go well, she'd throw them away tomorrow.

The clerk had disappeared into the back and now returned with several vases of colorful, speckled flowers that did indeed have the artful disarray of wildflowers. Moreover, they looked like Teddy to him, far more than the roses did. He nodded his agreement and then let the clerk select a bouquet. In the meantime, he roamed restlessly about the shop, then came to a halt before the strangest looking plant he'd ever seen. He had to touch it before he was convinced that it was real.

"It's a staghorn fern," the clerk said from behind him. "Despite its exotic appearance, it's really very hardy."

Graham thought that the name was very appropriate. From the first moment he'd seen it, the long, flat fronds had reminded him of antlers.

A few minutes later, he left the shop, clutching the day lily bouquet in one hand and the hanging basket containing the staghorn in the other. He almost laughed aloud at himself. Here he was, living in an apartment he hadn't even bothered to furnish properly, and he'd just bought a house plant. It didn't take much guesswork to know what had brought on this attack of domesticity.

THE UNPLEASANT, STENTORIAN SOUND of the doorbell had the sound of both impending doom and revived hope. Teddy took a deep, shuddering breath, opted for hope, and pushed herself toward the door.

When the door opened, Graham tried on a smile that he was sure looked ridiculous, and thrust out the bouquet. He felt like a kid on his first date and was sure that he must look the part, too. His throat felt tight and he feared that his tongue wouldn't work properly. And there she stood, poised and relaxed as ever, wearing the color he liked best on her and with her hair in a slightly longer, even more attractive length.

Teddy saw the flowers and was immediately lost in a memory of walks through the fields and forests of Matiscotta. She reached for the bouquet awkwardly, her fingertips brushed against his hand, and that electric current flowed anew.

"Thank you," she managed as she fingered the bouquet delicately. "I love daylilies because they remind me of wildflowers." Could he possibly have remembered that, or was it only wishful thinking on her part?

He surrendered them to her, electrified by the brief contact with her soft hand. His nervousness got lost in a wave of desire and he wondered what would happen if he just tore that blue dress off her right here and now. Civility was a very thin veneer over primeval urges at the moment, and it was wearing away with every second.

"I thought so, too," he replied, sounding almost normal to himself. "I remembered that you liked them. Have you been up to Matiscotta this summer?" There he went again: a reprise of the other night's idiocy.

She just shook her head, avoiding his gaze by staring at the bouquet that was even lovelier now because he had remembered.

"Ted isn't going to sell the house, is he?" Graham asked, disturbed by the possibility even as he knew he should be finding a less volatile subject of conversation for now. Among the many fantasies with which he'd tormented himself over the past year had been one featuring Teddy and him and their children spending summer vacations there.

"No, he won't sell it. We'll go back someday." She rushed to get this all out, then excused herself to get a vase for the flowers.

Graham watched her, wondering who the "we" would be. Had she shared his dreams, or was she just referring to herself and Ted?

He looked around her living room that was filled with plants and antique pieces he guessed might be family heirlooms. The overall impression was one of coziness, something he wouldn't have associated with her. He had guessed that she would favor bright, modern decor, and his mistake unnerved him.

In the kitchen, Teddy got out a lovely Waterford vase and, with shaking fingers began to arrange the bouquet. She was bemused by his apparent concern over the house on Matiscotta. Did it mean that he, too, had thought of returning there some day? Could they ever do that?

She looked up to find him standing in the kitchen doorway, watching her with that same quiet intensity she'd seen so often before. In her dreams she'd called it love, but now she wasn't so sure.

She picked up the vase quickly and slid past him to return to the living room. Keeping herself busy and observing the proprieties seemed her best course just now.

"Would you like a drink before we leave?"

"Uh, yes, fine," he responded, trailing along after her and jamming his hands into his pockets to keep them quiet. He was within one heartbeat of grabbing her and— "Wine or something stronger?" she asked, glad to have something else to do now that the flowers had been taken care of.

"Wine'll be fine," he said, following along after her again because he couldn't bear to let her out of his sight.

"Where are we having dinner?" she inquired as she got out the wine and glasses, wishing that he'd settle down even if she herself couldn't.

He thought about suggesting that they stay right here and order out for pizza after they..."It's a surprise."

She gave him a pleasantly startled glance over the rim of her wineglass. "Oh?"

"It's kind of different. I think you'll like it." On the other hand, maybe he'd made a big mistake. He'd never been there himself, but a friend had recommended it and he'd thought it sounded perfect. Now he thought he might be overdoing it, what with the flowers, too.

"Different how?" Teddy inquired. "You mean exotic food?" Her stomach, normally constructed of cast iron, had been queasy for the past two days.

Graham realized that he'd never even inquired about the cuisine. "No, I meant the atmosphere."

She laughed. "Is this repayment for my taking you to the lobster pound?"

"Not really, but I hope you like it as well as I liked the pound." He thought that talk of the past wasn't helping things along, but he didn't know how to move to the future.

"Dad called me this afternoon. I told him that I was seeing you tonight and he was pleased." That, she thought, was putting it mildly. He'd actually asked her to postpone the wedding until he was released.

"Does he have a release date yet?" Graham inquired.

Teddy was momentarily flustered by his uncanny sense of timing. "The parole board meets in two weeks, so he'll know right after that. I hope there's no problem." Her father didn't seem worried about it, but she was worrying enough for them both.

Graham heard that slight change in her voice that signaled her anguish and fear. He wanted to hold her and soothe her and tell her that she shouldn't worry so much about Ted. But he was afraid to make that first move, to shatter the fragile atmosphere.

"There won't be any problem, Teddy. He'll make it."

She responded to his words with a smile that he knew was pure bravado. As much as he'd hated to hurt Ted, he knew that the man had deserved it. But Teddy had been blameless, and yet she had probably suffered even more than her father. Because of him.

"Teddy," he said, choosing his words carefully, "if I could have done anything that would have changed it, I would have. You must know that."

She nodded slowly, then suddenly looked at him with that disconcertingly direct stare he hadn't yet seen this night. "Did you ever consider telling him who you were and preventing him from handing over those papers? After all, there was no hard evidence of that other time."

She had just asked the one question Graham had hoped to avoid. If he told her the truth, she might well throw him out right here and now. But he had no choice; there could be no more lies and deceptions between them.

"It crossed my mind, Teddy, but I never seriously considered it. I volunteered for that task force because I'm very concerned about the theft of American technology. It's the best thing this country has going for it and it's being stolen left and right." He paused, took a deep breath, then forged on.

"I probably could have gotten away with it, too, because all we had against Ted were vague suspicions. But I didn't do it and I don't regret it, regardless of what it cost me personally."

Teddy stared down at her empty wineglass, unable to meet his gaze. His answer had just confirmed what she'd suspected about him all along: that he was the very antithesis of the cynic he had tried to portray when she'd first met him.

"I'm sorry, Graham," she said softly, flicking her eyes to him and then quickly away again. "It wasn't a fair question. I've tried to be rational about it, but . . ."

Her voice trailed off into a thick silence that was weighted with ugly memories and a fear that they would always be there.

They left shortly thereafter for the restaurant, with both of them hoping desperately that a change of scenery would improve the situation. The evening had begun in desperation, and things were growing steadily worse.

Lost in her thoughts, Teddy paid scant attention to where they were going, except that she knew they were in Virginia. One suburban community tended to run into another in this area and she noticed that Graham didn't seem all that familiar with the route, either.

"Have you been to this restaurant before?" she asked, filled with an irrational urge to be going somewhere different, some place he hadn't taken other women.

He glanced at her briefly. "No. A friend recommended it and I thought you might enjoy it."

He didn't add that the friend, who was something of a playboy, had told him that it was the perfect place to begin a seduction. He now wondered if he should pretend he couldn't find it and go somewhere else instead. She might suspect him of just that, and Graham was a man with far more than mere seduction on his mind.

"There it is," he exclaimed with definitely mixed emotions.

Teddy peered through the windshield. They were at the edge of an older residential neighborhood filled with large, mostly Victorian-style homes. At first glance, the house appeared to be much like the others: a rather whimsical, turreted frame house, painted in a slate blue with cream-colored trim and a wide porch that ran the width of the front and disappeared around the sides. There were antique wicker tables and chairs set up on the porch, but only a few were occupied on this warm, muggy evening. A small sign in the midst of a flower bed stated its appropriate, if unimaginative, name: Victoriana.

Graham stopped the car before the canopied entrance and a white-jacketed attendant appeared to help her out of the car. As Graham handed over the keys and came up to join her, she smiled at him.

"I like it already. I just hope they've preserved the Victorian atmosphere inside, too."

Graham, who already knew they had, was greatly relieved.

The elegant appointed foyer divided two rooms that had once been parlors. Teddy saw to her delight that one still was, complete with dark, heavy Victorian furniture, velvet draperies in a deep crimson and papered walls. In it, couples sat talking over cocktails, their modern dress looking strangely out of place.

The other parlor had been converted into a dining room, but the atmosphere had been carefully preserved there, too. In both rooms and the foyer as well, the chief source of lighting were crystal wall sconces and chandeliers fitted with bulbs that flickered in a nearly perfect imitation of gaslight.

Teddy saw quickly that every table was occupied and hoped that meant they would be waiting in the parlor. But when Graham gave his name to the maitre d', they were promptly ushered up the wide staircase. Solemn portraits in antique frames watched over their progress.

The staircase ended in what Teddy could only think of as being a charming maze. Some walls had been removed and others had been left intact, creating cozy spaces for dining that afforded almost complete privacy. Huge potted palms hid some diners as well, and thick oriental carpeting muffled the sounds. As below, the lighting came from crystal wall sconces.

They were led to a table in a far corner, obviously the turret Teddy had seen from outside. The space was small, allowing only for a table for two, and silver and crystal gleamed in the seeming gaslight. More large palms at each end of the curved walls further heightened the nearly over-whelming sense of intimacy.

A waiter appeared immediately and took their cocktail orders, then disappeared to leave them alone in their charming nook. Graham continued to watch her nervously, wondering once more if he might have overdone it. But then he stopped worrying—and thinking, for that matter—as Teddy smiled at him.

"This is wonderful, Graham. Thank you for bringing me here." To her own ears, her speech sounded ridiculously formal, although the huskiness in her voice belied that.

Graham ignored the speech and concentrated instead on the huskiness. "I'm glad you like it."

But after this beginning, they both quickly found that they could not succumb to the romanticism of their sur-roundings. It almost seemed like a film set upon which two near-strangers had intruded. There were long silences they both struggled to fill, and others they tried hard to ignore. Each of them hoped fervently that the flickering lights were hiding their nervousness.

There were moments, however, when sensuality brushed against them with its soft heat and whispered darkly into their ears: moments when a comment or even a glance would remind them that it had once been different. The bittersweet past lingered, the unknown future threatened—and the present suffered.

They were both waiting, for what they couldn't say. Some sign, some irrefutable evidence that what had begun a year ago on Matiscotta Island could continue. Teddy would see, briefly, that dark intensity in Graham's gaze, then find it gone a moment later and think that perhaps she had only imagined it. Graham would sense that Teddy was about to abandon her first-date formality and become the warm, honest woman he remembered, but it never quite happened.

They lingered over the excellent dinner, then left the restaurant reluctantly. As soon as they were back at her home, Teddy once more became the gracious hostess, a role to which she clung with increasing desperation. Graham found himself disturbed by the coziness of the place, now that the surprise had worn off.

It occurred to him that in the past, he'd always enjoyed being in the home of a woman who had created something for herself, rather than one who gave the impression that her present life was nothing more than a temporary way station on the route to marriage.

But now, after listening to Teddy describe the new life she'd carved out for herself, and seeing it all around him here, he was beginning to feel that she was complete without him.

They decided on Irish coffees to top off the dinner, and Graham hung about in the kitchen while she prepared them, feeling ever more awkward and worried. But then he drew himself out of his self-pity long enough to notice the signs of nervousness in her, too. It was there in a surprising shyness and a certain lack of grace in her movements. He began to feel slightly better, although he still wasn't quite sure how to proceed.

Her sofa wasn't large, so Graham took a seat there, hoping that she would join him. But after fussing for a few moments with the daylily bouquet, she went instead to a chair. He found that choice to be both significant and ominous. With increasing desperation, he tried to find a way past all this awkwardness.

She began to talk about her father's plans to seek a teaching position and thanked him for having suggested it. He cut her off halfway through that polite speech.

"Teddy, I don't want to talk about your father. I want to talk about us."

She recoiled as though he had struck her, and only then did he realize how harsh his tone had been, the result of his frustration and anguish over the evening thus far. His expression and his voice softened.

"We have to find a way out of the past, Teddy."

After a moment, she nodded slowly but she avoided his gaze. "I know that, but it's proving to be far more difficult than I'd expected."

He relaxed. At least she wasn't questioning why they had to find their way out of that past. That was, to his mind, a small consolation.

"Why?" he asked, hoping she could answer a question he couldn't. He didn't understand why she was behaving like this and why he was permitting her to get away with it, either.

She glanced at him briefly, then looked quickly away again and shrugged. "I just keep thinking about how little we really know about each other and how long it's been."

He couldn't believe she really meant that. He knew every little detail about her, every nuance of speech and habit. He'd made a very serious and prolonged study of Teddy Bothern, firsthand and then from his memories.

"You're afraid," he stated flatly.

It worked. For the first time this evening, he saw a return of the old Teddy as she lifted her chin in defiance. "I am not. What could I possibly be afraid of?"

"Us," he stated in the same tone.

She said nothing as her gaze slid away. When Graham saw her begin to gnaw her lower lip, he could stand it no more.

He got up and walked over to her, then bent down to rest a hand on either arm of her chair.

"Look at me, Teddy," he commanded softly.

She hesitated for several heartbeats, then finally raised her head. He felt her fear and saw her hope.

"Teddy," he began, his voice gentle now, "what happened last summer is that two people met and fell in love. That's what's important now."

"We can't just pretend that nothing else happened, Graham," she protested weakly.

"We've paid for the rest of it, Teddy. Both of us."

Their faces remained scant inches apart. Their eyes were searching each other's faces, and both of them were holding their breaths. Finally, Graham straightened up from his awkward position and Teddy half rose toward him. He held out a hand to her and then drew her to her feet. Then he caressed the side of her face with the back of his hand and she turned to kiss his fingertips.

But the hesitance was still there for them both. Another small step had been taken, but each of them was still very careful, as though the other might be made of glass that could shatter from any sudden move. Graham led her to the sofa, where she curled into a corner. He sat down beside her, taking her hand.

"I've spent the past year waiting for our future, Teddy. Now it's here."

"I've spent it trying to ignore the future," she admitted softly. "I just wouldn't let myself think about us when Dad—"

He stopped her with a finger to her lips. "We're talking about us now, not Ted."

She nodded and he withdrew his finger, then began once again to caress her cheek softly. He felt the exact moment when she finally, completely, let go of that past, and moved toward her.

Teddy leaned toward him at the same moment, feeling the burden of the past lift from her just as his mouth covered hers with infinitely gentle warmth. He lifted her until she was cradled in his arms and continued to kiss her with a soft persuasiveness that melted slowly into raw hunger.

"I love you," he murmured against her ear. "Oh, God, how I love you."

"I love you, too, Graham," she whispered huskily. "That's why I've been so worried tonight. I was afraid that if anything went wrong, we'd never have another chance."

"I know," he said as he slid out from beneath her and stood up, then extended a hand down to her.

For a moment, she looked confused at his actions, and he realized that despite the admissions of love, a small amount of uncertainty remained.

He folded her into his arms and held her there silently, until he could feel the uncertainty leave her again. Then he buried his mouth in the soft curve of her neck. "Right now, I want to make love to you, and as soon as possible, I want to marry you."

She cupped his face and gently drew it to meet hers. "Yes, and yes."

She led him to her bedroom, but when they reached it, she stopped uncertainly in the doorway, while he advanced into the room.

Graham walked quickly back to her and took both her hands in his.

"Nervous?"

"No, of course not," she denied quickly.

He brushed his mouth briefly against hers. "Yes, you are. We both are—because neither of us has ever been in love before."

Then he felt her relax as he surrounded her with himself, sliding his hands down over her curves until he was urging them together in an erotic imitation of union. A softly pleading sound welled up in her that he answered with a deep groan.

"I need you so badly that I'm afraid I won't be able to go slowly," he admitted shakily.

"I'm not sure I could stand it if you did."

He reached for the back zipper of her dress, then slid it off her shoulders and let it fall to the floor. She fumbled eagerly with his shirt buttons, then pushed it off. The rest of their clothes followed in short order.

They moved into each other's arms with a sureness and an ease that belied the newness of it all. A year's worth of dreams and fantasies poured forth into reality. He quivered uncontrollably as her fingernails traced light paths along his thighs, and she moaned softly when his mouth closed around a button-hard nipple. They explored each other with exquisite thoroughness and sensitivity, sometimes seeming as though they had a lifetime's knowledge of each other, and other times exulting over new discoveries.

Their passion was equal, but Graham's patience proved the greater as Teddy reached for him and urged him to her. He held away, then drew her onto him instead. She hesitated tantalizingly before welcoming him into herself with a downward movement that met his thrust. Their eyes met for one brief moment before the explosion of passion blinded them and carried them both to a shattering, mindless ecstasy.

Afterward, he curved her against himself, content for the moment to caress her as the small aftershocks rippled through them both. He wondered now how he could ever have doubted that this moment would come. Then, in the next instant, he knew he wouldn't be totally certain that she was his until she wore his ring.

"Let's get married tomorrow," he said, kissing the curls that lay in disarray on his chest.

"Dad would like us to wait until he's released."

Graham considered that. He did owe Ted something, and besides, he wanted him there.

"It would be better that way, don't you think?" she asked. "That way, he can start his new life at the same time we start ours."

Graham buried his face in those soft, coppery curls and decided she was right—in every way.

COMING NEXT MONTH

#225 COMFORT AND JOY by Judith Arnold

Legal-aid lawyer Jesse Lawson thought Christmas was a time-wasting, energy-sapping distraction from life. Then he met Robin Greer—who showed him Christmas was laughter and love and sometimes...even miracles.

#226 SECOND TO NONE by Stella Cameron

Nanny Sophie Peters dreamed about a caring, trusting love, the kind her two small charges' parents shared. But Michael Harris's ploys and come-ons didn't promise that. Until he tossed away his bag of tricks and tried a new approach—honesty.

#227 KISSES IN THE RAIN by Pamela Browning

On the spur of the moment Martha Rose went to Ketchikan, Alaska, to open a Bagel Barn. But it was the town's most eligible bachelor, Nick Novak, who tempted her to stay. Nick was also the town's most talked about citizen; rumor surrounded his secret life. Cautious though he was, could he help but be fascinated by a creature of impulse?

#228 SEPTEMBER GLOW by Judith Yoder

The Golden Years had arrived! Retired Terrance Nelson had time on his hands now—but Rachel didn't. Working and raising a young son was all-consuming. Rachel wasn't looking for new challenges in her life, but years of experience had taught Terrance the art of persuasion....

ATTRACTIVE, SPACE SAVING BOOK RACK

Display your most prized novels on this handsome and sturdy book rack. The hand-rubbed walnut finish will blend into your library decor with quiet elegance, providing a practical organizer for your favorite hard-or soft-covered books.

Only $9.95

Approximately 16" x 8" when assembled

Assembles in seconds!

To order, rush your name, address and zip code, along with a check or money order for $10.70* ($9.95 plus 75¢ postage and handling) payable to *Harlequin Reader Service*:

Harlequin Reader Service
Book Rack Offer
901 Fuhrmann Blvd.
P.O. Box 1396
Buffalo, NY 14269-1396

Offer not available in Canada.

*New York and Iowa residents add appropriate sales tax.

BKR-1A

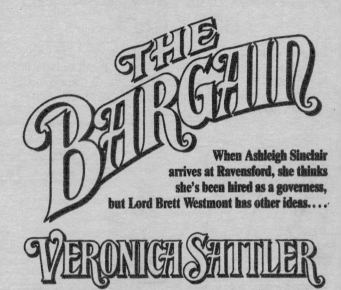